VEILED

THEY SAID CIVILITY REIGNED OVER DESIRE. THEY LIED.

STACEY ROURKE

DISCLAIMER:

Every action has an equal and opposite reaction.
Make note of the experiment days to line causes from the past to their effects in the present.

ONE
FORMULATED HYPOTHESIS

Hypothesis – The proposed explanation for a phenomenon that requires testing.

Oh how I missed the reoccurring dream that used to haunt me with its mundane regularity. In it, I took a running start over worn and splintered boards to throw myself off the end of a pier. Anticipating the rush of the icy water, my plummet downward lasted longer than I expected. Instinct screamed for me to tuck my body into a tight ball to brace for what was to come. Fighting that impulse, I straightened my spine and held firm. Plunging in with a spray of white foam, the chill of the sea shocked me to the bone. Still, despite that harsh bite of cold, I smiled and tipped my head skyward … because in my innocent, isolated world, I knew I was okay. I would break the surface of that watery tomb. The hands of my loved ones would encircle my extended wrists and draw me back into the light, cradling me in the warmth of their embrace.

That little bit of subconscious self-soothing came before I knew what a heartless bitch fate could be.

Now, I spiraled deeper and deeper into a realm the darkest, most vile minds couldn't fathom. Sinking into a toxic sludge from which there was no escape.

Here, no hands of salvation could find me and no hope could survive.

This was no dream behind the fluttering lids of a sweet and sheltered co-ed.

It was an ugly, gruesome death ... and I was its harbinger.

EXPERIMENT DAY 366: EFFECT

Cause & Effect – The basic principle of causality determines whether results and trends in an experiment are actually caused by the manipulation or whether other factors may underlie the process.

THERE'S SOMETHING TRULY liberating about walking into a room and knowing without a shadow of a doubt that you are the baddest bitch there. That undeniable truth struck me as I sashayed through the palace of designer duds and dripping diamonds.

"Get those wallets ready, ladies!" The evening's hostess—a retired television star from the 70s—pursed her lips coquettishly. "The next bachelor coming to the stage is none other than on-air vamp correspondent, *Mathieus Vaughn*. Mathieus was sired two hundred and seventy-six years ago, which has given him *plenty* of time to perfect his art of seduction, ladies. And remember, bidders, if the Nosferatu Presumption of Innocence Bill passes, he's planning to run for Congress. Play your cards right, and you could be a *congressman's wife*!" The stage lights glistened off her shimmering gown, which clung to her surgically maintained figure as if she had been dipped in gold-plating. "The bidding will start at one thousand dollars. Do I hear one thousand?"

While the bidding opened to the horny and rich, Mathieus posed and preened like the prize show pony he was. Flipping his hair, he puffed his chest and slathered on the charm.

Frustrated with their husband's long-since flaccid penises, the women in the crowd ate up his showy antics by the spoonful, driving the bids higher and higher. Their anxious giggles bounced off the ballroom walls, masking the loathing they harbored for each bitch that *dared* to outbid them.

The monetary equivalent of his charisma topped out just under the six-thousand-dollar mark.

Giddy with the power of her position, the nipped and tucked hostess twirled the gavel between her fingers. Once, she was idolized by teenage boys everywhere. Her bare midriff—absent of obscene flashes of belly button—and bright smile earned her the spot of America's sweetheart. Now, she got her much needed rush of attention with guest appearances, and high-paying events such as this. "We have five thousand, nine-hundred, and seventy-five. Do I hear six thousand? Going once … going twice … *sold*! Sold for five thousand, nine-hundred, and seventy-five dollars to the lovely lady in blue in the back!"

A smattering of polite applause emanated from the mass of women and their bitter libidos. The least he could have done, after working them all up into a lather, would have been to throw the active bidders a sympathy bone into their creaky, cob-web covered coochies. Be that as it may, only one lucky lady rushed the stage, frantically waving her arms as if her name had been called on *The Price is Right*.

Offering her a hand, Mathieus pulled the robust woman on stage like she weighed no more than a feather. His alabaster face didn't even redden at the strain—granted, blood hadn't pumped through his veins in a few hundred years, but the gesture was still a potent one to the romance deprived crowd which hooted in response.

The moment their palms touched, the lucky winner blushed a bright carnation pink. Fluttering her fake lashes, which had slipped awkwardly askew, she beamed up at his strikingly handsome face. Every romanticized vampire movie she ever double-fisted popcorn to flashed across her face as she stared into the sapphire pools of his gaze, wishing for their poetic eternity.

Side by side, they flirted and posed for pictures. Mathieus even went so far as to pantomime a vicious vampire sneer for a few clicks of the camera, pretending to bite his date's neck, much to the audience's uproarious delight.

Riding the high of their moment in the light, the couple was reluctantly ushered off stage to settle up her payment for one evening in his company.

"Next up ..." Positioning her bedazzled bifocals on the bridge of her nose, the once idolized starlet squinted to read the tiny print on an index card. "Oh, this is a good one! Our *next* eligible bachelor is the infamous newsman, Carter Westerly. Carter is very much a human, ladies, and came into fame as a hunky reporter for VNN, who then reported on the vampire initiative in a series of fun, risqué broadcasts. This guy isn't afraid to get his hands dirty, ladies. And, let me assure you, that can be a very, *very* good thing! Please help me welcome Mr. Westerly to the stage!"

To say he was received by a smattering of applause would be a kind over-exaggeration. A few palms found their way together, out of habit more than respect.

A room full of waning interest, yet I had found *exactly* what I came for.

Carter stumbled out on to the stage as if pushed, fumbling forward to get his feet under him. Someone had taken the time to dress him in a tux. It was an adorable gesture, really. Not unlike garnishing a Thanksgiving turkey before devouring its helpless carcass.

At a distance, he might almost have passed as dashing with his disheveled blond hair and sharp, chiseled jawline. I knew enough to look deeper than that—to the bruise-colored shadows lining his eyes, and the hollows of his cheeks gaunt with dehydration. His gaze didn't flick to the exits, as I anticipated. Instead, he stood with his arms swinging akimbo at his sides, scouring the room for who among them would free him by offering the mercy of a clean death.

"Isn't he a dish, ladies?" the hostess rasped into the mic. "The vamp mistresses in the room maybe interested to know that, rumor has it, our boy is *virgin* to the fang. With that in mind, how about if we kick the bidding off at one thousand dollars. Do I hear one thousand?"

Silence fell.

The only sounds echoing through the grand ballroom were the clink of champagne flutes meeting stainless steel trays and crystal baubles from the chandeliers clacking together as the central air blew through the overhead vents.

Clearing her throat, the hostess shifted her weight from one Jimmy Choo to the other. Batting her impossibly long lashes, she struggled to keep her plastered smile firmly in place. "How about seven-fifty? Do I hear seven hundred and fifty?"

Someone in the back coughed, only to quickly shake their head in affirmation it *wasn't* to be confused with a bid.

"Come on, ladies," the starlet would have cringed, if *Botox* allowed that caliber of facial movement, "he's an attractive guy. Imagine how good he would look mowing your lawn. At this price, it would be cheaper than most of our gardeners."

Her comment earned a light titter of laughter, yet still no bids.

"Five hundred? Any takers at five hundred?"

"One point four million." The ice of my tone sent shudders through the room, every gaze swiveling my way with fascinated interest.

"I-I'm not sure I heard that right." Cupping her hand behind her ear, the former bombshell inched to the edge of the stage. "It sounded like someone said—"

Draining the last of the Moët & Chandon Don Perignon from my glass, I set it on the table behind me and dabbed at my lips with a napkin embroidered with twenty-four karat gold.

Striding forward, the fabric of my gown shushed around my ankles. The crowd parted for me in breathless anticipation.

"One point four million," I clarified, stepping into the stage footlights which eagerly shifted in my direction.

Head held high, I allowed them a moment to take me in. The black mermaid-style dress clung to my skin in a lover's whisper, its plunging neckline hinting at my perfectly pert tits hidden from view. Under the glow of the lights my porcelain skin shimmered like freshly fallen snow, exposing me for what I truly was—flawless as a diamond, and equally indestructible. My short-sheered tresses were slicked back in a punk-coif. Full lips stained a delectable candy-apple red. I was a vision. An immortal goddess among lowly mortals. A … complete and total fraud.

"That's just fantastic!" the hostess gushed, her face brightening with a peaches and crème glow. "Thanks to you, The Vampire Society has *surpassed* its goal for this year's donation to Food for the Poor, a charity for orphaned and abandoned children. Let's give our bidder a round of applause while she makes her way to the stage!"

I was donating enough to charity to cancel out *their* need to do so. By the thunderous ovation I received, it became clear they saw me as Santa Claus, the Easter Bunny, and the fucking Tooth Fairy all rolled into one.

"Aren't you lovely," the hostess muttered through her plastic smile as I lifted the hem of my gown to step onto the stage. Up close, I could smell the toxins in her blood. If I had to guess, I would say a Vicodin and gin cocktail. "I'm sure our audience would love to know what plans you have for the delectable Mr. Westerly after placing such a generous bid on him?"

"That depends," I mused, hitching a brow in the direction of my bewildered prize, "on how well he takes direction."

The crowd responded with appreciative hoots and saucy catcalls. I fully intended to make them choke on them.

Whitewashing my face of all emotion, I let the chill of death seep into my tone and vine around each word in an audible threat. "Get on your knees."

The audience sucked in a shocked gasp, exchanging glances between them in their hunt to make sense of this sudden, taboo spectacle.

Carter's cerulean stare fixed on me, undoubtedly seeing me as just another vampress flexing her power to impress the weak and fragile humans. Despite the exhaustion weighing heavy on his sagging lids, one corner of his mouth tugged back in an arrogant half-grin. "I'm in a tuxedo. Such a thing would be as lowbrow as you flashing fang in front of this regal crowd."

"You think I need to show fang to gain your submission?" A snap of my fingers and a tablet was delivered into my waiting palm by a nameless face in the crowd, there solely to do my bidding. A careful click and swipe, and I showed Carter the screen. "Tell me, Mr. Westerly, do you know this young lady?"

Carter took a tentative step closer. His stare narrowed to focus, then widened with horrified realization. "That's my niece, Harper. If you lay one hand on her—"

"Harper," I interrupted, bored by any and all idle threats. "Quite the cutie, isn't she? I especially like her Pooh Bear pajamas. Now, if you would please direct your attention to the French doors behind her, and tell me what you see."

Zooming in the screen, I swiveled it back in his direction. I bit my lower lip, watching with delight as the tendons of his neck tensed, and his hands balled into defensive fists.

"Call them off," Carter snarled, nostrils flaring like a poked buffalo.

"Ah, so you *do* see my friend!" I declared in a victorious chirp. "That vamp prowling by the back window is a colleague of mine. He posed as a pizza man earlier at your sister's home, and she invited him in while she fetched the money. Can you imagine such blind trust in the world we live in? You *really* should have a talk with her."

No longer playing to the crowd, Carter dropped his voice to a raspy whisper. "What do you want?"

Arms falling to my sides, I reduced the shocked gasps and horrified sneers of the crowd to the meaningless drone of background noise

7

they were. "One word from me and my man will rip out Harper's throat while I pry your eyes open and make you watch. Now, with all due respect, Mr. Westerly, *take a knee.*"

Pressing his lips into a thin white line of vengeful hate, Carter did as directed. All the while he made a point of glaring murderous daggers in my direction.

"Good boy," I purred. Spinning on the ball of my foot, I snapped my fingers to my crew waiting in the wings. "*Bring him.*"

TWO

EXPERIMENT DAY 1: CAUSE

Control Group – A group that receives no treatment in order to compare to the treated group.

S pare me your shocked gasps. Yes, I know in that last snippet I come across as an unlikable bitch. But, before you get all judgmental, there's something you should know. I don't give two-shits about what you think. If that kind of spectacle gets your panties in a twist, you need to take another look around. There are far worse monsters than me in this world. How do I know? I've met them all, and done shots with more than a few.

No, I don't need your empathy. I know I'm the only one to blame for my plight in this miserable afterlife. Even now, thinking back to where it all started, I have a hard time drumming up even an ounce of self-pity. Oh, poor Vincenza. What could have possibly happened to blacken her young heart so? For starters? Love. Star-crossed, Hollywood contrived, Montague and Capulet bullshit. The media spoon-fed me stories of vampire hotties that wanted to love and worship their chosen mortal for *all eternity, and I strapped on a bib and gobbled that romanticized crap right up. The fact that my parents were adamantly anti-vamp registered with me as nothing more than icing on the cake of my rebellion.*

Don't misunderstand. Robert and Kathryn Larow weren't narrow minded. Quite the contrary, in fact. They were people of science who trusted confirmed facts over any syllable uttered by the media. That's right, I said were. Did ya catch that? If you thought this story would have a happy ending, you missed the blatant undertones.

Before the bottom dropped out of my world, my father had spent his life studying the science of politics, while my mother focused on biochemistry. They preached to my brother and me, before we were even at an age to understand what it meant, that people only think they know why things are the way they are. According to Ma and Pa Larow, the facts could only be confirmed through observation and validating experiments.

A year ago, on the kind of ordinarily dull night that used to make me think the spin of the world had slowed to a mind-numbing crawl, I became the experiment. Everything that followed has been a series of trials and tests. Causes and their effects on the very foundation my life had been built.

"WOULD YOU LISTEN to this guy?" My father, Senator Robert Thomas Larow, jabbed his hand in the direction of the flat-screen, his cheeks ruddy with frustration. "Using *the lion shall lie down with the lamb* in his rally speech? And these naïve humans are cheering and waving their Vampire Equality banners! If you follow the logic of this *insane* propaganda, he's saying that the lion—*that mighty king of beasts*—is going to lower itself to protecting and befriending the lambs. *That's not how nature works*! Go to a zoo! Watch *Animal Planet*! Lions *eat* lambs, and vampires *eat* humans! It's the basic fucking food chain!"

After cutting her steak into bite-sized pieces, my mother popped one medium-rare chunk into her mouth and chewed slowly. "I'm so glad you decided to turn the rally on during dinner," she deadpanned, washing her bite down with a sip of white wine. "Screamed profanities and watching my husband's blood pressure skyrocket adds a fun flavor of impending doom to the meal."

Taking the hint, Dad palmed the remote and made a great spectacle of turning the television off to appease his wife of twenty-two years.

She thanked him with a curt nod and a slight smile.

"This is *exactly* the kind of talk we need to squash *before* Finn gets here." Blushing at my vampire boyfriend's name, I snatched a second dinner roll from the basket in the center of the table and picked at it simply to have something to do with my fidgety hands.

Pause for backstory. Finn was a vampire, and my Nosferatu-opposed parents had agreed to meet my fanged beau. Their very natures demanded that they question and investigate every venue proposed. So, when their eldest offspring came home, claiming to be in love—ugh—with a vampire, they felt a tête á tête with the two-hundred-year-old suitor was in order. Giddy at the prospect, I secured the date with my love, Finn Danyor, who had once been a Roma traveler.

How did I fall for a vampire, despite my parents' previous and frequent warnings? That story you've heard a million times before. In the wise words of one Miss Avril Lavigne ... He was a boy. I was a girl. Can I make it any more obvious?

Finn was enchanting, sculpted perfection, and I had raging hormones and the false sense of security that nothing bad would ever happen to me.

Hearts fluttered—mine not his.

Things were groped—his not mine.

Fast-forward to me inviting him home to meet Mom and Dad, and begin what I was certain would be our happily ever after.

Sometimes being young and stupid is a formidable disability.

Slouched in his seat, my brother, Jeremy, snorted. "*Finn*? What kind of name is that? No real person is named Finn. That's the stage name of one of Nana's soap opera stars."

"*Hey*," I stabbed my fork in his direction, "don't criticize Nana's stories. That's all that got her through ..."

"Being married to Papi, God rest his soul," my entire family joined in, all of us crossing ourselves in well-practiced unison.

Our chorus of laughter rose in a happy symphony.

Leaning over the table, Dad gripped my hand and gave it a reassuring squeeze. "I promise not to get too political." He paused, eyebrows raised, waiting for me to take the bait.

"Unless …" I prompted, tongue in cheek.

"Unless I feel he's a threat to you in any way," Dad admitted, his expression equal parts sincerity and humor. "Then I will tie him up *Clockwork Orange* style and explore each and every one of the theories on vampire weaknesses in a slow and painful search for the most effective."

"Completely fair, and justified," I chuckled, patting his hand. "But he's a good guy. You'll see."

"Robert, totally off topic," Mom interrupted, draining the remaining wine from her glass, "but did you get a chance to glance over that list for the contractor? He's stopping by the lab tomorrow to pick it up. All of the changes need to be on there for him to put together the estimate."

"I still don't understand why we need to update the house. It's an unneeded expense," Dad grumbled, retracting his hand from mine to swab the steak juice from his plate with what remained of his dinner roll. Finding himself caught in the cross-hairs of Mom's murderous glare, he dutifully tagged on, "*But*, my wife's happiness with her new granite countertops is far more important than the food we will no longer be able to afford to put on them."

Clucking her tongue against the roof of her mouth, Mom rolled her russet eyes skyward. My bone-structure was a gift from her, yet I couldn't come close to harnessing her regal elegance. "Yes, *Senator*, we're practically destitute."

Dragging my last bite of steak through the salsa verde sauce Dad made, I rerouted the conversation to talking points more Vinx-beneficial. "*So* … did the attic happen to make that list?"

Mom and Dad groaned simultaneously. Jeremy let his forehead fall to the table with a smack.

"Really? We're back to *this*, Vincenza?" Pushing her finished plate aside, Mom leaned back in her chair. "For the life of me I can't figure out why that attic even appeals to you. There's nothing but dust bunnies and boxes of clutter we can't bring ourselves to throw away up there."

"Have you gone up there for anything more than grabbing the Christmas lights?" I gushed, flipping my curtain of blonde hair over my shoulder. "There are those three gorgeous arched windows right in the center of the space. If you stand right there, you can see the *entire* New Haven skyline. It would be an amazing master suite."

My mother and father exchanged matching flabbergasted stares.

"Hear that? That's the influence of *HGTV* on our offspring. She wants to move us into the attic, like long-forgotten trolls who just happen to pay all the bills." My father grinned to his bride.

My mother's fair complexion and sleek, raven tresses pleasantly contrasted his sun-kissed skin and flaxen hair. Much to my dismay, my own coloring favored the paternal side. Well … they did in life. But, I won't get ahead of myself.

Pursing her lips, Mom feigned being choked up with emotion. She fanned her hands at her eyes, waving away imaginary tears. "It's what we've always dreamed of!"

"I'm serious!" I giggled, fighting to maintain the persuasive tone of my campaign despite their antics. Gaze flicking to the window, I felt that familiar pull of magnetic longing. The sun was sinking in the sky. Finn would rise soon. I was moments from hearing his soft knock on the door and being gifted a glimpse of his intense, silver stare that never failed to enchant me. Finding myself suddenly parched, I cleared my throat and tried to recall where I was in my plea for prime real estate. "The attic is huge. You could keep half the space for storage, and the area leftover would still be twice the size of your bedroom now."

Leaning his elbows on the table, my dad stage-whispered to my mom, "Do you want to ask, or do you want me to?"

"By all means, go ahead." Trying unsuccessfully to stifle a grin, my mother leaned back in her chair and folded her arms over her chest.

Dad straightened his spine and fixed on a mock version of his senatorial façade. Pivoting his upper body my way, he addressed me as if finalizing the talking points of a new proposed bill. "Tell me, Miss Larow, if *we* move up to the attic, who gets our current master bedroom?"

Jeremy paused with another forkful of steak halfway to his mouth, glancing up from under his lashes with a sudden vested interest.

Matching my father's formal posture, I fixed my winning smile on him. "By age and the hierarchy of heirs, it rightfully goes to the first born … *me*."

"I say we go full Darwinian." Shoving the heaping bite into his mouth, Jeremy talked around it in a gross spray of food bits. "Survival of the fittest. We fight for it."

Rubbing her hand across my brother's back, Mom pressed her lips together in a thin line and shook her head. "Aw, we taught them scientific theories but *not* how to use a napkin."

Worst part of this whole ordinary moment of nothingness? Those would be the last words my mother would speak that weren't terrified shrieks tearing from her chest or a death rattle.

Picking up on the none-too-subtle hint, Jer sheepishly pulled his napkin from his lap to wipe his mouth.

The knock followed.

Its sharp rap ripped through our harmonious meal.

Intent announced like a clap of thunder before a brewing storm.

Twilight had muted the long afternoon shadows.

Still, it should have been too early for a vampire outing.

If my head wasn't clouded by all things Finn, I might have realized that.

Had my gaze swiveled even once to my mother or father, maybe I would have seen their trepidation, the way their bodies must have tensed with alarm despite their promise to me that they would keep an open mind. But, like I said, they were people of science. They knew the big, bad wolf was knocking on the door of their house made of sticks.

Not me. I didn't so much as hesitate when I leapt from my seat and scurried to let him in. "That must be Finn!"

Not by the hair on my chinny-chin-chin.

My father rose from his chair behind me. Physique toned by tennis, yet softened by a love of craft beers, his chest puffed with protective instinct. "Vincenza, wait a minute."

"And leave the guy standing out there sizzling?" I called over my shoulder, bare feet padding to the door. "He obviously got here early to make a good impression. That's those *manner* things you and Mom are always talking about."

Laughter bubbling from my lips, I closed my fingers around the brushed nickel doorknob and paused to check my appearance in the foyer mirror. Feeling my hair was looking a little flat, I dragged my fingers through it to fluff it. Looking back, that little act made about as much sense as applying lipgloss during a plane crash.

"Vinx, that's not how it works," my dad argued, his apprehensive stare twitching toward the door. "Vampires don't *choose* to stay inside before the sun sets. Their chemical makeup *insists* that they do."

His injection of common sense fell on deaf ears, my hand already turning the knob. Opening the door a crack, I peeked out to steal a glimpse of Finn's splendor just for myself before sharing him with my family. Instead, what awaited me squeezed the breath from my lungs in a shocked gasp.

Little pig, little pig, let me in …

Finn stood in the doorway with his head down, three additional vamps flanking him. One captured the meth-head tweaker look with his stringy-yellow hair and bony frame. The mocha beauty beside him reminded me of a deadly Black Mamba; hair wild and untamed, her lips curled from her teeth in a venomous hiss. A hulking albino rounded out the hive. Eyes glowing with crimson hate, his tongue—mutilated into a reptilian fork—flicked out between jagged fangs. The weak rays of the setting sun battered their skin, blistering and scorching any exposed flesh in angry slashes of red.

Slowly, Finn's head rose. What appeared to be genuine regret simmered in the pools of his wide, manic stare. "I'm truly sorry you opened the door."

With that, they charged.

Then, I'll huff, and I'll puff ...

The front door exploded inward, blown off its hinges in a shower of hardware and kindling. In a blur of speed, Finn lunged for me. Seizing me by the throat with one death-chilled hand, he pinned my back to his chest while his friends filled the foyer.

I didn't invite them in.

I didn't have to.

They were a hive, and he was their leader. When I opened the door to him, their invitation followed.

Nostrils flaring, my father barreled toward the intruders. "Get your fucking hands off my— *Agggghhhhh*!"

A blink, and the albino was latched on to my father's throat, shaking his head like an alligator preparing for a death roll. Slashes of gore painted the walls, pooling beneath my father's flailing feet.

Ears ringing, I gagged at the coppery stench that filled the room.

"I never wanted this," Finn whispered in my ear. His body trembled against mine as he dragged his tongue over my hammering pulse. "But ... I can't ... fight it."

Despite my own precarious position, adrenaline surged through me at the sight of the aptly nicknamed Black Mamba slithering in a slow circle around my younger brother. *"Don't touch him!"* I screamed, straining against Finn's unforgiving hold.

Running track had made Jeremy quick and agile. Unfortunately, he couldn't outrun a freight train. He bolted from his chair, but only made it two strides before she caught him. Seizing him by a handful of sandy-colored hair, she grabbed his chin and snapped his neck with a gruesome crack.

I watched the light fade behind my brother's eyes, his body crumbling to the floor like cast-aside trash.

"Jeremy! Baby, nooooo!" Folding to the floor, my mother's shoulders shook with the force of her sobs.

Sensing an opportunity, the scrawny tweaker pounced, drinking deep from Jeremy's throat.

"*Get off him!*" my mother howled. She scrambled on her hands and knees, to search the underside of the table for the loaded gun Dad duct-taped there. Calling it the only alarm system his family needed, he loaded it with silver-bullets that could kill vamps and humans alike. Her hands trembled in terror as she frantically scraped to free the weapon.

Seeing the gleam of metal, the monstrous albino charged.

Bang! Bang!

The first shot veered wide, shattering the dining room's bay window in a tinkling of shards. The second ripped a whole through the chest of the raging white bull. He exploded in a ball of fire, the flames from his execution singeing the wall behind him black.

"This isn't what I am," Finn murmured against my throat, his fangs raking over my skin. "I *never* would have hurt you, Vinx. Not ever."

I may have been a pining moron, but sentimental words uttered amid a massacre lost their poetry. Gripping the silver cross—passed down to me from my grandmother—strung around my neck, I yanked the chain free and swung blind. Its longest point stabbed into Finn's eye, sizzling and scorching through membrane and flesh. Roaring in pain, Finn stumbled back and lost hold of me.

"*You're dead, you human bitch!*" the Black Mamba spat, storming after me.

Swinging the chain out in a wide arc, I lashed at her. The silver cross hooked at the corner of her mouth, widening her smile in a spray of ash and smoldering skin. She grabbed her face, recoiling … at least for a beat.

Clambering to my mother's side, feet slipping in the thick slick of blood, I steadied myself with a hand against the wall. Bored with my brother, the tweaker had latched onto her, suckling from her neck in noisy slurps. Wrapping both arms around his head, I pressed the cross to his forehead and clamped it there. He reared back, screeching his anguish to the moon. Grinding my teeth, I pressed harder still, struggling not to gag as the metal burned through layer after layer of flesh, straight to bone. The scrawny vamp threw me off him, then retreated to the shadows to lick his wounds.

He wouldn't be gone long.

None of them would.

Gathering my mother in my arms, I tried to urge her slack frame up on to limp legs. "Come on, Mom. We have to go. I need you to help me!"

"*Vincenza*," she croaked, the artistry of Death painting the corners of her mouth a chilling cobalt. "You can't outrun them. Silver room divider … in the attic … block the door with it. Go … *run*!"

Her last act, before blood loss rolled her eyes back in her skull, was a quick glance where the gun had fallen.

"Mom? *Mama*?" Gently, I shook her, my wailing heart begging her eyes to open.

Shadows moved in the corner. A low, menacing vibrato snaked around me in a tightening noose. "I'm going to eat your liver, bitch, and keep you alive so you can watch me swallow each bite."

Spinning on my heel, I snatched the gun and sprinted for the stairs. I skidded around the corner separating the dining room from the stairwell in the foyer, and scaled the stairs two at a time. I made it to the halfway point, where my parents wedding picture hung on the wall in a simple silver frame, when a bony hand closed around my ankle and yanked my feet out from under me. The gun slipped from my fingers, thumping down one stair, then another. Knees smashing against the wood flooring, I fumbled for *anything* to anchor me before I slipped into the gaping jaws of death. Pain prickled through my legs, radiating up to my hips. Self-preservation demanded I ignore it. Snagging onto the railing, I gripped it in both hands and blindly kicked out. Cartilage crunched beneath my heel, a gush of sticky wetness coating my foot. The blow bought me a moment of freedom from the vamp's slipping hold. Dragging myself up, I palmed the gun and ran.

I rounded the bend at the top of the stairs, hobbling down the hall as fast as I could, and threw open the attic door. Slow and steady footfalls thumped in pursuit of me, not deeming me worthy of a high-speed chase. Their sound was muffled as I ascended the second set of stairs, drowned out by the pink fiberglass insulation surrounding me. By the time I burst out into the musty third story, the silence was deafening. The storm was coming for me; this was merely its taunting calm.

Spinning in a dazed and frantic circle, I tried to remember what random corner we shoved grandma's antique room divider into. It was a stunning piece, really. Comprised of four silver panels formed from individual tiles of pressed metal delicately welded together, the sections opened up accordion-style into a free-standing unit. If I could find it, I planned to bend it around the door, making a barricade they couldn't touch without scorching themselves. Funny how the appreciation for fine home décor goes right out the window in the face of certain death.

"Sniveling human slut," the tweaker growled from the top of the stairs. His gangly form lurked in the doorway. Black, tarry blood dripped from his chin, his broken nose flattened to his face. The skin on his forehead cracked and oozed, his skull exposed through the charred shape of my cross. "The only mercy I'll show you is *death*."

Releasing the safety, I leveled the gun and cradled it in both hands.

Prowling closer, he taunted, "You won't do it. I could admit I plan to fuck and suck you until there's nothing left, and you'd *still* be too pathetic to—"

The click of the gun's misfire cut him off.

"*Tsk, tsk, tsk.*" His tongue clucked against the roof of his mouth, fangs flashing in the moonlight filtering in through those windows I gushed about only moments before when life made sense. "Can't shoot it. What are you going to do now, little girl?"

"Stop!" My voice rose and fell with hiccupped sobs, tears blurring my vision. "Don't take another step."

"Or what?" Tipping his head, blond wisps of hair brushed his shoulder. "You'll throw it at me?"

Finn entered the room with the Black Mamba on his arm. Their wounds had all but vanished. The blood thirsty gleam in their eyes had not.

"Jump out the window, Vinx," Finn coached, his tone toeing the line of tender. "Try your luck with gravity. Because, if we get ahold of you ... you're already dead."

Hands shaking, I checked the chambers. One bullet. I had one bullet to defend myself from three vampires. Spinning the chamber, I locked it into place just as my father had taught me.

"Don't take another step," I warned with as much conviction as I could muster, trying to line up the sight with trembling arms.

Chin to his chest, the tweaker peered up at me, his glower dripping with jolly predatory amusement. "Little pig, little pig, let me in."

Click.

Empty chamber.

"Or, I'll huff and I'll puff ..." His jaws snapped in my direction.

Click.

"And I'll blow—"

BAM!

The bullet hit square in the center of his forehead, plowing him back in a fiery spray of bone and blood. He hit the arched windows in a reeling blaze, crashing through them on an expedited death march toward the ground.

For one beat of my racing heart, I stared through the shower of shattered glass into the vast nothingness of the night, shaking in stunned terror.

In the distance, sirens wailed.

The vast delight of my momentary victory met a violent end the second Finn's fangs sank into my neck. White hot needles of pain stabbed into me, radiating through my core. I tried to cry out, only to be silenced by his rough hand clamping over my mouth. Vamps can use their saliva to dull the ache of their bite and subdue their victim. Yet Finn couldn't be bothered with such courtesies. Weaving an arm around my waist, he pulled my body to his and buried his intrusive extensions deeper still. Blood gushed from the pinpoint wounds, streaming down my chest faster than he could lap it up.

I fought back with the effectiveness of a seal pup fending off a Great White. My clawing scrapes landed with little more than the irritation of a buzzing fly. What was left of my strength rapidly drained as my arms fell slack at my sides. I could feel myself fading, being erased from the life I once knew. Legs folding beneath me, Finn rode me to the ground, his fangs sawing through flesh to sever my artery. The side of my head bounced against the particle board floor. Having reached the limits of the human body's pain threshold, my nervous system gifted me the void of numbness.

As Finn withdrew and repositioned himself for a fresh strike, I lolled on to my back. Stars twinkled over New Haven, coaxing me into their peaceful oblivion. Each blink grew longer, my heavy lids whispering for me to succumb to the exhaustion.

They won the day, kid. My father's voice echoed through my mind, coaching me as he had after striking defeats in tennis tournaments or soccer games. *But next time you'll give 'em hell.*

The Black Mamba's face swam before my blurring vision. In the haze of my stupor, her features seemed flawlessly carved from impenetrable stone.

"Should we turn her?" Her voice seemed to come from miles and miles away, riding in on the night breeze to my own little island sanctuary in my mind where neither of them could hurt me.

Pulling back, Finn dropped from a crouch to his knees, the lower half of his face fully painted with my blood. "No. We were ordered to kill, not turn."

"That's a pity," the viper vampress purred, kneeling opposite of him. Catching a lock of my hair, she curled it around her finger and tugged it hard enough to snap strands from my scalp. "She would have made a lovely plaything."

Roused by their pedestaled position on the food chain, the vampires bowed their heads to feast. Each pull of their desire ushered me further into the dark abyss.

Consciousness waning, I closed my eyes and waited for death to gallop in and claim me.

Two blocks over, the southbound train whistle blew.

THREE

EXPERIMENT DAY 367: EFFECT

Apparency – Clear, understandable representation of the data.

Carter Westerly woke to a pudgy, little gremlin standing on his chest and licking his face. Ears forever perked with interest, the ebony fur-ball tilted his head and greeted our guest with a welcoming yip. His entire backside wagged in delight.

"Hello there," Carter rasped to his new friend, scratching the French Bulldog behind the ears while his own heavy lids fell shut again.

"That's Batdog," I offered from my cross-legged perch on the window seat. Balancing a plate on the palm of one hand, I expertly maneuvered a set of chopsticks with the other. I pinched a strip of thinly sliced raw tenderloin, dropped it on my tongue, and made yummy noises while I happily chewed.

Much to Batdog's disappointment, Carter rolled to the side and pushed himself up on one elbow. My poor pooch was left with no choice but to leap to the floor before getting squished. He punctuated his discontent with a potent and lingering dog fart.

"Where's Harper? Is my family safe?" Carter demanded, lip twitching back in an agitated sneer.

"Who?"

"Harper, my niece you threatened so I would submit and bow to you," he hissed.

Feeling my eyes widen, I blinked rapidly to maintain my cool façade. The majority of the night before was a blur to me … however, seeing as it resulted in the desired outcome, I was trying not to overthink the how or why. "She's fine. I never intended to harm any member of your family. Just wanted to put on a convincing show for the crowd." The lie flowed smoothly, made more believable by my silent vow to check on the status of this niece of his the first chance I got.

Dragging a hand over the rough stubble of his chin, Carter scanned his surroundings. Whatever he was anticipating waking up to, I highly doubt it included hardwood floors, craftsman style accents, or furniture that enveloped you like a cloud of comfort the moment rump met cushion. Odd as it may sound, it was the same home that had once belonged to my parents. A renovation overhaul had to be completed from top to bottom before I could step into the space and not be haunted by the grisly ghosts of the past. Although freakishly morbid, my bedroom was the same room I died in. What better place to sleep than the place where I met the eternal night?

All right, maybe it's a little creepy. Still, it worked for me.

"No one I love has been killed, and I woke up to a vampire that's not feeding on me. Is it premature to hope you bought me as a sex slave?" Swinging his legs off the couch, Carter eased himself up to sitting. The front of his dress shirt fell open, teasing at the muscular torso beneath.

One bluish-black eyebrow lifting in mild interest, I popped another sliver of meat into my mouth. "Is that all you think you're good for? Food or a fuck? You may have some self-esteem issues."

"No, I just believe in playing to my strengths." Rubbing the heels of his hands into his eye sockets to grind away the grogginess from the sedative he didn't know he ingested, Carter paused to leer my way. "Wanna see?"

Lips screwed to the side, I considered it for about a half a second before setting my plate aside and wiping my hands on the front of my black yoga pants. "Okay," I relented with a casual lift of my shoulder, "let's go."

Carter grabbed the open sides of his shirt, moving into position to shrug it off, but hesitated. "All right, but right after that you have to tell me your name."

Sucking air through my teeth, I cringed. "Oh. You're one of *those*. Sorry, I'm out. I don't dig clingers."

"Shame," Carter feigned disappointment and let his hands fall to his knees. "I was about to fall in love."

"The unrequited kind," I mused to my plate of morsels I gathered back into my greedy hands. "Ain't that a bitch?"

Pushing off the couch, Carter slowly prowled the room in search of some clue that would help him decipher what was going on. Batdog shadowed his every step like the noble sentry to the estate he was. "Okay, no names. How about a general observation? That was quite a performance you put on at the auction. I definitely didn't expect to become your house guest after that. Fixture in your torture chamber of sexual deviance was more the vibe I was getting."

Swallowing down my last bite, I gifted him with a playful wink. "*Acting*, my good sir. It was all part of the rescue mission."

"Rescue?" His brows knitted together tight.

I unfolded my legs, stretching them out and wiggling my toes. "*Aw*, I know. No one likes to be the damsel in distress. But yeah, I totally white-knighted your ass out of there."

"I was in … peril?" Carter's tone lifted just enough at the end to make it a question.

"After those news broadcasts you did implicating vampires in that blonde girl's death?" Shoving off my pillow seat, I floated up onto my toes and stretched my arms wide over my head. "You might as well have tattooed '*Bite me, asshole*' on your neck. Although, if you *do* decide to do that, make sure the punctuation is right. One missing comma, and you come across as a pervert."

Turning in an abrupt about-face, Carter's arms fell to his sides, his shoulders sagging. "I consider myself a reasonably astute fella, but I have no idea what the hell is going on right now."

"You're overwhelmed with gratitude." I shrugged, the wide-neck of my oversized sweatshirt slipping off one shoulder. "It happens."

The lock of the front door clicked open, sending a soft night breeze tossing through the room. Micah Walker stepped into the foyer with an exhausted sigh. Dropping her satchel on the side table, she kicked off her hideous orthopedic shoes and strode into the living room we occupied still clad in her lab coat and scrubs.

Gaze flicking from me, to Carter, and back again, she wilted me with her glare. "You were supposed to wait for me. We agreed to talk to him together in case he freaked out. I thought after your little performance at the auction we agreed a more planned approach was necessary."

"I was going to freak out?"

"It was possible." Purposely avoiding Micah's judgmental glower, I chose to address Carter instead. "If you did, I had this move prepared to subdue you with a chopstick. It was going to be sweet."

One corner of his mouth tugged back in a half-grin. "I'm sorry to ruin your fun with my calm bewilderment."

"Ah, there's still time," I mused. Unable to prolong the wrath of Mics a moment longer, I met her stare head on. "I told you, I'm sorry about the auction. I truly don't know what came over me. Maybe it's a side effect of being dead. Even so, we achieved our goal, so I say we count it in the win column."

Crossing her arms over her chest, the corners of her mouth tugged into a frown. "His niece is fine, by the way. *I* checked."

Carter cleared his throat in a subtle reminder of my earlier declaration of the same.

"Now you have proof," I countered. "You were going to take the word of a dead chick? Damn, dude, babies born yesterday are marveling at your gullibility." Craning to see past Mics, I rerouted the conversation by sniffing the air. "Any chance you hit the butcher shop on the way home? I'm still starving. I mean, I'm not partial to the taste of human, but you two are starting to smell like a burger and fries."

Pursing her lips, Micah rolled her russet eyes. In another world, she could have been a Rastafarian goddess with her waist-length dreads, caramel complexion, and exotically beautiful features. In this one, she was a lab rat who had even *less* of a life than I did.

Get it? Because, technically, I'm dead. There's a little afterlife humor for ya, folks! What fun is being dead if you can't joke about it?

"If there's one thing you should know about Vinx, it's that she's a slave to her appetites. Hunger being the most prevalent and pushy one." Shrugging off her lab coat, she tossed it over the back of the gray and white striped over-stuffed arm chair.

"Beautiful and lacking inhibitions? I died at that auction, didn't I? This is Heaven." The moment the words slipped from his mouth, Carter held up a hand to halt us. "You know what? Don't tell me. Just let me have this."

Distracted from their banter by the hunger burning through my veins, I fixed my penetrating stare on Micah. She folded under it with a groan. "There's a bag in the hall. Steaks and a gallon of pig's blood. I hope it's fatty and goes straight to your ass."

"Me too! I'd be hot as hell with a thick J-Lo bootie." Arching my back to stick out my flat, white-girl butt, I sashayed toward the foyer to claim my second dinner.

"Carter, it's nice to meet you in person after all this time." Micah playfully swatted at me as I passed. "I apologize for my colleague. It seems a lack of couth is a side effect of the serum."

Eyes narrowing, Carter offered Micah his hand. "Your voice is familiar, but I don't believe I've had the pleasure."

"I'm Micah Walker, from the Yale Institute, Mr. Westerly. We've spoken on the phone several times." Taking his hand in hers, the two exchanged an all-business shake.

"Micah?" Flaxen brows disappearing into his hairline, Carter's head whipped in my direction. "Then this ... *she* is your pseudo-vamp? She looks so ... *real.*"

I probably should've been offended. Be that as it may, I had cracked open the pigs blood a beat beforehand and was currently licking a dollop of it off my finger. It was so good; I couldn't even pretend to care in the slightest what they were blathering about.

Cheeks reddening with pride, Micah beamed at his recollection of her accomplishment. "She is indeed. Would you like to examine her?"

The white Styrofoam container, full of nourishing slop, was halfway to my mouth when the offering up of my person gave me pause. "Not really in the mood for a probing, if that matters to anyone."

Ignoring my request, Micah caught his elbow and ushered Carter my way. "The news segments you've done on the vampire initiative have been explosive. They invited you into their fold, thinking they could entice you into running fluff pieces. Instead, you hinted at cover-ups and conspiracies. You were on the right track, Carter, and *that's* why they forced you underground."

Something flashed across Carter's features before I could slap a label on it. Whatever it was carried twinges of guilt.

Too caught up in her own ramble to notice, Micah gushed on, "Vinx's antics at the auction *proved* that your safety was of no concern to them. I believe that's because their ultimate goal was to silence you. With us, you can get your voice back! We can expose the truth to the world!"

"What you're suggesting is insanely dangerous." Forehead pinched with concern, Carter's jaw tensed. "How good is this mask of hers that you think she can pull it off?"

In a blur of speed no human eye could track, I sat down my blood—careful not to spill a drop—and lunged. Fangs lengthening from my gum-line, my forearms slammed into Carter's chest. I curled my fingers into the fabric of his shirt and rode him to the ground. Pinning him there, the tips of my incisors pressed to the pulse point in his neck with just enough pressure to dimple the skin without breaking through.

"No, no, it's convincing." Carter gulped at the ceiling. "Consider me convinced, and in need of a change of pants. I do feel the need to make the counterpoint, though, that you could be a vamp with a vendetta, looking to use my connections to break into the inner circle. How do I know I'm not getting played?"

I slid my knees on either side of his hips, sat up, and peered down at him. "Put your hand on my chest."

Without hesitation, he obliged.

"That's my tit. I meant over my heart."

"Your directions were unclear." With a devilish grin crinkling the corners of his eyes, he redirected his wandering digits. After an awkward beat, Carter dragged his tongue over his bottom lip. "I ... uh ... gotta say, I got more out of feeling you up."

"Give it a minute. Sometimes it takes a while." Flattening his palm, I pressed it harder to my breastbone.

"I've had nights like that," he deadpanned.

Beneath the fortress of my rib cage came a faint, barely detectable thump. "It's sluggish, and way too irregular to keep a normal human alive, but it's there."

Carter blinked up at me as if seeing me for the first time. His chest swelled with excitement—as did other parts south of the border I happened to be sitting on. "We could really do this. You could get us in. And, I know just what to do to have *them* seek *you* out, with the keys to kingdom in hand ..."

FOUR
EXPERIMENT DAY 2: CAUSE

Heuristic Technique - Any approach to problem solving, learning, or discovery that employs a practical method not guaranteed to be optimal.

V lad the Impaler.
    Prince of House Draculesti.
    Son of the Dragon.
First of the vampire bloodline.
Under his teachings and affliction blood meant not only life, but power.
This lesson was lost to me as archaic folklore, until I awoke with fire in my veins and my body revolting against me.

Lungs constricted in a vise grip of pain, my back arched off the table I was bound to, an anguished roar tearing its way from my throat.

"Vincenza, can you hear me?" a female voice bellowed all around me.

My head whipped in one direction, then another in search of my captor. I found her by the door—her skin the hue of melted caramel; her hair a wild mane of thick rope braids.

Eyes spastically twitching over her, I missed no detail or subtle nuance. She had a small, pink chicken pox scar above her lip. Her pores permeated with the enticing aroma of fear. A bead of perspiration dotted her temple, slowly streaking toward her jawline.

My gaze traveled down of its own accord, drawn to the steady pulse of her blood pumping through her veins. I could see it through her flesh, its strobe a magnetic invitation.

Fresh pain stabbed into my top teeth, red-hot pokers drilling to the bone. Mouth agape, I screamed at the ceiling as canine incisors gored their way through my gums, bursting forth in a frothy spray of saliva and blood.

"*What have you done to me?*" I shrieked, fighting against my restraints. "*You should have left me there to die!*"

"Miss Larow, do you know where you are?" the woman asked. Her professional façade was off-set by a thin gold hoop decorating the edge of her nostril. "We are in a lab at Yale University. I imagine you visited your mother here before?"

Chest rising and falling in frantic pants, my eyes rolled to take in all around me. She was right. It wasn't a hospital, but one of the labs my mother frequented. The domed observatory: whitewashed cement walls and cold, stainless fixtures and tables.

Perplexing as that information was, a spider in the corner diverted my attention. I could hear it chomping on a fly with the deafening ruckus of screws and bolts thrown into a blender.

I could draw only one conclusion from the evidence provided.

Monsters slaughtered my family with wild abandon, and now ... I was one of them.

Tears streamed down my cheeks in torrents, blurring my vision with a crimson haze.

"*Please, just kill me,*" I beseeched the stranger.

Swallowing hard, she approached me with measured steps. "Your body is undergoing changes, but this isn't the transformation you think it is. My name is Micah Walker, and I would very much like to explain to you what's happening … if you'll let me."

As I ground my teeth together, freshly sprouted fangs stabbed into my lower lip with a gush of coppery warmth.

"I *know* what is happening." I yanked one wrist up with all my might, breaking free from the metal cuff pinning my arm to the table. Rising on my elbow, I made short work of the remaining shackle. "And I will *not* become one of them. Either kill me or show me the sun. Either way, this ends now. *I will not become a monster!*"

Rounding my back, I bounded off the table and landed in a low, menacing crouch.

Despite her brave front, Micah stumbled back. One hand raised to halt my advance. "Okay, easy now. You see that yellow button by the door?"

Barely a twitch of my head, and I zeroed in on it.

"That opens up the dome ceiling. It's two thirty-three in the afternoon. If I hit that button, this whole room will be flooded with sunlight. If that's what you want, I'll do it. But *only* if you promise to listen to what I have to say afterwards."

"Afterwards I'll be a pile of ash," I snarled.

"Then I guess you have nothing to lose." Micah inched back a step, then another.

As her hand reached for the yellow button of impending doom, I squeezed my eyes shut. Silently, I prayed to be reunited with my family in a place of peace, far from the terrors of this world.

Overhead a motor whirred in flurry of clicks and grinding gears. The ceiling retracted, sliding down the sidewalls to open in a cavernous maw. Sunlight warmed my skin in what I thought would be the kiss of death. Shielding myself behind my arm, I braced for the pain … that never came.

Prying open one eye, I risked a peek. I turned my hand over in front of me, marveling at the sunlight radiated off my skin without harm. Every scar, freckle, and blemish was gone. What remained was porcelain vampirical perfection.

On my feet in a blink, I stared her down. "What have you done to me? What am I?"

Folding her hands in front of her, Micah tilted her head. "Up for listening now?"

Instinct curled my top lip from my teeth in a menacing threat. "*Talk!*"

Jerking at my demonic rasp, she hid her trembling hands in the pockets of her lab coat. "You didn't drink vampire blood. The hive that attacked your family left you for dead. When police arrived on the scene, a couple of the officers supportive of our cause contacted the lab. Your mother is behind what's happening to you now, Vincenza. You were injected with a serum she created. Without it, you would be dead."

The incessant drumming of her heart assaulted my senses. Hooking my hands behind my head, I shielded my ears with my forearms and folded to the ground. Blood-tinged tears dripped from my chin, painting the tile floor.

"Her miraculous development has dramatically decreased your organ functions. Your heart will only beat once or twice an hour, if that. Not enough to be detected by the most astute Nosferatu. You require less than ten percent of the oxygenation needed to sustain human life. To the outside world, you're a vampire freed from their aversions to sunlight and silver."

"*Shut up!*" I screamed, her every syllable stabbing into my brain. "*Why?* Why would you do this? I was *dead!* A rotting corpse on my way to oblivion! *Why did you drag me back?*"

Her footsteps clapped against the ground with a thunderous echo, each step jarring me to the bone. Stopping close enough for me to smell the nauseating stench of black coffee she drank to wash down red-pepper humus, Micah crouched beside me. Her voice dropped to a whisper that still resonated through my skull like a shout in a temple. "Your parents were part of an underground collation. They designed this serum to allow a chosen specimen to infiltrate vampire society and expose the truth behind their political propaganda."

I lunged without thinking. Seizing Micah by the throat, I lifted her from the ground with one hand. With an enraged scream ripping from my dying lungs, I slammed her against the wall hard enough to rattle her teeth.

"Why me?" I demanded, my face mere inches from hers.

"Your name was never mentioned as a potential candidate," she gasped, her fingers grappling to loosen my hold. "If your parents had their way ... this would have never come near you. But when they wheeled you into my lab ..."

I could feel the bird-like delicacy of her bones. One pulse of my hand and I would crush the life out of her. Somewhere deep within me, tendrils of darkness tempted me to give in to the chaos. Unable to trust myself, I dropped her to the ground in an unceremonious heap. Turning my back, I fought to regain control.

Micah panted to catch her breath, gazing upon me not with accusation, but compassionate understanding. "Kate and Robert meant the world to me. I couldn't let them down by letting you die."

Whirling on her, even I didn't recognize the throaty growl that rumbled from my chest. "*So, you turned me into a demon? Is that honoring their memory?*"

"What you're going through now?" Dragging her braids over one shoulder, Micah tipped her head to the side and pulled her lab coat away from her neck.

Instantly, I recoiled. The heat of her blood called to my chilled flesh with every palpitation.

"It was supposed to be me," Micah finished, seemingly oblivious to my pained reaction.

She held the pose, waiting for me to get over my own bullshit enough to notice the scars covering her neck. Ten sets of puncture wounds clustered near her jugular in a pattern that looked like the points of a star.

I knew those markings. They had been plastered over every news segment and magazine cover not that long ago.

"The Scarlett Star." Digging through the foggy mess of my muddled mind, I plucked her media moniker.

Jaw tightening, Micah let her braids swing back into place. "Daughter of a judge at a known vampire bar wearing red-lipstick and a low-cut top. The media said I was asking for it. Your mother and father took my side even when my own family shunned me for the scandal I caused and how it sullied my father's political aspirations. Your parents were good people. I owed it to them to save your life in whatever way I could."

A fresh wave of anguish slammed into me, driving me down on one hip. I could feel my bones hardening, the last of my pliable humanity morphing into unyielding stone.

"This ... was meant for you?" I panted, no actual breath leaving my stationary lungs.

"It was," she confirmed with a dip of her chin. Adjusting her position, she pulled a penlight from her pocket and shined it into my eyes. "But when I saw what they had done to all of you, I knew this calling wasn't meant for me. This pain you're feeling, Vincenza? It's temporary. The scars the vampires marred on your soul will last forever."

The light of her pen in the bright room expanded my pupils farther, allowing me to see every vein feeding her body and where her blood surged the strongest.

Shrieking at the torturous longing I couldn't comprehend, I curled into a ball and shielded myself behind my arms.

Micah hung back, granting me the mercy of space. "I was ready for this change. I prepared myself. Even so, I couldn't let you die. Now, *you* are the weapon of the rising revolution. I can use my knowledge and training to help you harness this, Vincenza. But first, you have to stop screaming."

FIVE
EXPERIMENT DAY 376: EFFECT

Falsification of a Statement – the inherent possibility that the statement can be proven wrong.

Scream for me, baby," the muscle-bound Viking growled. Catching his buxom human plaything by the waist, he wove his hand into her hair. Forcing her head back, he bared fang.

"Oh no!" she gasped as his razor-sharp teeth pierced her supple flesh with a deep thrust. Her weak protest quickly morphed to moans of pleasure, her long legs locking around his hips to pin him to her. "Oh … oh, yes!"

Clicking the pause button on the remote control, I spoke directly into the camera. "This is the exact kind of soft-porn villainization I'm talking about. *Humans* are responsible for creating these stereotypes of us and feeding that hype for their own entertainment purposes. Who, then, is the *real* victim in this hurtful misrepresentation?"

"You can't be serious!" the pasty-faced, NPI opposer bellowed, his scalp reddening under his horrible comb-over. "This quote-on-quote example you brought is a television show on a cable network. It's fluff in the face of serious issues! What we are talking about here is a complete integration of vampires into mainstream society without the benefit of registration of any kind. That's the equivalent of abolishing the sexual predators list and allowing deviants to work in schools, wear a badge, or even administer medications. It's not safe, and the human race needs to stand together for our own protection."

Elbows on the desk provided for our televised debate, I crossed my arms and tilted my head in the direction of the sweaty little man. "Comparing us to aberrant criminals? How do you justify making such a bold leap?"

"With centuries of murders, torture, and feedings!" he exploded, hopping in his seat as if suppressing the urge to leap onto the tabletop and douse me with holy water. "All of these vile acts have been committed under the teachings of your demonic demi-god, Vlad Draculesti. Your immortal *Lord Impaler*."

One corner of my mouth tugged back in a knowing smirk. "And no one has ever killed, maimed, or committed genocide in the name of Christ?"

"It's a sorry argument to use our history against us!"

"*Yes, it is!*" I vehemently agreed. "And yet that is *exactly* what humans subject us to. You fault us for the mistakes our kind has made in the past, mocking our deity without truly understanding his teachings. Meanwhile, you fetishize our culture and use it in your foreplay. Statistically speaking, human on human deaths outweigh vampire-on-human deaths twenty-three hundred to one. And why is that? Because humans take their passions too far, while when we pair with a human we focus on building a lasting relationship built on trust, safety, and security."

"*Humans you keep around for feeding and screwing!*" my opponent hollered, spittle bubbling in the corners of his mouth. "You're vicious killers!"

"My apologies to our viewers for that use of inappropriate language," the prim and poised moderator stated into the camera before fixing her critical gaze on the frothing conservative. "Mayor Donaldson, I again ask you to control these outbursts or we will have no choice but to conclude our debate."

Before his mouth could open to protest further, I leaned in and caught him with my narrowed gaze. "Show me proof. Where is the recorded documentation of these crimes you're accusing us of? I tell you what, while you hunt to find that, I will wander into any costume shop or Halloween store and snag a set of fangs and a gothic cape that misrepresent us as night prowling fiends. The so-called facts you are basing your viewpoint on are myths formulated by your own kind to make us these legendary creatures that go bump in the night. Thank you, for granting me more power than I can fathom. That said, you should know I can't turn into a bat, I spend as much time in front of the mirror as the next gal, and I enjoy a few extra shakes of garlic on my pasta. I'm not a monster, Mayor Donaldson. I am a vampire citizen who wants the same rights you take for granted."

"I'm afraid we are out of time for this segment," the moderator interjected. Pushing her glasses farther up the bridge of her nose with the tip of her index finger, she spoke directly to the camera. "When we return, we will be joined by representatives from the Environmental Protection Agency and the Center of Disease Control and Prevention to debate the benefits and risks of adding fluoride and vitamins to our public water system. We'll be right back after a message from our sponsor, Everlasting Beauty Cosmetics—get that flawless vampire look while your heart is still beating."

"*Annnnd* ... we're clear," the camera man directed, dropping his headphones around his neck for the break.

"Even the God damn *sponsor* is a vamp lover!" the troll of a mayor spat, shoving his chair back from the table.

"It was a pleasure to meet you," I called after him, my flat tone a statement to the contrary.

"Rot in hell, devil bitch." Striding away, his comb-over bouncing in the breeze, he flipped me off over his head.

"Sorry about him," the moderator said with a grimace. "You probably encounter intolerance like that all the time."

"I don't fit in to any crowd anymore," I admitted with a stark truthfulness, offering her a tight-lipped smile.

"If it makes you feel any better, you were amazing against him. He came across like a bigoted prick."

Leaning over the desk, I dropped my voice to a whisper. "I don't think that was an act."

Her head listed to the side and she gazed into my eyes, sinking into the dangerous waters of the titillating undead. I had watched it happen many times before. That and a public nudity display by a brazen barista were why I couldn't go back to my favorite coffee shop.

Lips parting in a breathy sigh, a ruddy blush filled her cheeks. "I hope he didn't tarnish your experience of being on the show. I'd *love* for you to ... *come* again."

"It would be my pleasure. Thanks again for having me." Unclipping my mic, I set it on the desk. Experience taught me in situations like this it was best to get some needed distance and fast. Unfortunately, my polite exit was thwarted by the randy reporter catching my wrist.

Draping herself across the desk, her heaving cleavage strained against the fabric of her blouse. "The subtle approach doesn't work with you. I like that. I'm not afraid to work for what I want. How's this: we go back to my dressing room and I let you bite me *wherever* you want?"

"Camelia, we're back in thirty," the cameraman said, trying to pretend he *wasn't* eavesdropping. The anxious sheen of sweat coating his brow and tightening of his trousers hinted otherwise.

Dropping fang, I gifted her with the full vampire thrill. Excitement shuddered through her, her nipples poking through the thin fabric of her silk button-down.

As I dragged my tongue over the tip of one jagged tooth, I let my stare wander the length of her. "You deserve more than thirty seconds of rushed ecstasy, Camelia. Enjoy the rest of your show. I'm sure we'll see each other again."

Leaving her marinating in her own desire, I sauntered off set with my heels clicking against the cracked and peeling linoleum.

Carter met me at the door. Wisps of blond hair fell across his forehead as he shook his head with a mock pout. "Did I just lose my top spot of available options when you decide to take a human *luv-ah*?"

I froze the second the door clicked shut behind me. "Wait, we aren't sleeping together?" Staring at the wall, I narrowed my eyes. "Huh. Who the hell was that guy, then?"

"Cute. You were fantastic up there, by the way. Not that you need me to tell you that." Resuming our stride, we headed back down the narrow hall that led us in.

Pausing at the coatrack, I grabbed my black trench coat and tossed it over my arm. "Thank you, but I can't take the credit. That guy was a moron, and I had a diligent coach who drilled me day and night—only not in the fun way."

Hiking one flaxen brow, Carter pressed his index finger to his lips. "I was trying to pay you a compliment, and now anything I say in response will end up sounding filthy. Happy to help you cram? Totally vulgar."

"Screw vamp strength, inappropriate innuendos are my true gift." Dragging my fingers through the silky tresses of my chin-length bob, I battled looming exhaustion from waiting too long between feedings. And by too long, I mean it had been a whole forty-five minutes. "Remind me why facing off with that horrid little man on a public broadcast channel was beneficial to our cause? Seems to me we need a geyser of media attention, not this puny little trickle."

Carter cast his stare down the hallway in one direction, then the other, and stepped in close enough for me to smell the hint of copper from where he cut himself shaving that morning. "Vamp society keeps their finger to the pulse of all aspects of the media, monitoring their budding reputation without fail. What you did today was show them there's a fresh face in vampire politics. One brilliant, beautiful, and ready to be plucked."

"It always comes back to *plucking* with you," I mused just as my phone vibrated in the pocket of my coat.

"That would be them." Carter nodded at the buzzing phone with a victorious grin.

"Or Micah. I used the coconut oil she cooks with to get a bur out of Batdog's fur. She's going to be pissed when she finds those little black hairs in the jar. Not going to lie, I was kind of hoping to be there to see that." Digging the device from the confines of the fabric, I clicked it to life and pressed it to my ear. "Hello?"

"Good evening, may I speak to Vincenza Larow, please?" a commanding voice, smooth as warm maple syrup, requested.

"This is Vincenza."

"Miss Larow, my name is Rau Mihnea. I am the head of the coalition striving to get the Nosferatu Presumption of Innocence Bill passed. I just watched your debate and was compelled to contact you with accolades for an exceptional performance. The vampire community is fortunate to have you on our side."

Tapping me on the shoulder, Carter mouthed, *Who is it?*

"Why thank you, *Mr. Mihnea.*" I pointedly said his name to answer the question of my blatant eavesdropper. "I appreciate the show of support."

Carter's eyes bulged, his jaw swinging slack as he did a little dance on the balls of his feet. *Rau Mihnea?* he lipped.

Nodding in confirmation, I redirected my attention to what was happening on the other end of the line.

"We are always on the lookout for fresh voices to further our cause." Papers shuffled, accompanied by the click of a pen. "Tell me, have you ever been to a rally? We are marching in Washington DC next week to raise awareness for our agenda. I would be honored to have you join us."

Beside me, Carter leapt into an impromptu game of charades. Lips curled back from his teeth, he held up his hands like claws. When that only earned a confused scowl from me, he tried again. Shielding the lower half of his face behind his bent elbow, he wiggled his eyebrows. Scratching my head, I shrugged. In a final attempt, he mimed a pregnant belly then gestured outward with one hand in a wide wave from the region of his crotch.

"Mr. Mihnea, can you hold for one minute? I'm about to go through a tunnel and don't want to lose you." Muting the phone, I blinked in Carter's direction. "What the hell are you doing?"

"That's Rau Mihnea!" he gushed. "The one and only son of Vlad Draculesti. *His dad is friggin' Dracula!*"

Maintaining slightly exasperated eye contact with my giddy side-kick, I unmuted Rau. "Mr. Mihnea, I would love to join you. Would it be possible for me to bring a friend?"

"*Bring a friend?*" Carter hissed in an urgent whisper. "What is this? A ten-year old's pajama party? *Why would you ask that?*"

"Bring as many as you would like," Rau chuckled. "The more bodies moving on Washington, the better. I'll get with you later in the week with the details."

"Fantastic! The invitation is very kind of you."

"Did he say yes?" Carter pried, practically bouncing where he stood. "Micah's stupid. Take *me!*"

Slapping in his general direction, I turned my back to him in attempt to keep an iota of my professionalism intact. "Do you need my email or contact information?"

Rau guffawed, the boom of his laughter causing me to pull the phone away from my ear. "I do so enjoy interacting with young ones such as yourself who have yet to learn the extent of vampirism. Have no fear, *infans*, we can *always* find our own."

Statement looming with the threat of a shark's dorsal fin breaking the surface of still waters, the line went dead.

Pocketing my phone, I turned to Carter with my folded hands pressed to my lips. "It seems the vampires are going to Washington."

He puffed out his cheeks and exhaled through pursed lips. "I have never been more terrified of being right in my entire life."

SIX

EXPERIMENT DAY 33: CAUSE

Hindsight Bias – The inclination after an event to see the outcome as being predictable despite objective basis.

The two police officers sent to teach me basic self-defense moves stood in the corner of the lab, whispering to Micah. All three of their concerned gazes shifted my way. After forty-five minutes of prodding, they still hadn't lured me from the floor. Sitting with my legs tucked tight to my chest, I pressed my forehead to my knees and let everything around me meld into monotone white-noise. How long I sat like that, I couldn't say. Time became irrelevant when I woke up, lost in a world I no longer fit into.

"Vincenza?" Micah's voice was muddled, as if I had truly sunk to the depths of despair with its weight crushing in from all sides. "Can you look at me?"

My head rose like a leaden anchor. Blinking Micah's way, I tried to focus on her blurring silhouette as she knelt beside me.

"Our boys in blue say your training didn't go well today. Why do you think that is?"

"Not a vampire," I murmured, my tongue thick and swollen.

"That's right. You're not. But you *are* a being with strength, reflexes … and *needs*."

Sensing where this conversation was headed, I placed one palm on the floor and scooted in a half circle to turn my back on her.

"You haven't eaten anything in days."

"I can't stomach regular food."

"We talked about this. There are alternatives we can try. You just have to be open to it."

Deficient of the strength to argue, my only response came in the form of my head dropping back to my knees.

"Vinx." Micah edged in closer. The fact that she smelled as enticing as Thanksgiving dinner made my empty stomach roll with revulsion. "We can work on this. Let's find a solution."

"No." My voice came muffled within the cocoon of my arms. "I'm not an experiment."

Silly little pseudo-vamp. That's exactly what you are.

Micah fell silent, seemingly choosing her next words with careful deliberation. When she opened her mouth to speak, her tongue clucked against the roof of her mouth. "I didn't want it to come to this. I really didn't. But I'm afraid you've left me with no choice."

Pulling a pair of surgical scissors from the pocket of her lab coat, she dragged their point across her palm. Flesh split in a shallow crevice bubbled with drops of ruby.

I watched her blood drip on the linoleum with mild interest. "The palm is a stupid place to cut yourself. That's going to crack back open every time you move your fingers."

Without a word, she extended her hand to me in offering.

She expected … what? A sudden loss of control and building frenzy?

"I am *not* a vampire," I clarified yet again, and folded in on myself.

"No, you're not." Disappointment sagging her tone, Micah pulled a handkerchief from her pocket and wrapped it around her hand. "You're a college girl who has been trapped in a lab for a month, sleeping on a cot in the breakroom. It's time we changed that, get you back among the living."

But I'm not living. *I'd fit in better in a graveyard.*

"The Yale labs acquired facilities we're going to use as our own little dormitory," Micah explained. "Part of it was designed with you in mind. While construction isn't quite done, it would do you good to get out of here for a while. What do you say? You up for a field trip?"

Head lolling to the side, I peered her way in between heavy blinks. "At this new place ... do I have to sleep in a coffin?"

The corner of her mouth twitched in an almost smile. "No, but you *do* have to ride in a car with UV tempered glass to keep up appearances." Grabbing my arm, Micah helped me up on unsteady legs. Hit by a heady whiff of my pungent funk, her nose crinkled. "*Whoa*, how about a shower first? I think bathing is the only thing you've held out on longer than food. You smell like sour milk poured on a shitty diaper."

OF ALL THE vampire lore I wished were true, there was none more so than the absence of a reflection. Fresh from the shower, which offered temporary relief from the constant chill of my flesh, I stared at the stranger in the mirror with unbridled loathing.

The blonde girl with an easy smile that met me at every reflective surface had vanished. In her place stood a black swan of threatening elegance. Any trace of who I had been was wiped away like steam from the mirror.

The scar above my lip from when I fell off my bike as a kid.

The shamrock tattoo on my hip I hid from my parents.

The evidence from where my throat had been ripped open by vicious beasts.

All ... *gone.*

Something in the transition stained my hair a deep, inky black. Unable to get all the matted blood out of it, Micah resorted to cutting my tresses into a blunt, chin-length bob. Turning my head one way then the other, I sucked in my cheeks. Maybe starvation was to blame for my gaunt appearance, but my features seemed sharpened to a deadly edge. The look in my eye more feral. Every inch of me was an enigma, even to me.

When it came down to it, there was only one thing I knew for *certain* about the new girl staring back at me: she was born into this world under a shroud of blood and chaos.

MOONLIGHT REFLECTED OFF the thin layer of snow and ice covering the ground. Tree branches, naked of their leaves, slashed at the night sky like wrathful demonic claws. Street lights changed from red to green, guiding forth the quests of the living. Televisions flickered inside homes, spewing images of a happy, safe, cotton candy world. Diner workers slopped greasy comfort food onto heaping plates for hungry patrons that figured the health of their hearts to be tomorrow's problem. With every image that blurred past the car window, I became more aware of how life pressed on, while I remained locked in the purgatory of my own displaced uncertainty.

The click of a gun chamber being loaded and locked, pulled my attention from the window to where Micah sat beside me. One of her seemingly endless supply of minions acted as our chauffer in this mad charade.

"I don't want you to be alarmed," Micah explained, her hand curling around the grip. "No. You know what? Fuck that. Be alarmed. I have loaded this tranquilizer gun with enough juice to neutralize an entire herd of elephants. So, if you start feeling froggy, know that I can and *will* shoot you."

Dragging my gaze from the gleaming metal to her face, I blinked my detached confusion. "Why would I feel froggy?"

Micah dropped the gun into her lap, mouth swinging open like a loose screen door in her search for the proper words. "Vinx, do you not recognize where we are? This street should look familiar to you."

Glancing back out the tinted window, I watched the row of houses parade by. "Looks like about a million streets just like it across the country. Cookie cutter homes filled with toys and trinkets to distract us from a world slowly imploding in on itself."

"When this is over, you should look into becoming a motivational speaker," Micah jabbed. Dragging her tongue over her lower lip, she added, "At the risk of being the catalyst that sets you off ..."

"You want to use the gun," I interrupted. "I can smell your rush of endorphins and estrogen when you grasp it. It borders on a sexual high."

"That's ... invasive." Clearing her throat, Micah sought to reclaim an ounce of her floundering professionalism. "As I was saying, you may want to take another look. This is the street you grew up on. Your parents' house is on the next block."

Only when she pointed it out, did clarity cut through my numb fog. There was the sidewalk I learned to ride my bike. That was the massive oak tree that was always "safe" when the neighborhood kids played tag. The yellow colonial-style house on the left had belonged to Jake Thomas' family. He was my first kiss, freshmen year after the homecoming dance. The stop sign we were idling up to had been the scene of my fender-bender when I borrowed the Buick without asking. All were memories from another life, when my heart beat with more than a sporadic, lethargic lurch.

"Why would memory-soaked real estate agitate me?"

Micah's face folded with confusion. "I don't know, Tin Man. Maybe because the grisly scene of where their family's death occurred would gut a normal person. For someone who protests she's not a vampire, you sure as hell aren't acting human."

Was I supposed to protest? What would be the point? She was right. I was nothing.

"Compelling counterpoint," Micah interjected into my vacant silence. "I do feel obligated, though, to point out that you may feel different when we get inside. You being legally dead, your parents' house was left to the Yale Science and Quantitative Reasoning Labs. We really *are* turning it into dormitories specifically for our secret operation—aka, you. That said, if it's too much for you to stay there I will happily take the big-ass suite we designed with you in mind."

"Thank you," I muttered. The sentiment wasn't heartfelt, but I knew it was expected.

Micah ground her teeth together, frustration building. "Look, I get that you're stuck in this broody, melancholy loop. Even so, when we get inside, you may find yourself facing some bottled-up emotions. You need to embrace them, Vinx. Because if you starve, the vampires who killed your family win. Don't give them that. When we get there ... *try.* Try to feel something."

"Because you really want to shoot me?" A flick of my head tossed a rogue strand of hair from my eyes.

Filling her lungs, Micah's shoulders sagged with mock revelation. "God help me, I really do."

As the car turned into the driveway, gravel crunching under the tires, I tipped my chin to take in the craftsman-style two-story. In the dark, it looked as I remembered. But inside, true horror had forever tainted what it once was.

Just like me.

"I'll try not to disappoint you," I murmured to the night.

Pushing open the car doors, Micah and I ventured inside. Any similarity to the Casa de Larow I knew ended at the door. No trace of our lives there, or the hellish events that unfolded, remained. The foyer wall that divided the entryway from the dining room had been knocked out, welcoming us into an open concept kitchen and eating area. The furniture still had the tags on it. Freshly installed reclaimed pine flooring had yet to earn a scuff or footprint. Wandering inside, I dragged my fingers over the white and gray speckled granite countertops and surveyed the espresso cabinetry. "My parents were going to have the kitchen redone. White cabinets with butcher block counters."

"You doing okay?" Micah asked with a scientist's interest.

Head floating in clouds of detachment, I turned to face her, my hands falling limp to my sides. "I'm sorry, Mics. There's nothing here for me. Not anymore."

Chewing on her lower lip, I could see her plugging in various figures trying to solve my perplexing equation. "Then, I guess there's no reason you can't stay here. Come on. I'll show you to your room."

Dutifully, I fell into step behind her. Pausing over the exact spots where my family members had fallen, I waited to feel *something*. To have my heart shredded at the loss of them, just so I knew the infernal muscle still worked.

Nothing.

My prison of emptiness refused to crack.

In attempt to spur some form of emoting, I narrated as I walked. "My father was the first to die. The largest of the Nosferatu punctured his jugular. He bled out right here. Jeremy fell there, after having his neck snapped by a black vampress. My mother retrieved the gun under the table …" My throat tightened for a split second, the feeling passing in a blink before I could name it. "She fired two shots and took down one of the vamps before she was attacked. The scrawny vampire chased me up these stairs. He grabbed my ankle here. I felt his fangs graze the back of my leg. Somehow, I kicked him off me and made it to the attic."

No sooner did I step into the redesigned attic space, then Micah spun on me.

"Oh my God, you have to stop!" Tears zigzagged over her cheeks, raining down on the plush, newly installed carpet. "You made your point, you're a heartless *ghoul*! Believe it or not, I *cared* about these people! They were good to me when my own family treated me like dog shit. Stop rehashing the details of their deaths like a fucking crime scene investigator!"

"You don't think I'd cry if I could? My soul is *screaming* to mourn for them, but I can't even muster the emotions."

Two blocks over, a train whistle blew.

An audible reminder of the moment of my death.

External silence preempted the monsoon of stopped up emotion crashing in from all sides. All the grief, the hate, and the loathing flooded in. The spigot tapped and gushing.

Venturing farther into the renovated oasis, I located the spot forever stained by my stolen essence. Red-tinged tears blurred my vision, my voice choked from my anguish-constricted throat. "This is where the boy I thought I loved attacked me. He leaned over my crumpled body to lick my blood off another vampire's face. I invited him into my life, and he destroyed it." Flames of rage ignited in my core, threatening to consume me. Dropping fang, my gaze swiveled to Micah. "You want me to be your weapon? Fine. But *only* if I get to find and kill each and every one of the monsters responsible for killing my family."

Free hand closing around the grip of the tranquilizer gun, Micah brought her sliced palm to her mouth, and tore the bandage off with her teeth. "Seems to me if that's your goal you need to eat."

I was on her in a blink, cracking open her wound with the tip of my fang before closing my mouth over it and drinking deep.

That exuberance lasted a fraction of a second.

Gagging, I pulled back. It took three hard swallows to force down the rusty taste in my mouth. "That's …"

How do you tell someone they taste terrible without offending them?

"… an acquired taste. Can we try *literally* anything else?"

Clicking off the safety, Micah pressed the tranquilizer gun to my temple. "Vampires drink blood, and we need you to be convincing. We will find you something more appealing when your strength is up. But for now … *try again.*"

"This dynamic shifted quickly." Lip curling in disgust, I did as directed and bowed my head.

SEVEN

EXPERIMENT DAY 383: EFFECT

Placebo – A substance or treatment with no active therapeutic effect.

H ow exactly do we have access to a private jet?" Running my hands over the armrests of my seat, I wriggled my butt farther into the supple white leather cushion.

"Our benefactors have deep pockets," Micah muttered, not looking up from the tablet she was toiling over.

"My chair is squishy. Is your chair squishy?" I asked Carter, a jolly lilt of excitement bubbling through my tone.

Before he could answer, Micah let her tablet fall to her lap and glared up at me with a potent dose of judgmental side-eye. "Vincenza, we have a job to do. Could you try to focus please?"

"*You* have a job to do," I corrected. "*I* am dead. Funny how that shifted my priorities. Did you know I was valedictorian? Was on the dean's list all four semesters of college I survived. I was driven. Really going places. Now? Now, I'm doing this." Pushing off the wall, I spun my chair in a circle. "Wheeeeeee!"

Snorting with laughter, Carter hid his smirk behind his hand. Micah's scowl snapped his way. "Don't encourage her."

"I'm pretty sure she needs no encouragement," he chuckled.

I tossed him a wink, then treated myself to a second twirl.

Unbuckling her seatbelt, Micah closed the distance between us and caught my chair before I could go for the triple-rotation. "We are about to step into a den of vipers. Can you at least *pretend* to take this seriously?"

Dropping fang, I tipped my chin to snarl up at her from under my brow. "The captain hasn't turned off the fasten seatbelt sign. You should take your seat."

We held each other's stare for a beat, waiting for the other to break.

Micah was the first to crack, a smile curling up the corners of her mouth.

"You're an asshole." Laughing, she patted my cheek and returned to her chair. "But, God help me, I love ya."

"We're headed to vamp territory." I gazed out the window, watching the Washington DC skyline swell beneath us. "I believe prayers like that should be offered up to *Vlad*."

"Very true." Planting his heels in the lush eggshell carpet, Carter leaned over me to marvel at the landscape ... and, most likely, try to sneak a peek down my blouse. "The second the wheels of this plane hit the ground, we need to be all Team Vamp all the time. Their mission is our mission."

My shoulders sagged, and I slapped him with an exasperated glance. "Three hundred and eighty-three days, that's how long I've had every detail of the vampire agenda drilled into my head. If I don't have it by now, I'm not going to get it."

Filling her lungs to capacity, Micah exhaled through flared nostrils. "There had to be a more uplifting way to word that."

"Breathe, Mics," I lobbed back with a carefree shrug. "We got this."

Oh, how wrong I was ...

LIPS CURLING FROM my teeth, I let myself be jostled through the stifling crowd. Shoulder to shoulder, smelling the farts and funk of strangers, I moved with the masses toward the raised platform which marked the first official stop of the rally.

Holding on to my elbow so she didn't lose me in the crowd, Micah yelled to be heard over the buzz of the excited horde, "The event kicks off with a speech by Rau Mihnea. Then, we start the march up Constitution Avenue to the Supreme Court and Capitol Building. Along the way there will be historic exhibits and speakers."

Face white-washed of emotion, I blinked in her direction. "But is there cotton candy? Because that's really the only reason I'm here."

"Did someone mention cotton candy?" Carter asked, randomly clapping at whatever the announcer leaving the platform had said. "I could totally go for some spun sugary goodness right now."

Eyebrows raising to my hairline, I stared Micah's way, waiting for her to validate our unified craving. Instead, she groaned and rolled her eyes skyward. "I shouldn't have to say this to two grown-ass people, but ... if you're good, and we see a vendor, I will get you some."

"Score!" I crowed. Following suit with the crowd, I applauded a smoldering silver-fox that took the stage. He wore blue jeans, but in an ironic way that made me think the fabric had never touched his skin before. The top two buttons of his shirt hung open, a thin smattering of black and silver chest hair visible beneath. The look was topped off by a navy-blue blazer with the collar popped. Combine that with his *come and get me* smirk, and it didn't matter what age you were—if you enjoyed the male form, you were digging his vibe.

"Look at all of these beautiful faces," the speaker drawled into his microphone; the hint of an accent I couldn't place added a bit of flavor to his timbre. "So many of you pouring out to support our cause. And it is *ours*, isn't it? All vampires can trace our lineage back to Vlad Draculesti, of House Dracule, can't we? We pay reverence to him as the first of our kind." Pacing the stage with casual ease, he made eye contact with as many of his listeners as he could. "*I am the sole being to wander this planet that would ever know him as *Papa*."

A shocked gasp rippled through the crowd as it registered who the man speaking *truly* was.

"Vlad had only one child. Mihnea cel Rau ..." The speaker dragged his hand over his chin, offering us a beguiling grin. "Flipping my first and last name was a convenience to all those who were brutalized attempting that pronunciation."

"That's Rau Mihnea?" I asked, leaning in to Micah as the crowd tittered with polite laughter.

"Sure is." Chewing on the inside of her cheek, Micah scanned the twenty-something age girls beside us as they fanned themselves and practically swooned. "I don't know how politically charged they are, but he's got a large portion of this crowd itching to be liberated from their drawers."

Nodding his appreciation to the audience, Rau continued. "My father was a good man, no matter what others may claim. He sacrificed everything to keep his family and his kingdom safe. What he became because of it ..." swallowing hard, he wet his lips, "he loathed to the depths of his soul. I loved and admired my father, and longed to stay by his side for the rest of eternity. Even so, Papa wouldn't hear of turning me. That is how deeply he despised the monster within him. He sent me away to a monastery run by Father Van Helsing, that I may be raised far from his curse."

If I had to guess, there had to be close to a million bodies crammed into the Capitol. All fell silent while Rau unburdened his soul.

"It was the finest sliver of a margin of vampires that were willing to go against the whims of Vlad, I can tell you that." Looping one thumb in the front pocket of his jeans, Rau sauntered from one corner of the platform to the other. "I searched far and wide for most of my human life, getting rejected time and time again. My luck changed when I found one of father's cast-offs in an alley, practically starving. Her conscience weighed so heavy on her that she couldn't bring herself to feed. Unfortunately, it had been so long since she'd eaten she appeared more monster than eternal beauty that comes to mind when we think of the Nosferatu. I have no doubt that others viewed her as a beast. To me, she was an angel of mercy who bestowed me with the gift my tortured soul yearned for. The night I awoke, my transformation complete, I rushed to Papa's side to regale him with the news." Lifting his chin to the crowd, blood-tinged tears filled the vampire lord's eyes. "My father … wept. So broken was he that his only son had become the same type of immortal anomaly as he, that Vlad stopped eating. Since that day, he has slept in stone back home in Romania, watched and protected by his Magi. *He* is my inspiration for the Nosferatu Presumption of Innocence Bill. For *him*, I want to remove the stigma accompanying the vampire title. I want to create a new reality, one in which we can prosper and be proud of what we are. Then, I will wake my father and welcome him to the new world *we* have created for him."

Thunderous applause and a chorus of catcalls seconded that proclamation.

"That said," Rau queried the throng, "how do we do that? Well, brothers and sisters, our demands are simple ones. Today, we march for equal rights! To be able to protect our country by our service in the military. To vote for our elected officials, or be able to hold office ourselves. To be protected from discrimination by government backed legislation. To be safe from violent oppression. And, to enjoy the same equal housing opportunities that so many citizens take for granted. Ours are not lofty demands, my friends. They are morsels of humanity that we shouldn't be denied simply because of our cultural differences."

A second round of hoots and applause.

"With each step of this march," Rau bellowed over the smothering noise, "we must steel our spines with pride and conviction, acknowledging that we are not inflicted, but atoned from a society that chooses to paint us as frenzied monsters. For too long we have been held back by the misconceptions of the masses. Today, we scream for the world to truly *see* us." Throwing his free arm out wide, Rau's head fell back. His deep tremor boomed to the heavens, "Forget your stereotypes and constricting labels! This is me! Take me as I am, for I will accept you just the same." His hands fell to his sides with a slap, and he slowly raised the mic to his lips, giving the audience a chance to simmer in the potency of his message. "My brothers and sisters, we march today for a better tomorrow. Now, without further ado, I invite you all to take a walk with me that will resonate through history."

Wrapping her scarf in a second loop around her neck, Micah crossed her arms over her chest and ran her hands up and down the arms of her wool coat to fight off the evening chill. "The orchestration of this entire endeavor is really quite impressive. Even down to planning this during the Winter Solstice—the shortest day of the year. The sun setting at five pm allows the vamps to be out at a prime marching time to effect the flow of end-of-the-day traffic. Brilliant strategizing, really."

"Shut the hell up!" Carter yelped, clapping a hand over his mouth.

Pursing her lips, Micah gave him a fraction of a second to take that back before she checked him.

"Not you," Carter clarified. "Rau! He's coming over here. He sees us, and he is *definitely* walking in this direction. Oh … my … God. I may vomit." Raising both hands in front of him, he turned them over as if hoping an answer was written somewhere on his skin. "What do I normally do with my hands? Do they just hang at my sides? That doesn't seem right. I can't remember proper hand protocol. There's a chance I'm freaking out."

"A chance?" Micah countered with a snort.

"I had no idea he was a Rau groupie. Did you?" I asked, bumping Micah's elbow with mine.

"Not a clue." Mics shook her head, braids swaying beneath her knit cap. "Had I, I wouldn't have done anything different. This may be one of my favorite things *ever*."

Rau woven through the crowd, shaking hands and greeting attendees until he landed directly in front of me with his hand extended in welcome. "Miss Larow. I am so happy you made it. Your debate last week was truly inspired."

He was flanked by a trio of bodies that stood shoulder to shoulder in an impenetrable wall behind him. Their gazes remained on a constant swivel for any and all potential threats.

"The pleasure's all mine!" I said, a few decibels louder than necessary. Taking his hand, I tugged him in close to whisper, "I don't mean to alarm you, but you're being followed. Blink twice if you need me to create a diversion so you can escape."

Rau's head fell back in a chuckle. Clapping his other hand over the back of mine, he gave a gentle squeeze of appreciation. "You are a delight, Vincenza. May I call you by your given name?" At my nod, he pressed on. "These are the triplets, my ever-attentive security detail."

"How do you tell them apart?" Carter deadpanned, lips pinched tight in eager anticipation of the laugh he was *certain* his comment would earn.

Clearing his throat, Rau blinked Carter's way while wearing a mask of stoicism. "It's quite simple really. One is a muscular Caucasian male, one a mountainous black man, and the other an Asian woman that I believe to have once been a trained assassin. But, if I forget that, I put a different color dot on each of their foreheads so I don't mix them up."

The most painfully awkward silence *ever* followed.

Breaking the hush with a heart-felt boom of laughter, Rau chucked Carter's shoulder with the side of his fist. "Having a bit of fun with you, of course. This Asian beauty is Elodie, the pale fellow is Thomas, and my enormous friend here is Duncan. And, *you* would be Carter Westerly. It is good to see you up and around. I heard about the struggles you endured. There is no stronger man than he who prevails over adversity."

Adversity? Your kind locked him up and tried to sell him to the highest bidder, I thought, keeping my jaw locked tight before the accusation tumbled from my lips unchecked. *Save the considerate act for someone that* doesn't *know you're a parasite.*

Glancing to Carter, I expected his outrage over that comment to trump my own. To my surprise and confusion, something closely resembling guilt flashed across his face.

"I'm doing much better. Thank you," he mumbled, a hot blush spreading from his neck up to his earlobes.

Throwing his arms out wide, Rau turned on Micah as if she were the prodigal child returning.

"And Micah Walker." Stepping forward, he cradled her face between his palms. Eyes bulging, Mics froze. In my mind, I watched the interaction play out like an uneasy antelope being licked by a lion.

"I see you, Micah," Rau rambled in a hushed whisper. "And I am honored to have you here after the hell you endured. The fact that you would even consider coming out in support of the NPI Bill is a true testimony to your character. You give me hope, of the kind of open-minded acceptance that mankind is capable of. Know that."

"Thanks." Micah's lips were puckered into fish lips by the heels of Rau's hands.

"Uh, Lord Mihnea?" Duncan injected, his hands clasped behind his billboard-sized back. "She was brutalized by ten vampires. Squeezing her face might be off-putting to the girl."

"Oh, of course! My apologies." Rau released Micah as if worried his touch had scorched her. "The security detail is just a rouse. The real job of my triplets is to keep me from committing this kind of social faux pas."

Polite chuckles fizzled through our little huddle while the crowd around us swelled and churned with the flow of their political current.

"Before I get the opportunity to embarrass myself further, I should join the march." Rau turned on the ball of his foot, his inviting smile oozing charisma. "It would be my privilege to have the three of you at my side."

I would have filled my lungs with a calming breath, if those sluggish lumps of tissue rattling around my ribcage were capable of such an act. As it was, I took my cue from Micah, who stepped forward with her head held high. "Lord Mihnea, shadowing you is *exactly* why we're here."

"**OUR FANGS ARE** not a movie prop! Exploiting vamps needs to stop!"

"Our fangs are not a movie prop! Exploiting vamps needs to stop!"

Over and over the crowd chanted, waving their signs that screamed *Freedom for Fangs, Undead Lives Matter, Back the Vamp*, and any other cute catch phrase they could think up.

Ever the belle of the ball, Rau marched down the center of Constitution Avenue, smiling and waving to the reporters and spectators watching along the route. The first tent our horde passed was one with treasured historical artifacts encased in glass. The crowning jewel of the display was the chest plate of Vlad Draculesti, engraved with a dragon, its thick neck arced to strike. Microphone in hand, a human Barbie doll acted as tour guide for the historical sampling.

"History calls Vlad the Impaler." Tour Guide Barbie beamed as if her face was frozen that way. "In reality, he was the ruler of Wallachia—a region of Romania. It was his job to protect his people from the Ottoman Empire. And, I don't mean the furniture, folks. This isn't a Disney movie."

The people clustered in the tent chuckled, while the triplet I now knew as Elodie huffed her contempt.

"Let them make a joke like that about Christians and the streets would run red with blood," she grumbled, tossing glossy black bangs from her eyes.

Hmmm ... was that a hint of dissention in the ranks? Seems to me someone needs to fan the flames of those smoldering embers of contempt.

As we continued our march, the tour guide's droning faded behind us. "Here, we have the clay goblet from which Vlad drank the blood of the demon, Orlok, which led to him rising as history's very first vampire."

"Check out the human getting the *Donator Tresâ*." I jerked my chin toward a brunette seated in the booth we were sauntering past. "Think she has any idea what that actually means?"

Perched on a high stool, the girl in question held perfectly still while a thin strip of black leather was braided into the hair at her right temple by nimble vamp fingers. At the end of the decoration, a lone raven feather was fixed to swing just above her shoulder blade.

"Are you kidding?" Elodie mused with a humorless laugh, her thin lips pinched tight. "To her, that's just a pretty accessory to show her support for a cause she couldn't begin to understand."

"Where as those of us who have taken the time to educate ourselves know that the *Donator Tresâ* was a symbol of the Wallachia people after Vlad's transformation," Micah interjected, critical gaze fixed on the demonstration. "It showed their support for the yolk he took up to protect them all. By wearing it, they were offering up their blood to help fuel his immortal conquest to protect them. I wonder if the vamp performing it knows the curve of the feather is supposed to point *in* toward the jugular. Or, doesn't she care to offer authenticity to a sorority girl that is probably just here in search of a sparkly Cullen she can bang?"

Slim upper body swiveling in Micah's direction, genuine appreciation softened Elodie's critical features. "See? That is *exactly* what I mean. If you're going to be an activist, at least take the time to educate yourself. Otherwise, you come across as a dumbass following the crowd like brainless cattle. You're pretty okay for a human."

Pretty okay.

It was far from a standing ovation, but we eagerly took it as a foothold in the ladder of Nosferatu acceptance that would elevate us to the answers we needed.

From the curbside, a helmet-haired reporter spoke directly into a camera with all that was unfolding in this ground-breaking movement. "Capitalizing on mainstream media, the Nosferatu community has used their visibility to call what is estimated to be over a million and a half bodies out to support their cause. Spear-headed by Rau Mihnea, the purpose of this march is to end widespread discrimination—including demolishing current legislation which excuses hate crimes against undead Americans. Their goal today is to build and invigorate local and national support for the Nosferatu Presumption of Innocence Bill. Look for the NPI Bill on our ballot this November."

A shiver prickled down my spine at the idea of the bill passing. Vampire teachers, doctors, and local officials. Might as well set fire in the streets and watch the world burn. Disguising my physical reaction as a casual toss of my hair, I offered a tight-lipped smile to the white boy triplet, Thomas, who was staring intently in my direction.

Before he could return the acknowledgment in anyway, a series of pops crackled through the street. Chaos erupted. People shrieked, diving for cover. Duncan was on Rau in a blur of inhuman speed. Forcing the vampire lord's head down, he ushered him toward the nearest building, using his own mammoth frame as a shield. Thomas and Elodie vanished into the frantic masses, on desperate search for … something. Even then, I had no idea what was happening.

The sound of gunfire was unfamiliar in my Ivy League world.

My gaze was still rolling over the crashing waves of the sea of bodies in search for clues or explanations, when Carter's frantic pleas cut through my mental fog. "Vinx! *Vincenza*! I need help. We're losing her!"

Brow puckered with confusion, my head seemed to turn in slow motion in the midst of a fast-forward scene. Micah was slumped on the ground, her head cradled in Carter's lap. Skin drained ashen, her teeth chattered as shock set in. Tilting my head, I struggled to make sense of what I was seeing. The thick weave of her coat had changed colors, morphing from cloudy gray to sticky crimson. Blood. So much blood. A pool of it seeping out around them from a crater of torn tissue and mangled flesh pulsating in Micah's chest. Pushing his hands down hard against the wound, Carter tried unsuccessfully to slow its demanding gush.

In the distance, sirens wailed.

"Bullets. That noise was gunfire." Stumbling forward a step, my feeble mind whirred to catch up.

"Yes! Those were bullets. And *this* is a bullet *hole*! Now help me, damn it!" Carter shrieked, the tendons of his neck bulging.

"Is this your human?" a vampress asked. Brushing past me, she knelt beside Micah and took her hand. Ginger waves cascaded down her back, her expression soft and serene as she checked for a pulse.

"She's my … Micah," I rasped.

"I hate to tell you this," brushing away a braid that had fallen in Micah's face, the vampress glanced my way with what appeared to be genuine sorrow, "but your Micah will be dead before an ambulance can arrive. If she ever expressed desire to be changed, you need to do it now or it will be too late."

"Can you *do* that?" Carter asked, his tortured expression pleading for confirmation.

"I-I don't know," I stammered, my inoperative heart shattering under the weight of my own inadequacy.

"Of course, she can," the helpful vamp intervened on my behalf. "And I will walk her through the process."

"My blood!" I erupted, the realization slamming into me. "I can heal her!"

Staring into Micah's stilling face, the undead good Samaritan shook her head. "It's too late for that. She's too far gone. Your only choices now are to turn her, or let her pass."

"The ambulance can't get through," a random bystander shouted. "There's too many people."

Voice dropping to a desperate plea, I beseeched the fanged predator currently playing Florence Nightingale to my friend. "I've never had a progeny before. Please … *you* do it."

Whispers rippled through the crowd—judging all aspects of my looming failures, no doubt. From my potentially fatal hesitancy, to the act of making a life altering decision for another person.

The vampress peered my way. Alabaster skin glowing under the street lights, she closer resembled an angel than a creature of the night. "This sweet child deserves a sire that loves and cares for her. Not an eternal bond to a stranger. If she is to be granted rebirth, honor her with *your* bite and blood."

"Vinx, *please*. She's so cold." Carter's voice broke with emotion, Micah's blood smeared across his cheek where he had wiped away a rogue tear.

I'd like to say it was a complex reasoning that drove my leaden feet forward. The truth was far more humble. I had lost so many people I loved, I couldn't lose another. She may wake and hate me forever, but she would *wake*.

Falling to my knees beside her, I let my fangs lengthen from my gum line and tenderly wove my fingers into the thick ropes of her hair.

Tipping her head back with care, I bowed my head to whisper against her cheek, "I'm so sorry, Mics."

Further words failing me, I squeezed my eyes shut on a rush of blood-tinged tears and sank my fangs into her fading pulse. Struggling not to gag on the metallic warmth that exploded in my mouth, I swallowed hard to force it down. A simple taste, enough to meld our life forces, did the job. Pulling back, I dragged one lengthened fang over my wrist and split the skin in a cerise gash. Enveloped in my embrace, I held Micah against my chest and eased ruby droplets over her graying lips. Holding her tight, I waited for her heart to slow ... and everything to change.

EIGHT
EXPERIMENT DAY 94: CAUSE

Observation – The active acquisition of information.

Leather bound books were splayed across the dining room table in a stifling forest of knowledge. Legs curled under me, I plucked another cutlet strip from the platter at my elbow and plopped it on my tongue while trying to make sense of the letters blurring before my sleepy eyes.

A ceramic mug thumped down on the table beside me, balanced between Micah's splayed fingers. In her opposite hand, she cradled a mug of her own, the steam from her tea tickling over her cheeks as she sipped from the rim. "Drink that. You look like death, and not in the spry, reanimated way."

Mouth swinging open in a wide maw, the yawn that escaped me tittered on the brink of record-breaking. My lips closed in a series of noisy smacks, and I peered up into the face of my torturer. "Not *actually* being a vampire, the fact that you're insisting I get on their sleep schedule borders on cruel and unusual punishment."

Over the months that had passed, Micah and I settled into what had once been my family home. A fact which sounded far more macabre than it was. On the outside, the craftsman bungalow was the same sanctuary I sought refuge in since I was a little girl. Inside, everything was unrecognizable from what it used to be.

That was a concept I could relate to.

Setting her mug on the table, Micah pulled her braids from her face and secured them on top of her head with a stretched-out hair tie. "Because, outside of these walls you're a vampire. That ruse would be far less convincing if you were spotted walking to the local coffee shop at two in the afternoon *not* engulfed in flames."

"I know your mouth is moving, but all I heard was '*Yadda-yadda-yadda, I'm the sleep Nazi*'."

"There's nothing more pathetic than the pouting undead," she lobbed back.

"Your *face* is pathetic," I grumbled, only to immediately be struck by a guilty wave of female solidarity. "That's not true. Your face is lovely. It's your personality that sucks."

"Remember when you first changed and were emotionally crippled?" Mics asked. Snatching a tissue from the box on the counter, she dabbed at her nose, careful of her hoop. "Moments like this make me miss those days."

With a huff of laughter, I tossed back a swig from my mug. The moment the lukewarm concoction flooded my mouth, my face crumbled in disgust. Choking it down, I dragged my tongue over the roof of my mouth to try and wipe away the haunting taste. "*Ugh!* Did you mix human blood into my bovine again?"

Easing into her seat, Micah pulled a thick text with a tattered crimson cover toward her and flipped open its dusty cover. "I did, and I will continue to do so. You have to be able to stomach blood. There's no such thing as a vegan vamp."

"I *can* stomach blood! Pigs, cows, deer—all yummy. That's why we keep that stockpiled in the fridge. Mixing human into it is like frosting a cake with unsweetened baking chocolate and expecting me *not* to notice. Can't miss the ick!"

Dropping the leather-bound book into her lap, Micah shriveled me with a glare. "We plan to inject you right into the belly of the beast. You will be completely surrounded and far enough into their world that *no one* will be able to help you. In that deep, what do you think would happen if they so much as *suspected* you weren't one hundred percent vampire?"

I weighed her words for a beat, my fingernail clicking against the handle of the mug. Finding this to be an argument I could never win, I scooped up my grisly cocktail and drained it in a gulp. I met Micah's stare across the table, denying myself even a hint of a grimace.

"Good girl." Adjusting her glasses, Micah returned her attentions to the books.

"Don't think this is the last time I contest this issue, if for no other reason than my enjoyment of how your nostrils twitch when you're annoyed."

Micah's chestnut gaze flicked my way over the lavender frame of her glasses. "Isn't that a constant state I'm in since we moved in together?"

"Don't pretend you don't love me." I *tsk*ed, clucking my tongue against the roof of my mouth.

Grabbing her tea, she indulged herself in another slow sip. "I'd love you more if you would study, like you're supposed to."

Elbows on the table, I dragged my hands over my face, my hope being the mountain of books would miraculously disappear. No such spectacular phenomenon occurred. "I took a college course on the history of Modernism and Postmodernism in Eastern Europe before I was turned. That was like a raunchy Jackie Collins novel compared to this. Why do I have to know every subtle fact, figure, nuance, and oddity of vampire history? I mean, I haven't met a ton of vamps, but the few I've encountered weren't exactly road scholars."

"They were lawless thugs. You need to be able to rub elbows with politicians without making an ignorant comment that insults their entire system of beliefs." Closing the book, Micah slid it across the table to my growing pile. "That's a good one. It has some solid information about vampires during the Age of Enlightenment which, from what I can gather, was Mardi Gras for blood suckers."

"Vampire sacraments, testaments from those fortunate few who walked beside Vlad." I flipped through the musty pages, scanning for crucial details until I went cross-eyed. Which didn't take long. "Basically, I'm prepping for vampire catechism."

Shuffling through the mess of papers and books, Micah decided on a small, blue leather bound. "I wouldn't know. I'm Buddhist."

My shoulders lifted in a befuddled shrug. "Then the Buddhist equivalent. What would that be? Like jolly bellies and elves?"

Shaking her head, Micah didn't even bother to look up. "You're thinking of Santa, not Buddha. That's offensive as all shit. I'm getting you a whole other set of books to educate your dumb ass when we're done here. *Ow*! Fuck!"

While the taste for human blood didn't appeal to me, its smell still riled the creature within. Pupils dilating, my head snapped up. My gaze fixed on the rubies budding from the tiny slice in Micah's fingertip.

"You okay?" I asked, wetting my suddenly parched lips.

"Yeah, stupid paper cut," she grumbled, popping her finger in her mouth to clean it off.

"C-can I try something?" I tentatively ventured, rubbing my hands up and down the thighs of my black leggings. "A little experiment?"

"Who am I to hinder science?" she mused, head tilting with interest.

My chair squeaked across the hardwood floors as I pushed back from the table. "Fangs in the room, don't freak out," I warned, my incisors stretching from my gums.

"We share a bathroom. I've watched you floss. Why would I freak out?" Micah scowled, lips twisting to the side. Freeing her hair from its tie, she soothed her braids over one shoulder.

"Besides the panicked endorphin rush I can smell whenever I show fang? How about you instinctively covering your scars whenever I get a little long in the tooth?" Squatting down beside her, I extended my hand for her injured finger. "I know there are some wounds that can never heal, but *you* should know I would never hurt you. Like it or not, you're all I've got now, Mics."

Tensed muscles relaxing a fraction of a degree, Micah offered me her hand.

"Thank you. Now, all I'm going to do is ... *devour your soul!*" I hissed in the most God awful pantomimed snarl ever attempted.

Micah blinked in my direction. "You're an ass."

"True story." Bringing my own finger to my fang, I ground it into the point of my tooth until blood burst from my skin.

Micah winced, retracting her hand slightly.

"I just want to see if I can heal you," I explained.

Her hand returned in silent submission to science.

Gently cradling her hand, I coaxed a drop of my blood into her shallow cut. Not sure how the process worked, I massaged it in for good measure. Under the scrutiny of our stares, the slice vanished.

"It worked!" I beamed, grinning up at my flabbergasted friend. "Which apparently, you did not expect."

"No ... I didn't ... it couldn't," Micah oh-so-eloquently stammered. "I didn't expect your blood to be such a close replica for the real thing. It's astounding."

"Do you think I could change someone?" I whispered, as if the walls would tattle my query to the outside world.

Shoving her glasses farther up the bridge of her nose, Micah swiveled her legs my way and peered down at her blemish-free finger. "Scientifically speaking, if your blood can mimic healing properties of this magnitude, likelihood is high that this would carry over into the regeneration necessary to sire someone."

Pushing off the floor, I paced to the far side of the dining room. As I gnawed on my lower lip, a taboo idea formed on my tongue with an acidic sting. "My parents were preparing you for the serum.

You *had* to be mentally preparing yourself for it. Is this what you want? Do you ... want me to change you? Or, try to at least?"

A moment passed in silence.

Pushing her braids back, Micah exposed the lacework pattern of her scars. With one finger, she delicately traced over each of the violent slashes and punctures. "There was a time when I wanted that power and strength more than anything. I never again wanted to enter a room and feel vulnerable or afraid. I didn't want to have to glance over my shoulder in parking lots every time I heard footsteps. I longed ... for a life without fear. But, you know what? That doesn't exist. I look at all you're going through and I see how terrified you are of yourself. You shrink when your fangs drop unexpectedly. I watch you cut and prepare your food to look like delectable sushi platters and *not* the raw meat your body sings for."

My gaze flicked to the thin strips of meat and chopsticks beside me.

Understanding softening her features, Micah pressed on. "Through you I've learned that no matter where we go, or what we do, there are always monsters to fear. The worst of which being the ones haunting us from within. What we are doing now has meaning. For the first time since my attack, I feel like I'm making a difference. This whole operation could prevent other girls from being victimized like I was. And when the day finally comes that we blow the lid off of this, I want to do it as Micah—the girl they called the Scarlett Star. Because, no matter what any misogynistic judge or reporter said, I wasn't '*asking for it*'." She air-quoted the archaic claim. "If a situation ever arises, Vinx, don't be selfish. Let me go. The world couldn't handle the second-coming of Micah Walker."

How right she was.

NINE
EXPERIMENT DAY 383 CONTINUED: EFFECT

Replication – If an experiment cannot be repeated to produce the same results, this implies that the original results might have been in error.

"Could you tell which direction the shots were fired from?" the wiry officer asked, his pen scratching over his notepad.

"I didn't even know someone was shooting," I mumbled, voice devoid of emotion as I stared down at Mics on her pedestaled slab. Still and lifeless, her warm caramel complexion had drained to a milky mocha. No pinch of color filled her cheeks. No pink flush of life kissed her lips.

"We had just turned from Constitution Avenue onto South East 1st Street. The shots seemed to come from the south-west side of the road, on top of one of the buildings." Carter grasped his blood-covered coat between white-knuckled fists, unable to wear the soiled article yet unwilling to let it go.

Closing his pad, the police officer tucked it in the breast pocket of his shirt. "That coincides with the majority of eye witness accounts.

From what we have learned so far, this seems to be a random hate crime directed at Rau Mihnea. The shooter even posted footage live on social media announcing his intent. Your friend just had the unfortunate luck of being close to Mr. Mihnea when the maniac opened fire into the crowd."

A flash of yellow beckoned my stare to the DOA tag dangling from Micah's toe. Such a sunny color in the dank, dreary morgue. "Did they find him? The shooter?"

"Turned his gun on himself." The officer cast his stare in one direction then the other, checking for anyone listening in. In a room full of dead bodies, the gesture reeked of irony. One hand smoothed over his thick mustache. "I guess he wanted to finish himself off before the vampires he had been targeting could get ahold of him for a little retribution. That's a pity, if you ask me. I can't support vigilante justice, but that guy had it coming in spades."

Dragging the back of my knuckle down the side of Micah's face, I gently traced her jawline to the point of her chin. She was cold. Ice cold. "They would have torn him apart without even dropping fang."

"Probably." The officer's chin dipped in a brief nod. Peering down at Micah, his bushy eyebrows knitted together with something that resembled compassion. "Will she rise? As a vampress, I mean?"

I could feel the heat of Carter's intense gaze burning into me at the question posed and couldn't bring myself to meet his stare.

"I don't know," I answered honestly, my mind clicking through the formulas and equations in the same fashion my mother had taught me. Consider all obstacles, factor all variables. "There are too many components for me to even make an educated guess. I gave her blood, but was it enough? If it was adequate, did it get into her system in time?"

Swallowing hard, the officer's voice dropped to a whisper. "And if it didn't? What happens then?"

My head lifted with the reluctance of rusted metal. "If she was already brain dead when the blood reached her, she would rise as one of the Nosferatu our world is too terrified to speak of—those that live only to feed. They feel nothing. Fear nothing. From the moment they rise, the clock is ticking. The only thing vampires and humans agree upon is that these beasts have to be put down *immediately*. They will kill without discrimination, or mercy. Every second they are allowed to exist, gives them further chance to increase the body count of their slaughter."

Adjusting his hat, the officer whistled through his teeth and took a few cautious steps back. "Let's hope it doesn't come to that. You both have my card. If you can think of anything else that could be useful, please give me a call. I know our cultures believe in different things, but my prayers are with you and your friend."

"Thank you," Carter said, wiping at a tear with the back of his hand, his cheeks gaunt with sorrow.

A shroud of silence fell, broken only by the sharp clap of the officer's shoes against the cement floor and the clank of the door banging shut behind him.

The void I found myself in threatened to swallow me whole, plunging me to a purgatory of endless torment that a beast like me deserved.

Clearing his throat, Carter disturbed the heavy hush of my melancholy. "You did what you had to for Micah, Vinx. Whether this works or not, you're a hero."

"This wasn't for Micah." Tilting my head, I stared down at her, wishing her eyes would open just one more time in that critical glare I had come to count on. "It was for me. She would have wanted the chance to finally find peace."

"You have no way of knowing that."

"Oh, I do," I countered, my eyebrows lifting to my hairline. "She told me. She flat out said that she would rather die than be a vampire. But I was too selfish to let her go. I put my own foolish needs first and ignored her wishes. I'm a lot of things, Carter. A hero isn't one of them."

"Awkward, this is. Knocked, I should have," someone muttered from behind us, doing a pretty convincing Yoda impression.

Carter and I turned to find a newcomer whose small stature was strikingly reminiscent to the infamous green Jedi. Awkwardly shifting his weight, he shoved his hands into the pocket of the lab coat that hung down to his shins. His bald head was perfectly spherical, as were the spectacles balanced on the bridge of his nose.

"Holy shit," Carter muttered under his breath, "it's Bunsen Honeydew."

"It's Gordy, actually." Nose crinkling to correct his slipping glasses, he shoved his hand forward only to immediately pull back. "No," he quietly coached himself, "you are a *doctor* now. If you don't honor your own accomplishments, no one will." Pulling himself to his full height—which I guessed to be about four-foot-three—he offered his hand again with notable conviction. "I am Dr. Gordon Ringle, it is a pleasure to meet you."

I didn't take his hand, but pressed my lips into a thin line and let my stare fall to Micah.

Gordy's hand fell to his side with a slap. "I said *pleasure* while your friend is on a slab in the morgue. This is going horribly. Maybe I can go out and come back in? We can start over?"

Carter rounded the slab by Micah's feet, taking a protective stance beside me, his arms crossed firmly over his chest. "Excuse us for not being in a jovial mood. How about if you tell us what the hell you want?"

"I-I'm here for her," Gordy squeaked, jabbing a finger in Micah's direction.

Icy fear racing down my spine, my fingers gripped the end of the slab as if to anchor me to that spot. "No! You can't have her! You can't do an autopsy. *Not yet.*"

I wasn't aware my fangs had extended until Gordy pulled back, palms raising to pump the conversational brakes. "Whoa! We just took a warp speed jump to the wrong conclusion! I was sent by one of the benefactors to your cause. I'm here to help! I'm here to bring her back!"

My incisors retracted with a sharp snap. "I gave her my blood," I confessed, as if the success of his mission rested on that one piece of information.

"Yes, so I heard, and saw on every media stream available. You're a bit of a celebrity now. If I could ..." Gordy tried to fumble his way between Carter and I, before slamming into the impenetrable wall of our resistance. "I'll just go around. As I was saying, I am aware you gave her your blood, and I think that may have bought us the time needed."

Following Gordy with a critical gaze, Carter leaned his knuckles on the table next to Micah's hip. "Time needed for what?"

In place of an answer, Gordy plucked a penlight from the pocket of his lab coat. Prying open one of Micah's lids with the side of his thumb, he shined the light directly into her eye. My mouth fell open as her pupil dilated in response.

"Ah! Just as I thought!" Little legs scurrying across the floor, Gordy waddled as quickly as he could to a medical bag he dropped by the door when he came in. "Your blood can do many things, Miss Larow, but making a vampire is not one of them," he explained in his toddle back to the slab. "However, its healing properties *were* able to delay what would have been her inevitable death. You bought us time. Ran defense, as it were. Now it's time for me to run the ball in for a touchdown by giving her the serum."

"You're the quarterback? You strike me as more of a kicker." A lilt of hope lightened Carter's tone, still his posture remained stiff and tight with the fear of trusting too much.

Glaring up over the frames of his glasses, Gordy's shoulders sagged in exasperation. "You wanna stand here and insult me, or get out of the way and let me Frankenstein your friend back to life? Your choice."

My eyes locked with Carter's, a million unspoken questions passing between us.

Seeing the blind leap of faith as our only option, I wet my lips to croak, "Let's step outside and let the man work."

THE CHILL OF the night air cooled my skin which scorched with regret. Raking my fingers through my hair, I tipped my face to the delicate snowflakes drifting down. The heavy iron door of the morgue banged shut behind Carter, gravel crunching under his feet as he closed the space between us.

"What do I do if she dies?" I asked the universe, understanding for the first time how much Mics had tethered me to some semblance of normalcy.

Out of the corner of my eye, I caught a glimpse of Carter lifting his hand to reach for me. Second guessing himself, he retracted the wandering appendage and tucked it in the pockets of his slacks before it could betray him again. Despite the cold, his gore-splattered coat still hung over his forearm. "You'll go on. You'll stay the course, because that's what Mics would have wanted."

Chin trembling, bloody tears filled my eyes. My quaking lips parted, searching for some words to express the soul crushing anguish sawing through my gut with a dull blade.

There were none.

Language was inadequate in my spiral into eternal solitude.

What I needed, more than anything, was connection. Simple *touch*.

I spun without thinking, folding into Carter. Reveling in the thump of his heart beating against my cheek, I nestled into the warmth of his chest.

Without hesitation, his embrace enveloped me. Still, my despair screamed that he wasn't close enough. The smothering walls of loneliness were closing in from all sides. Clawing at his arms, I drew his chest to mine—my fantastical hope being that his heart could prompt the indolent lump in my chest to beat, even once, in a reminder that I was more than a shell. That life *hadn't* forsaken me. Tipping his chin, Carter's forehead found mine. I heard his pulse catch in a stutter-beat, then launch through his veins in a raging current. The tip of my nose brushed his cheek, tempting his mouth to mine. With each wavering exhale, his breath on my skin sent cascades of warmth tingling through me. Lips parting in a breathy sigh, I tilted my face to his. His fingernails dragged down my back, seizing my waist with a firm, yet gentle, insistence. Pulling me to him, our bodies molding together, he paused to breathe me in deep. Nothing except a thin veil of sizzling desire separated us, our gazes locked in seductive invitation.

The buzz of my phone in my coat pocket injected a dose of reality into the fantasy I longed to lose myself in.

"Ignore it," I encouraged, knowing already that—for him, at least—the spell of the moment had been broken.

Closing his eyes for a beat, Carter's hands shifted to the curve of my hip bones to softly push me away. "When this happens, and it *will*," he murmured in a throaty whisper, "it will be because it's what we both want. Not a desperate act of losing ourselves in a moment of need."

He reached down, fingers skimming my thigh, plucked my vibrating phone from my pocket, and dropped it in my hand.

"If that's one of our benefactors, ask for two rooms for the night. I've exhausted the last of my willpower." Primal craving darkening his cerulean stare to a stormy sapphire, he took a step back. His chin lifted in encouragement for me to answer the phone.

I blinked hard at the device in my palm, attempting to clear away the lusty pheromone haze enough to recall how the contraption I held worked. Turning my back to Carter, I thumbed the screen and pressed the phone to my ear. "Hello?"

"Miss Larow." Rau's velvet timbre poured from the line like decadent melted chocolate. "I reached out to you the very second the circuits were clear. I feel simply dreadful about what happened to your friend. And for you, poor child, to have to sire someone for the first time in such a violent and abysmal situation."

Nails of contempt scraped down my throat as I swallowed down his offered concern. *My friend.* My friend who would be alive and well had she not made the mistake of occupying the same space as the political poser on the other end of that line.

"I appreciate you taking the time to call." Clearing my throat, I tried to keep abject loathing from dripping from my tone. "Today has been a nightmare, to say the least. I had never ..."

Drank a friend's blood while the world watched.

"… changed anyone before. It was a mad scramble to find a safe place for her rebirth." As I stared out at the trees across the street, a ruffle of feathers caught my attention. Adjusting its position on a forking branch, a tar black crow tilted its head with an avian twitch, considering me with one beady eye.

The pause on the other end of the line dragged on, as if the vampire lord was devouring my words and savoring their taste. "Your love for Micah will transform into kindness and compassion for her as your progeny. From what I have gathered, that was a consideration you weren't shown by your own maker."

He knew so much about everyone, and everything. Was it possible he knew my truth? No. It couldn't be. Micah had been so careful, down to the meticulous planning of every detail.

"None of us get to choose how we come into the world, Mr. Mihnea. All we can hope for is to do right by others, even when we weren't shown that same consideration." As if satisfied by my answer, the crow took to flight. Its wings beat a methodic chorus against the night sky.

"Too true, too true." Ice clinked against a glass on Rau's end of the line. "I'm sure you have much to do in preparation for the awakening of your newborn. It's rude of me to keep you. Please, contact me when she's settled. Put an old man's mind to ease that all is well."

"I absolutely will," I lied. It was me that signed on to delve into the Nosferatu world. Not Mics. If I had my way, that would be the last time she was within throwing distance of a real vampire. Then again, I seldom got my way.

"Wonderful, and if you're both feeling up for it, you could join me at the *Afişare Mare* next month."

"*Afişare Mare?*" I repeated, trying to make sense of words that hit my ear in a muddled mess.

Head snapping in my direction, Carter's eyes bulged.

"That name is a mouthful, I know. Blame my sentimental heart for feeling the need to fall back on Romanian from time to time. It translates to the *grand display*, and I am using it as an opportunity to introduce some of the beauty of our culture to mainstream society. It's a black-tie event, by invitation only, which I am hosting at the Lockwood-Mathews Mansion I recently acquired. If you'd like, I would be honored to send you an invitation."

"An invitation?" I parroted, spinning on the ball of my foot in search of Carter's coaching.

Lips pursed tight, he nodded his exuberance.

"Yes, I would love to be a part of that. How better to further our cause than to show people what we are truly all about?" *Or in my case, what we pretend to be so magnificently that we even have ourselves fooled.*

"Fantastic. I'll have Duncan drop an invitation by. May the strength of Vlad be with you and your progeny, Miss Larow. Be well."

Thumbing the call to an end, I chucked my phone into my pocket and raked blood-encrusted fingers through my hair, tugging at the strands with more force than necessary. This was just beginning, and look how far askew our axis had slipped.

TEN

EXPERIMENT DAY 126: CAUSE

Credibility – Refers to the quality or trustworthiness or a piece of qualitive research.

With more excitement than was really warranted or necessary, I carefully arranged the giant bowl of fresh and fluffy popcorn on the coffee table. Then, situated myself on the couch with my legs crossed under me. Wriggling into the cushions, I found my perfect level of bootie comfort. That night was one to commemorate. After more than four months of nonstop physical and mental training, Micah invited me to a night in and a movie. The simple idea of it rang in my ears with the promise of nirvana. I even dug through the bins of my boxed up human life in search of my favorite sassy gnome pajamas. Yanking the hair-tie off my wrist, I knotted my short strands in a ridiculous sprout of a high ponytail and let my gaze travel over the rarely used living room. Micah's work files tucked away? Check. A plentiful bounty of snacks? Check. All I needed was Mics and her film selection. I was hoping for something classic 80s.

Bonus points if it starred any member of the Brat Pack. Scooping my drink off the coffee table, I settled in to wait, my fingernails tapping against the side of the ceramic *Scientists do it … periodically* mug.

Normalcy, however fleeting it may be, had been accomplished.

For an instant, at least, life seemed blissfully *mundane*.

Like those hideous sweaters grandma used to make at Christmas: itchy, ill-fitting, and yet somehow comforting to the soul.

"Oh, good. You're already here." Micah's clipped tone was all business as she strode straight for the flat screen, disc in hand. Clad in her usual attire of drab scrubs, she could have been coming home from work or getting ready for bed. To her, scrubs were all purpose.

Practically giggling with delight, I hugged my mug to my chest and prepared for the opening credits. None came. Instead, the screen flickered to life on a fuzzy, black and white image. Bodies milled on a dance floor: people sipping drinks and writhing to silent music. There was no sound. The footage was seemingly shot from one camera angle. Chewing on my lower lip, I tilted my head and tried to make sense of what I was seeing.

"Is this supposed to look like a small budget film? Like *Blair Witch*?" I ventured, hunting for plot amongst the popping and locking forms.

"No." Micah pulled her chin to her neck, seemingly taken aback by the question. "It's a security tape from a club."

Only then did she notice the stage I set. Pressing pause on the remote, her posture straightened, arms falling slack to her sides. My face would've burned with a hot blush if my sluggish pulse allowed such a thing. The whole thing reeked of the kind of painfully awkward moment when a girl realizes a guy she friend-zoned arranged an elaborate date.

Shifting her weight from one foot to the other, Mics wet her lips and laced her fingers in front of her. "What … did you think we were doing tonight?"

"Movie night?" Shoulders sagging, my lingering hope deflated.

Blinking my way, Micah's mouth fell open. "I, *uh* … lined up an informant. He's a reporter hired by the vampire coalition to, basically, make them look as beneficial to mankind as Habitat for Humanity. I got this disc from him today. It's linked to a missing persons case."

"But ... I made snacks," I countered, my rebuttal landing closer to a plaintive whine. "Regular popcorn for you, and kernels dipped in pig's blood for me."

"First of all ... *ew*." Micah halted further culinary description with one raised finger. "Secondly, this isn't Sigma Ki on a Friday night. We're staging a political uprising, remember?"

Staring down at my pajama pants, I threw out the only card left in my hand. "But, I dug out my *Gnomes Just Wanna Have Fun* jammies."

Pushing one wayward braid behind her ear, Mics did her best not to openly laugh at my expense. "This isn't a girls' night, Vinx. We're training you to be a *weapon*."

Resting the base of the mug against my crossed feet, I dragged one finger around its rim. "The last moment of fun I had was a dinner with my family. We laughed. We joked. Then, I watched them die and got my throat ripped out. If fun of any kind perished that same day, what the hell are we fighting for? What's the point of any of this?"

Head falling back, she groaned her exasperation at the ceiling. "I thought vampires were supposed to be broody, not melodramatic."

"I surpass all labels." I shrugged.

"Fine." Micah's eyebrows disappeared into her hairline, as if she was trying to reason with an obstinate child—which she was. "Let me tell you about the missing girl, and then we'll watch *Sixteen Candles*."

Chin lifting with interest, I narrowed my gaze to kick off negotiations. "Make it *The Breakfast Club*, and you have a deal."

Without a word, Micah offered me her hand to shake on the terms.

Our palms met and the deal was struck.

"So ..." I grabbed a handful of popcorn from the bowl and settled back into the cushions. Dipping one kernel in my mug of blood, I popped it in my mouth. When I discovered it to be every bit as gross as it sounds, I spit it right back out and pressed on like nothing happened. "Tell me about the girl."

Turning her face to the screen, Micah hit play once more. Her features, pinched tight with concentration, were illuminated by the television's soft glow. "You'll understand more if you watch."

In the video footage, a sinewy blonde sauntered on to the dance floor. Hands thrown over her head, she gyrated her hips in tempting invitation. Swaying to a beat denied to our ears, one strap of her slip dress fell off her shoulder. So much exposed flesh, the monster within me could feel the ominous swell of danger closing in around her. A moment later, the crowd around the girl was forced aside by a swarm of vamps rancid with bad intention.

Oblivious to the sharks circling her, the girl danced on. Tossing her hair, she wriggled her ass as the cloud of death closed in. A bald vamp, who had to be nearly seven feet tall, with a swastika tattooed on the back of his neck, was the first to strike. Stepping in at an intimate proximity, he gripped the girl by the hips and ground his arousal against her. Her attempts to push him away landed with all the power of a fly on the back of horse. Hooting and jeering, the rest of his hive swarmed. Breaking free, because the disgusting supremacist allowed her to, the blonde spun in search of escape. Caught in a huddle of groping hands and exposed fang, freedom taunted her from only an arm's distance away.

Horrified spectators, stepping in and out of frame, tried to intercede on the terrified girl's behalf. Their own fear of finding themselves thrust into her place prevented them from being of any real use. Shrinking his quaking victim with his glare, the bald vamp wove a hand into her hair, wrenching her head back hard enough to rip a scream from her lungs. Lips peeling back to reveal viciously curved fangs, he bowed his ravenous maw to her pounding pulse.

I gripped my mug in a tight two-handed hold, and my gaze swept to Mics who stood still as stone. "How can you watch this? It *has* to hit a sour note of similarity."

"Keep watching," Micah murmured, her attention transfixed.

Just as the towering vamp's fangs brushed exposed flesh, a male form darted into view. Flinging the hungry vampire off his potential prey with one hand, the newcomer positioned himself between the two. It seemed a hive that size could've taken down one would-be hero with ease. Instead, they immediately put their hands up in defeat and backed away. Wrapping a protective arm around the sobbing girl, the man ushered her toward the nearest exit. A second before they disappeared from frame, the knight in shining armor glanced directly at the camera. Micah pressed paused on the remote to hold him there.

Mug thumping down on the coffee table, I inched to the edge of the sofa to squint at the screen. "Is that ... another vampire?"

Dressed in a dashing three-piece suit, the chivalrous gent's lip twitched just enough to hint at a pair of menacing incisors beneath.

Micah clicked off the TV and turned to face me with her lips pinched tight. "That's not just *any* vampire. That's Rau Mihnea, head of the vampire coalition. No Nosferatu makes a move anywhere within his domain without approval from *him*."

"Hence them backing off with their tails tucked." Resting my elbows on my knees, I drummed one finger against my chin. "If he wields that kind of power, he may know where Finn and his hive are."

"Possibly. I'm guessing Mr. Mihnea's fountain of knowledge is an untapped geyser of secrets." Pulling a manila folder out from behind the TV, she tossed it on the table in front of me. Cut-up scraps of newspaper spilled out in a scattering of data snippets. "He became quite the hero after that little show. Every local news station and paper wanted his firsthand account of what happened."

"If he's so wise and powerful, why would vamps in his region risk such a public display of douche baggery? It doesn't make sense," I pointed out, chewing on the inside of my cheek.

"It does if the whole thing was staged." Leaning over the table, glasses drifting down the bridge of her nose, Micah shuffled through the news clippings until she found what she was looking for. She pushed it toward me and tapped it with her index finger. The picture that accompanied the article was of Rau and that same pretty blonde arm in arm, adorned in formal attire and beaming smiles. "This was taken just two months after the alleged attack. This lovely lady—whose name is Joselyn by the way—publicly paired with Rau. For nearly two years every ribbon cutting he attended, every yacht christening that demanded his presence, she was on his arm batting her lashes in adoration. As someone who has suffered an *actual* vampire attack, I can tell you I have no desire to take High Tea with a blood sucker. I stay as far away from them as possible. No offense."

Retrieving my mug, my mouth twisted into a grimace as I brought it to my lips. "A little taken."

"My point is," Micah pushed on as if she hadn't just insulted my dietary restrictions, "whatever kept her locked to Rau's side, it landed her here last week."

Plucking one last article from the file, she placed it in my outstretched palm.

"Body pulled from Candlewood Lake," I read aloud, glancing up to gauge if Micah expected me to keep going.

"Spoiler alert, it was Joselyn." Turning on her heel, Micah paced the length of the living room. With determined strides, she marched from the couch, to the French doors, and back again. "They found her floating in the river, wearing nothing but a masquerade mask. She had been drained of blood by two deep punctures in her jugular. The media claimed that the thugs from the video came back for a little revenge. There were even reports that Rau handled their egregious offense by driving a silver stake through the heart of all those involved."

Sensing her heavy pause, I prompted her with a, "But ..."

"The informant I mentioned? He said no such punishment was doled out. At least not in the public execution style you would expect for killing the boss man's arm candy." Micah rounded the table, flopping down on the couch beside me.

Staring at the Modge Podge collection of articles, I tried to make sense of the splayed out puzzle it presented. "What does all of this mean to that mega-brain of yours? How does this give us anything to go on?"

She rocked forward and treated herself to a handful of popcorn. "It gives us *her* to go on. She dove into the vampire world, Vinx. And whatever she saw got her killed. If we follow the trip she took down the rabbit hole, we might just be able to expose *why*."

"All right!" I chirped, practically bouncing in my seat. "That actually gives us a place to start, above lab time and extensive reading."

"It gives us something to *investigate*," Mics corrected, talking around her mouthful. "We haven't even tested your disguise up against a true Nosferatu yet. We're at the threshold of the truly dangerous shit, but we're not quite ready to cross that line."

Sinking back into the cushions, I folded my arms over my chest. "You tell me—oh, Wise One—what *am* I ready for?"

Snatching a DVD case from the table, she waved it between us, her face brightening with a rarely seen smile. "Hanging with *The Breakfast Club*. *That* rare little treat you are beyond ready for."

ELEVEN
EXPERIMENT DAY 384: EFFECT

Uncertainty – a situation which involves imperfect and/or unknown information.

Eighteen hours. That's how long Carter and I waited to learn if our friend had lived or died. Rotating from our spot hunkered shoulder to shoulder on the curb, to alternating naps in the backseat of the rental car, we maintained our constant vigil. Trips to the restroom, or for a much-needed caffeine fix, were done in shifts. When those doors creaked open with an update, we damned sure weren't going to miss it. Every second that ticked by seemed to drive another nail of finality into Micah's looming coffin.

Dragging a hand over the rough stubble of his jawline, Carter stretched his legs out into the street in front of him. His gaze, puffy and bloodshot, shifted from the heavy clouds overhead, to my face. He dug into the pocket of the coat he reluctantly shrugged back into, and pulled out a pair of aviator sunglasses. "The sun staying hidden behind the clouds is allowing you to keep up pretenses, but you should still put these on." At my hesitation he added, "Micah would want you to."

Leaning into him, I tipped my chin his way, allowing him to slide the frames up the bridge of my nose.

"How much longer do we give her?" he asked, voice raspy from exhaustion.

I wanted to answer, to explain that while *I* had been out for days, vampire awakenings typically take between twelve to twenty-four hours. Unfortunately, I lacked the capabilities to form words. My attention was locked on the throbbing pulse of Carter's neck. Mouth suddenly parched, my veins burned with the demanding reminder that it had been nearly twenty-four hours since I last fed.

"No way of knowing," I managed. Breathing in the scent of his blood, an audible sigh escaped my trembling lips.

Tensing, Carter's upper body pivoted to get a better look at me. "Are you okay? You sound … weird."

When I felt my incisors swelling from my gums, I shoved myself off the curb to grant him the safety of distance. "I haven't eaten," I explained, turning my face from him to hide the shame of my predatory longing. "I didn't expect this to be an overnighter, so I left all my blood bags on the plane."

Pushing off the ground, Carter brushed off his hands on the back of his slacks. He peered up at me from under his lashes, shoved his sleeve up his forearm, and offered me his wrist.

Mouth aching with hunger, I shook my head with an adamant twitch, averting my stare to the cracked concrete beneath my feet. "No, thank you. I don't really have the taste for human blood, I just get a bit … *peckish* when I go too long between feedings."

Carter's extended arm wavered, but didn't retract. "Weren't you the one who explained to the officer, with the 70s porn mustache, that there is always a chance that a vamp could come back *wrong*? What if she does and you're too weak to stop her? You can think I'm being noble and chivalrous if you want. To me, it's loading the only weapon I have. Go ahead, Vincenza. It's okay."

Tentatively, I peered his way, only to be met by his ironclad resolve. Mouth watering, I risked a step closer. "I've only ever fed from Micah, and that was under controlled circumstances."

"Controlled how?"

"She had a gun to my head."

"So, the severe level of control then." He laughed. Tilting his head, he added, "I trust you. No heavy weaponry required."

"I'm glad one of us trusts me." Wetting my lips, I focused on the forking blue veins pulsing beneath the surface of his skin. So faint. So inviting. "I'm not sure I'll know when to stop."

Closing the distance between us, Carter brushed his hand down the side of my face, his wrist coming to rest mere millimeters from my mouth. "We'll learn together," he murmured.

My lips curled from my teeth, and my swollen gums felt the snap of the day's chill. As one fanged grazed his pulse point, I pulled back the fraction of an inch my willpower would allow. "I can numb it. You don't have to feel any pain."

"No," Carter refuted with surprising conviction. "I … want this."

Stares locked, we silently dared each other to back down. Neither did.

Focused on the welcoming pools of his cerulean gaze, I bowed my head. Gently as I could, I applied the needed pressure. My fangs broke through in a gush of coppery warmth.

Mouth falling open, a husky moan rumbled from his chest.

I sealed my lips around the wound, drinking in one deep pull, then another.

Sucking air through his teeth, Carter's breath caught.

Hard as it was, I pulled back. "Does it hurt? Do you want me to stop?"

"No," he rumbled. Weaving his hand in my hair, he guided my head back to his dripping wrist. "Take what you need."

While the taste didn't appeal to me, his passionate consent lit a fire in my core that radiated through me in tingling fingers of longing. Gifting him my mouth, I drank deep, swallowing his metallic essence in urgent gulps.

Sexually speaking, I never considered myself worldly. I had lovers, but this was something altogether different. What passed between us ran deeper than naked, writhing flesh.

It was real.

Primitive.

Full of a heady intoxication compelling enough to distract me from our watch ... until a bloodcurdling scream sliced from the morgue. Pulling back, my tongue darted out to seal the puncture wounds.

"Micah!" I barked. In a blink I was at the door, yanking it open on reluctant hinges to bolt inside.

A blazing ruby glare greeted me into nightmarish gore. Micah hunched over Gordy's lifeless body, blood pooling at her feet. The scene was bumped to a new level of weird by Gordy's pants being around his ankles, his shriveled manhood sagging to the side like a dead slug.

"What's happ— *Whoa!*" Carter jogged up behind me, where I halted him with one extended arm.

Micah moved in a blur of speed and fangs. Darting around me, she seized Carter by the front of his rumpled shirt and shoved him against the wall, knocking the air from his lungs. Lips curling in a vicious hiss, she arched back to strike.

I hooked my forearm around her throat and heaved her off him, flinging her to the floor in a splay of limbs. Bounding to her feet, she hit a low crouch. Her wild, feral glower flicked around the room, seeking retribution ... or escape. The moment our eyes met, an animalistic growl bubbled from her chest. Losing myself to instinct, I flashed fang in a challenging sneer.

Something that resembled comprehension sharpened Micah's hateful stare.

"*You promised me,*" she spat. Loathing snaked between her words, coating her tone with venom.

"I know what you're feeling." Positioning myself between her and Carter, I risked a step closer. "Colors are too bright. The quietest noise rings through your head like a shout. You can even smell the flask of bourbon Carter *thinks* he has hidden in his back pocket. There's power surging through your veins, and how much you dig it scares the shit out of you. I *know*, Mics, and I *will* help you. You didn't let me become a monster, and I won't let you. What happened here ... this isn't you."

"Not a monster?" Her snarl morphed into a manic smile. Floating to full height, she glided body-skimming close with an ethereal grace. "You turned me into the thing I hate most in the world. You're the very *definition* of a monster. And now, thanks to you, so am I. I'm the thing humans fear. The ghostly image that goes bump in the night. In honor of my second birthday, I feel like stretching my fangs. If you want to stop me, *Mommy Dearest*, I suggest you keep up."

Weaving around me, she streaked for the door and threw it open with enough force to make it bounce on the hinges. She tossed a taunting glare over her shoulder before vanishing into the land of the living.

"We probably should have locked that door." Carter pointed out the obvious, his brow puckered with concern.

"She won't get far. But, first ..." I raised my wrist to my mouth and dragged my fang across my skin, splitting it in a clean slice. Shoving the crimson gash Carter's way, my voice hardened to steel. "Drink."

"A world of no. But thanks." Carter cringed.

"The smell of my blood on you will repel Micah," I explained, offering the mercy of my flesh a second time. "It's the only protection I can offer you. Please. Hurry before the wound closes."

Clasping my wrist, Carter's tongue flicked over the shrinking ruby stream. His body convulsed in euphoric shudders the second he swallowed.

Threading my fingers into the silky locks of his hair, I brought his forehead to mine and fought the desire to taste myself on his supple lips. "Lock yourself in here. Don't open the door for anyone but me."

Wrenching open the door, I sniffed the air in search of Micah's scent.

"Vincenza!" Carter called after me. "Come back safe."

Hand hooked on the door frame, I caught sight of a crow lifting from a branch. Its wings beat a drum solo against the wind, shifting my eyeline in the direction of a trail of chaos.

"That's the standard plan," I mused and rappelled myself off the concrete wall.

MICAH'S PATH OF destruction was easy to follow. A street light had been ripped from the pavement and speared through a truck windshield. Screaming security alarms wailed from a boutique shop where the door had been kicked in, and a few of the mannequins stripped down and ransacked. Smoke rose from the hood of a car with its fender caved it—the driver paced the sidewalk beside it, ranting on his phone about the "crazed nurse" who jumped in front of him. Bystanders lingered, none of them bleeding. None clinging to life. Micah may have been a tornado of annihilation, but she hadn't killed again ... *yet.*

Sniffing the breeze, I found her scent—antiseptic soap and the rusty stench of human blood. It led me to a nondescript brick building with a flashing neon sign that introduced it as The Purring Kitty Gentlemen's Club. The tattered sandwich board by the door announced it to be Nickel Shots Day. Five cent booze, bouncing boobies, and a baby vamp: that seemed the recipe for cataclysmic disaster.

Pulling open the door, I was slapped in the face by a thick fog of testosterone musk and stale beer. Bawdy R&B music thumped into my temples like railroad spikes. Soles of my shoes sticking to the floor, I *prayed* all I was stepping in was spilled liqueur. On the stage, bored looking dancers shimmied and gyrated through routines they could probably do in their sleep.

I felt her before I saw her, her presence shuddering through me. Moving in the shadows, Mics coiled around me like a tightening noose.

"Took you long enough to catch up," she rasped against my ear, her fingertips dancing across my shoulder blades in her orbit around me. "All those hours of training were a waste. You move like a geriatric sloth."

"Nice outfit," I snorted, gaze traveling the length of her. Her detour at the boutique allowed her the opportunity to trade gore-stained scrubs for snakeskin leggings, a black mesh crop top, and thigh-high red platform boots. "You managed to be the tackiest thing in a strip club. That's downright impressive."

"Did I disappoint you, *Mommy*?" she asked with a faux pout, batting her lashes coquettishly. "Let me make it up to you."

As her pinkie finger linked with mine, I bristled. Accepting this for the trap that it most definitely was, I let her lead me to the VIP room blocked off by a red velvet curtain. Pushing it aside in a rustle of fabric, Micah with the blood red eyes ushered me into the den of debauchery. Our stripper tour guide for the journey waited inside. Frizzy red hair puffed around her face like cotton candy, and the curves of her buxom frame glistened with a thick sheen of body glitter.

"An all-girl party?" The redhead's smile widened with genuine delight. "Those are *always* a treat. Well, ladies, my name is Chantel. And if you two take a seat, I would *love* to work my magic for you."

A cold fist of unease tightened in my gut, sending prickles of warning skittering up my spine. "Mics, what the hell are we doing here?"

"I'm exploring my new nature," she taunted, sashaying to one zebra-print upholstered chair to claim it as her throne. "And *you're* here to witness my coming out party."

"Coming out party?" Chantel repeated, rolling her hips on Micah's lap with her bedazzled bra in the face of the newborn pseudo-vamp. "Congratulations, girl!"

"Thank you, my dear. It isn't the life I would have chosen for myself, but the hand of fate had other plans." Micah's stare pointedly locked with mine, stabbing in the dagger of guilt to the tune of Shakira's "Loca." Wetting her full lips, she dragged her attentions back to the hardworking dancer. "If I were to tell you my friend and I were vampires, would you believe me?"

With a bemused huff of laughter, Chantel indulged Micah's little game. "If it wasn't mid-day on a Tuesday, absolutely. Those red contacts are really convincing."

Gripping Chantel's waist hard enough to bruise flesh, Micah forced her down on her lap. "Our kind is changing ... evolving. We're the next generation of terrible."

"Whatever you say, doll." Chantel tried to laugh off Micah's antics, but the thin bead of sweat trickling down her spine reeked of fear.

Tilting her head, Micah searched the stripper's face as if considering her for the first time. When her mouth opened, words tumbled out in a hollow echo. "If I told you I wanted to bring you to the euphoric brink where pleasure and pain meet, would you let me?"

As she posed the question, Micah's fangs stretched from her gum line. Their gazes melded in a hypnotized stare; neither so much as blinked or twitched.

"Yes," Chantel vacantly responded, her hands snaking around Micah's neck.

At my scholarly mentor's insistence, I once read about a rare breed of vampire with the capability to enthrall their victims into a completely submissive state. Until that moment, I thought that to be a fictitious rumor. While Micah's gaze drifted down Chantel's swan-like neck, fixating on the sweet spot where her pulse thumped a steady chorus, the dancer sat astride her blank and transfixed.

Edging into the room, my fingernails sliced into the fabric of the empty chair I bumped into. "Mics, what are you doing?"

Whatever dark alley of her mind she wandered into, my query could no longer reach her. With blood-tinged tears spilling over her lashes, she mimicked a cruel command once imposed on her.

"*Beg me*," she demanded, her voice betraying her by cracking. "Beg me to hurt you ... and make it convincing."

"I want ... you ... to ravage me," Chantel uttered with robotic obedience. The dam of her own tears broke free, sending torrents of watery pain zig-zagging down her cheeks. "Tear my throat out. Take what you want."

"Such a good little girl." Playing her part in the grisly memory from her past, Micah pressed one dagger-like fingernail to the vulnerable flesh of Chantel's cleavage. Firm and consistent pressure split her skin in a cerise streak, blood bubbling from the wound. "And good girls get a reward."

Chantel whimpered through tightly pinched lips, the absence of freewill anchoring her in that spot without the hope of escape.

"Mmmmm." Licking the blood off her finger, Micah's pupils dilated with desire.

Shoving the chair aside, I bounced it off the wall to clear it from my path. While it crumbled to kindling, I hooked the dazed dancer under the arms and flung her off Micah's lap. Her faculties returned the moment she crumbled to the floor, her heavily mascaraed eyes blinking our way with equal parts terror and relief.

Dropping fang, my face contorted in a beastly snarl. "*Run.*"

Her insanely high heels scraped against the floor in a desperate hunt for traction the same moment Micah lunged for my throat. Catching the upper body of my progeny, I used her momentum to spin us both around. We crashed to the floor in a violent blur of gnashing teeth, biting, and snapping at any and all exposed skin. Pinning her arms to the ground with my knees, I quickly discovered the sire rule was true even for pseudo-vamps. Her strength was no match for mine.

"*Micah*!" Palms pressed to her shoulders, I pulled my chin to my chest to avoid the gnashing strikes of her rapacious jaws. "This isn't you! You can fight this. You can get control."

Lifting her head off the ground the small allowance I granted her, her murderous glare plowed into me. "This is *exactly* what I am. I'm the monster *you* made me. The same kind of despicable beast that made me *beg* before he and his buddies sank their teeth into my flesh *over and over again*."

"And that makes it okay to kill a scientist and traumatize an exotic dancer?"

"I woke up to the scientist taking incredibly *unscientific* liberties with my body," Mics spat, lip twitching at the memory.

"Oh, Gordy." I cringed. "That's why his pants were down."

"That's why his pants were down, and that's why I went for his throat. Is this the part where you tell me that was wrong?"

"No," I countered, loosening my grip on her shoulders in the slightest degree. "Guy tries to rape an unconscious vampire, and he's going to get what's coming to him. But what about the girl? What makes it okay to hurt her like that? Why would you want to curse her to the same nightmares that haunt you?"

The blaze of her rage simmering down to crackling embers, she sagged under my weight. Red eyes blinked back to a warm chestnut, which I took to mean coherency had won the day. "No one deserves that. *No one.*"

"That's right. They don't." Looping my fingers into the mesh of her shirt, I lifted her up and bounced her head off the floor to ensure she was listening. "Consider this your one and only *Get Out of Jail Free Card.* Your devil bitch act ends now."

Brows hitched, the fires of challenge burned behind her stare. "And why would I listen to you?"

Leaning down, I whispered against her cheek, "I'm your sire. I'm older than you, stronger than you, and I *will* take you down before you can even drop fang. We have a job to do. One that you have been hell-bent insistent on. Remember that? Is it ringing any bells for you?"

Body falling slack beneath me, pure and genuine loathing radiated from Micah's every pore. "I want to expose the truth behind the vampire coalition, but don't think for a minute I will *ever* forgive you for doing this to me."

"I'll take it," I relented. Climbing off her, I offered my steaming progeny a hand up.

"I don't want your fucking hand," she grumbled, taking it anyway to help guide her up onto those ridiculous boots.

"Your resolve is admirable."

"Bottle that resolve and shove it up your ass," she politely suggested.

"There! That's them!" Chantel shoved the curtain aside, pointing us out to the cluster of security following her. "That's the *cipa* who attacked me and her *dupa* friend!"

Micah's expression cleared, a flicker of her former self shining through. "You're Polish? I never would have guessed that."

"Out!" the burly guard with acne scars and ruddy cheeks demanded, jamming his thumb toward the exit. "Vampires out in the daylight is a new breed of bullshit! As the owner of this establishment, I have the right to kick your asses out of here, and no NPI Bill will ever change that! Now, get the hell out."

A low rumble bubbling from Micah's chest, I shoved her toward the exit before she could counter his point with hostile negotiations.

Sauntering past, I offered him a toothy grin, the glittering club lights reflecting off my exposed fangs. "I do hope we have your vote on election day." I winked and followed my baby vamp out.

TWELVE
EXPERIMENT DAY 149: CAUSE

Contingency – Statues of proposition that are neither true under every possible valuation nor false.

I f this is another lecture about symphony etiquette or what fork to use, I swear to God—"

"Vlad," Micah interrupted. Glancing up from the file she was reading, the frames of her glasses slid halfway down the bridge of her nose. "Vampires pray to Vlad, not God."

"I swear to *Vlad*," I corrected, slathering on the sarcasm, "I will knock you off that chair, break off one of its legs, and stake myself with it. You said *months* ago we were going to pursue the missing girl lead. Yet here we are, staring at the same four walls I have come to loathe with a fiery passion that burns deep in my blackened soul."

"Be more melodramatic, *please*." Micah clucked her tongue against the roof of her mouth, eyes rolling skyward. "I haven't met my daily quota of whine yet."

"You meant that as the one with the H, not the drink, didn't you?" I asked, in order to determine how offended I should be.

"H, not drink," Mics confirmed with a curt nod. Crossing her arms, she hugged the file in her hands to her chest. "Because I feel you are failing to realize that when we do this—when we send you down Joselyn's path—we will be dropping you into a minefield. One wrong step, and you're dead. In this case, that means being poised, respectful, and able to matriculate among them. Preferably *without* carnage or bloodshed."

Shoulders slumping, my lip curled in disgust. "You lost me at that last part."

Filling her lungs to capacity, Micah exhaled through pursed lips. She turned on the ball of her foot, the soles of her orthopedic shoes meeting the floor in muted thumps in her stride toward the door at the far side of the lab. "No matter how repugnant you find them, you have to learn to play nice. *That* is our drill for today."

When she swiped her ID card, the door slid open with a whispered *shush*.

"If you wheel in a tea set, I'm leaving." I sauntered over to the wall and let my head fall back against the painted cement blocks. "Last time you didn't even have cream. What are we, heathens?"

Poking her head out into the back hall of our facility, Micah spoke to one of her many lab-hands. "Number 730, could you bring our guest in, please?"

"730 holds his breath whenever he's around me," I mused to the ceiling. "I think he thinks what I have is an airborne virus. Whatever happened to 675? I liked him. He hit that good butcher shop in town for my steak and blood. The quality is totally worth the drive."

"Our primary benefactor doesn't want us getting too attached. You know that. They are afraid that kind of connection could be a liability to the security of our operation. Hence the 'No Names, Only ID Numbers' rule." Micah stepped back into the lab, leaving the door open behind her for 730 and our mystery guest.

730—a mountain of a man with a bushy soul patch and receding hairline—ambled in, shoving a gaunt and scruffy vampire in front of him. The vamp reeked of garbage and piss, an odd combination considering the latter was a function his own body could no longer manage. Sucking on one of *my* blood bags, he stumbled forward. Greasy hair darted off his head like porcupine spikes. His denim shirt and brown work pants were as stained and filthy as he was. If I had to guess, I would say neither had been cleaned in months. Yellow-rimmed eyes swung lazily in one direction, then the other. By the looks of his sunken cheeks and skeletal frame, a strong wind could take him down.

I didn't want to give that random gust the chance.

He was a vampire.

My muscles twitched with longing to paint the floor with his blood.

Shoving off the wall, I bolted forward only to be blocked by Micah's outstretched arm.

"Your objective is *not* to hurt him," she stated, locking stares with me to drive the message home. "Try to suppress your hatred and impulses. Talk to him. Make introductions. The sooner you can be civil, the sooner you can get out of the lab."

"Yesssss." S's slurring between lengthened incisors, I snapped my jaws in open threat. The hobo-vamp didn't even flinch. "Let's pretend we're civilized."

"Off to a great start," Mics grumbled, patting my shoulder. "Vinx, this is Vesbon. He doesn't abide by the Nosferatu rules of conduct. In some ways, I'm sure he considers himself a rebel to their cause. In actuality, he's known as a *scavenger* in the vampire hierarchy—aka a bottom-feeder. Hunting and rules aren't exactly his forte. Instead, he follows the stench of death and gobbles up whatever is left over. In his case, that usually means roadkill and other assorted vermin."

Combat-ready pose faltering, I shivered at that gruesome mental picture.

"Still think he's public enemy number one?" Pulling a pen from the pocket of her lab coat, Mics scribbled a note into the file. "730 and I are going to step outside to give you two a little time to get acquainted. This room will be monitored. I suggest you kids *play nice.*"

Keeping her warning glare fixed on me, she mind-melded the importance of achieving a passable level of decorum. Right up until the door clapped shut behind her.

For her, the tortured Scarlett Star, I would try. At least for a minute ...

"A scavenger, huh?" I muttered, in place of a standard greeting. My chin jerked in the smelly vamp's direction. "That's gotta be slim-pickings as of late. I'm guessing you're *not* a fan of the NPI Bill?"

Finishing the blood bag with a noisy slurp, Vesbon tossed it aside and wiped his mouth on the back of his hand. His discarded trash flopped to the floor, a few remaining ruby droplets slopping out onto the otherwise spotless linoleum.

Only then did his heavy-lidded gaze sweep my way, attempting to focus as he swayed on unsteady feet. If I had to guess, I would say the only thing he had to drink for a few months prior to that had been from a bottle in a brown paper bag.

"Hey, I know you," he slurred, jabbing a bobbing hand in my direction ... sort of.

Dragging my hands through my short-sheered hair, I tried to breathe through my mouth to avoid his stench. A pointless task with heightened senses. "I highly doubt we have *ever* traveled in the same social circles."

"No, no," he argued, wagging his grimy finger. "The hair is shorter and darker. Oh, and you're a vamp now. Still, I remember your smell. Even now, living in the darkness, the scent of sunshine lingers on your skin. I tasted you once, girl. You were as sweet as sugar-covered strawberries on a hot summer day."

Jaw set on edge, I rolled my shoulders to shrug off the shivers from his repellent existence. "I wasn't a fang slut. Two vamps bit me. That's it. Neither of which were you."

"You wouldn't remember me." Staggering a wide circle around the perimeter of the lab, Vesbon's vacant stare wandered up the walls to the glass dome that crowned it. "You had one foot through the pearly gates when I sniffed you out. *Mmmm*, the smell of all that carnage—that gushing pool of temptation—lured me to the house. I must have been a good boy, because it was my most mouth-watering fantasy come to life."

"Stop talking." I forced the words through clenched teeth. Whether he had actually stumbled upon the massacre that claimed my family or not, I had no way to know. Mentally, I tried to assure myself it didn't matter. If he *had*, he was nothing more than the crow picking at the corpse of the squirrel after the semi-truck ran it over. Unfortunately, that did nothing to suppress my growing urge to rip his head from his shoulders and fling it across the room like a shot put.

If he heard me, he didn't let on, but continued his stroll down memory lane. "I can't tell you where I holed up to escape the sun yesterday, or when I had eaten last before that bag your friend treated me to. What I do remember, in wonderful detail, is that bloody utopia I stumbled into, as if Vlad himself gifted it to me. Three bodies downstairs, one up. Two already dead, the others on their way. I got little more than a taste out of you. Whoever enjoyed your feast was the greedy type."

"*Shut ... up*." The words snuck from my lips in a barely audible hiss. Back rounding, my shoulders rose to my ears.

"On my hands and knees, I lapped blood off the floor. There was enough to keep me full for weeks."

"You *need* to stop," I warned, the last of my resolve slipping away like granules of sand through my fingers.

In the hall outside, a swipe card buzzed, being denied access to open the door.

"What the hell? Get it open! *Now!*" Micah yelled from the other side. "*Vinx!* Vincenza, I didn't know. I'm sorry! Stay with me, don't listen to him. We can get you through this."

"I couldn't let myself get filled up there, though." Finally turning my way, a malicious smile twined at the corners of Vesbon's thin lips. "Not with the boy laying there, whimpering for mercy."

Jeremy.

The vamp bitch snapped his neck. Had she not killed him? Was he laying there paralyzed, powerless to do anything while this twitchy parasite fed on him?

"Vincenza, focus on me! I'm right here." Micah banged on the door, the sound of her voice drowned out by the sirens of rage blaring in my mind.

My gaze dragged to Vesbon in slow motion.

"Did you touch him?" I asked, tone hauntingly vacant of emotion.

Vesbon's gray, lump of a tongue flicked out to wet his lips. Eyes closing, he plunged headlong into the blissful recollection.

"I did so much more than that. There was enough fight left in him to cry for help. Not that anyone came. They never do." Adopting a sing-song cadence, he chirped, *"Not until ole' Vesbon's through!"*

While his mouth was still moving, I couldn't make out the words over the roar inside of my skull. Black tendrils of hate curled around the edges of my vision; coaxing ... prodding ... begging me to act on my darkest delight.

Micah's fists hammered harder still, rattling the door on its track. "Remember why we are doing this, Vinx! You're going to be faced with far worse. Don't give in to his taunting."

Vampires can't tolerate silver. But I was no vampire. Shortly after I moved back into the house, Micah gave me a few boxes of my belongings she had pulled from storage. At the bottom of a tote full of toiletries, I found a sterling silver nail file that once belonged to my grandmother. A rose-gold orchid vined up the handle. Beautiful as it was, it was deadly in the right hands. *My* hands. Since that moment, I kept it with me at all times, nestled somewhere on my person. As Vesbon rambled on, the cold chill of it warmed my hip, where I stowed it in the waistband of my stretchy workout pants. Fingers twitching, my hand itched to close around the file and introduce it to chatty Vesbon in a flurry of violent slashes.

"Ah! I still have my souvenir!" Vesbon boasted. Digging into the pocket of his soiled trousers, he held up his treasure for me to see. A small chunk of rotting, putrefied earlobe, decorated with a thin gold hoop, dangled between his pinched fingers.

Ice seeped through my veins, seizing my heart in an unforgiving fist of sorrow. The last time I stared directly at that same earring, I was flicking it with my forefinger just to annoy Jeremy because he ate the last bag of microwave popcorn. There it hung, a hunk of decomposing flesh that was all that was left of my brother.

In the silence of that moment, the last thread of my reservation ... *snapped.*

The file *shush*ed free from my waistband, eager to greet my palm. One slash, straight across the throat, sliced a gaping smile that belched a cape of tar-like blood down Vesbon's front. Flipping the file into an overhand grip, I swung wide. The second strike sunk into the worthless lump of his heart. Tissue squished beneath my thrust, the file stabbing in, handle deep. Pulling back for a third blow, Vesbon denied me the pleasure —miserable beast that he was—by exploding into a flurry of fiery ash.

While I covered my mouth with the crook of my elbow to avoid inhaling the toxic vamp, the door finally stuttered open. Sprinting into the room, Micah and 730 pulled up short at the settling cloud of vamp dust. Blinking my way, shock and horror jockeyed for primary emotion etched into Micah's aghast features.

"On the upside," I offered, one shoulder rising and falling in a tight shrug, "he *totally* believed I was a real vampire. That's good, right?"

THIRTEEN
EXPERIMENT DAY 400: EFFECT

Peer review – Evaluation by one or more people of similar competence.

Welcome to the historic Lockwood-Mathews Mansion!" Dressed in a white suit, paired with a plum button-down, Duncan— the colossal triplet—threw the doors to the grand estate open wide. Stepping back, he welcomed the waiting masses in with a formal wave of his arm. The crowd around me moved in a steady surge, excitement swirling in a titter of anxious whispers.

Hand on my elbow so he didn't lose me in the crush, Carter sucked air through his teeth. "These Washington bureaucrats came here to see Bela Lugosi, and Ricardo Montalbán opened the door." Hitching one eye-brow he attempted Montalbán's well-known accent, "Ah, yes, Tattoo, the humans expect the malevolence of a *Dark Shadows* episode. We will confuse and enchant them with bright colors, clever lighting, and an excess of alcohol."

Lifting my knees higher beneath the shimmering ivory fabric of my silk sheath dress, I tugged the heels of my designer shoes out of the grassy terrain. Extra outdoor lighting had been positioned around the immaculately landscaped grounds, brightening twilight's subtle cloak to the glow of late afternoon. "Skip the alcohol, my rapid healing makes it damned near impossible to maintain a buzz for longer than a minute. I would be far more enchanted by patio pavers to save my Louboutin's."

Not that the rolling grounds of the estate weren't magnificent; every inch of it exuded regal elegance. A massive porch ran the length of the mansion. Roofline peaks jutted toward the sky like fingers reaching for the angels. It was old school elegance thrust into the modern day bore.

Beside the etched glass doors of the main entrance, a reporter in a sharp red pants suit with black piping stepped in front of a middle-aged pretty boy with a chin dimple.

"Representative Alfonso Markus," the reporter rambled at top speed, shoving a microphone in his face as her camera-man jogged to keep up. "What brought you to the Lockwood-Mathews Mansion today? Can we expect an endorsement from you for the NPI Bill?"

"It's a little early for me to make an endorsement," he said without breaking stride, a practiced smile sliding across his nipped and tucked face. "But I will say that the NPI Bill affects us all, and we should educate ourselves before casting our votes in either direction."

With gentle insistence, he pushed the microphone aside and excused himself into the threshold of the vampire manor.

Back straightening, Carter craned his neck to scan the throng being herded in like cattle. "Your boy Rau has friends in high places. It's a who's who of the political elite here. That's Supreme Court Justice Nathaniel Dean." He jerked his head in the direction of a man with a basset hound face and puffy gray hair. "He fought tooth and nail to prevent gay marriage from becoming legal ... despite his own inklings toward those possessing the Y chromosome. And the hobbit looking guy with the wide-rimmed glasses? That's Lawrence Rawling, the county commissioner. He was placed in that job after the previously seated commissioner was fired following Micah's unfortunate incident which earned her the title as the Scarlett Star."

Bristling at the mention of Micah's name, I said a silent prayer that she would stay home and inside as promised, and *not* slaughter 842 and 657 who were stationed at the house as guards. "Two of many," I mumbled, jaw locked tight with the tension of the topic. "Think this bill has a better chance than we thought?"

With the wide maw of the mansion's opulent entrance looming before us, Carter's gaze traveled the length of me with appreciation. "I think ... we're at a stately manor, swarming with the flawless beauty of immortals, and *still* you manage to be the most stunning creature in the room. I am one lucky son of a bitch to get to walk in with you on my arm."

If my blood pumped normally, I may have blushed. As it was, I gifted him a playful grin while lifting the hem of my dress enough to grant me the motion to step up onto the stoop. "Put him in a suit and instantly he's gifted with the 007 charm."

There were roughly a hundred of us being corralled into the foyer, decorated with rich mahogany and precious antiques. Dressed in a fitted silver suit complemented by a pale pink shirt, triplet Thomas closed the doors behind the last of the stragglers and nodded to Elodie at the base of the grand stairs. At the march, she had been dressed in all black, her expression fixed and stern. Now, the rough edges of her style had been smoothed over for the sake of the skittish humans. Black hair piled on top of her head, a white chiffon dress with tiny pink roses whispered over her curves.

Hands folded demurely in front of her, she addressed the crowd with an easy smile. "Welcome, friends. All of us at the Vampire Coalition are delighted to have you join us. Now, it is my great honor to introduce your host for the evening, activist and political pioneer, Rau Mihnea."

Pivoting her upper body, she tipped her face to the top of the stairs and led the room in a polite round of applause. The silhouette of Rau's frame appeared down the hall. Building anticipation with his measured stride, his presence swelled before us.

At the summit of the stairs, he paused to let the room drink him in. This was no cloaked creature of the night. This was a charismatic business man in a tan sport coat and robin's egg blue shirt. Shaking my head, I marveled at their impressive staging. They took rebranding to a whole new level.

Eyes crinkling with a subtle grin, the vampire lord made eye contact with each of his guests, easing down the stairs as he spoke. "I am humbled to have you all join me tonight. When I first made the decision to host this gathering, I feared no humans would attend. That the media had so swayed public opinion, blind fear would prevent any chance of an alliance. Yet, here you all are, dressed to impress and eager to learn about a culture often misconstrued. I invite you now to follow my lovely assistant, Elodie, into the ballroom. Our exhibits and artifacts are on display there. We will begin our demonstrations shortly."

At the bottom of the stairs, a receiving line formed of visitors eager to shake Rau's hand before wandering off to peruse the sights. The line moved in a steady course, shoes scuffing over the speckled marble floor, until Representative Markus reached our host. At his elbow stood a lanky bald man who looked as though he made a career sucking the tartness out of lemons.

"Representative Markus, Mr. Rutherford, always a pleasure." Rau shook their hands one after the other, looking each in the eye for a pointed acknowledgment. "After our previous discussions about your reservations, I'm happy to see you coming out to gain more insight into the culture of the Nosferatu."

"Don't confuse this with us supporting you or your bill," the bald man I now knew as Rutherford snipped, wiping his palm on his pant leg as if worried Rau's touch contaminated him. "This is a fact-finding mission. Nothing else."

"Easy, Neil!" Representative Markus chuckled, tipping his head in apology to Rau. "It seems my friend here hasn't quite reached the level of open-mindedness one would hope after you opened the doors of your lovely home to us. While my own hesitations and doubts are still in place, I *am* interested to learn more about your society of vampires and why, after all these centuries, you suddenly want so badly to integrate into our community."

Seeing an opportunity to educate for his cause, Rau rocked back on his heels and folded his hands in front of him. "Only through an open dialogue can we reach mutual understanding. May I ask what qualms you have with the vampire integration?"

"For starters," Rutherford grumbled, "more than once I have had bodies on my table with mysterious bite marks on their necks. Never are charges filed. Not *once* has the public been notified of a potential threat."

"Oh boy," Carter sucked air through his teeth, grimacing on Rau's behalf. From our front row seat as the very next people in line, we got the treat of catching every awkward moment of the exchange. "I thought I recognized that guy. That's Neil Rutherford, the county coroner. Vampires and the keeper of the dead in the same space. That's a terrifying prospect."

Head listing to the side, I sized the angry-looking man up as the scrappy type. "If this goes south, I hope they opt for bloodshed. Debates are a tedious torture no being should be subjected to."

Carter considered me through narrowed eyes. "And if that were to happen, whose side would you be on?"

Snagging glasses of champagne for us both from a passing tray, I gifted him with a toothy grin. "That's easy, my own. But I would let you huddle behind me in fear."

"That may be the sweetest thing you've ever said to me," Carter *tsk*ed in over-exaggerated appreciation, accepting the elegant stemware I offered.

"Low standards and a hot ass. You just might be my perfect man," I teased, bringing my glass to my lips to hide a flirty smirk.

Back straightening, which only accentuated the expert cut of his tailored suit, Carter adjusted his silver-blue tie. "Keep talking like that and I'm going to get all school-girl giddy and forget we're here on business," he muttered, a devilish grin stealing across his handsome features.

As the crowd around us thinned, we seemed the only ones that hadn't gone silent. The rest of the dawdlers hovered close by, itching to catch every word of the potentially volatile political exchange.

Wetting his lips, ever present mask of composure firmly in place, Rau met Rutherford's accusation head on. "On the rare occasion our coalition learns of a possible offense by one of our own, an investigation is immediately launched. If the accused party or parties are found guilty, it is dealt with internally with severe, and often fatal, repercussions. We have a zero-tolerance policy for feeding on the unwilling, Mr. Rutherford, and it's a decree we do *not* bend on."

"With all due respect," one corner of Markus's mouth tugged back in a casual half-grin, "that's part of the problem. Your kind want to join our society, yet still continue to police your own. If you don't respect the laws, rules, and regulations as the rest of us do, how can you ever truly assimilate?"

"Representative Markus, we already live by your laws. We choose to, just to walk among you. But yes, we do police our own because your methods of imprisonment and recourse are not Nosferatu effective. Until the time that law enforcement includes vampire police, or silver holding cells and restraints, we have no choice but to continue to supervise and regulate our own."

"I couldn't agree more." Rutherford's lip curled in distaste. "Our officers *should* carry vampire weapons of mass destruction. That and riot gear for the day we chase you all back into the shadows."

The air was sucked from the room in a shocked intake of breath by stunned onlookers.

All eyes swiveled to Rau who turned to frosty stone under the scrutiny.

The silence was broken by Markus' mouth opening with a pop. "I've known you for nearly thirty years, Neil, and I never knew you to be capable of such blatantly disrespectful bigotry." Turning to Rau, he added, "My deepest apologies to you, Mr. Mihnea. I would not have made him my plus one for this event if I knew him capable of behaving in such a fashion. Perhaps you could have one of your aides show him out so as not to further tarnish the evening for the rest of us."

"And this would be of no insult to you?" Rau confirmed before acting.

Silently, Rutherford glowered, jaw clenched and nostrils flaring.

"Not in the least. As a matter of fact," rising on the balls of his feet, Markus caught Duncan's eye and waved him over, "I'll lead the effort myself so nothing is misconstrued. My good sir, would you please escort my friend here out? It seems he remembered the dress code, but forgot his manners."

Uneasy laughter bubbled through the huddle of lookie-loos as Duncan reached for Rutherford's arm.

"Don't you dare touch me, you unholy beast!" the enraged coroner barked, snatching his arm away. "I can show myself out of this glorified freak show."

Casting a final scowl in Markus' direction, Rutherford stomped out, with the crowd parting to escape his wrath, and slammed the door behind him.

"What did you say this would be?" Leaning against Carter's chest, I gifted myself an enticing whiff of his eucalyptus shower gel as I whispered in his ear, "A stuffy gathering full of pompous windbags?"

"I stand corrected." The warm tips of his fingers brushed the small of my back where my gown dipped to the rise of my hips. "This keeps up and we might see someone drop fang before daybreak."

"There now," Markus beamed, clapping a supportive hand on Rau's shoulder, "we can move on and have a pleasant evening. I'll leave you to your waiting guests, and see you inside."

Turning on his heel, Markus followed the path Elodie had led into the ballroom.

Carter and I waited a beat for Rau's stare to tear from the retreating state representative, and fall on us. Lucky for him his next guests weren't unfamiliar humans. They would have taken one look at the unchecked darkness swirling in his gaze, and all his professional pretenses would be shattered.

In a series of rapid blinks, he forced his façade back into place and offered us his hand and a smile. "Vincenza, Carter, you are a welcome sight. Your progeny—"

"She couldn't make it tonight," I interrupted, hating the mention of her slipping from his tongue. It was because of *him* the change was forced upon her. "Adjusting to rebirth has taken its toll of her, I'm afraid."

"Quite the opposite, my dear." Rau's grin brightened with genuine amusement. "In fact, if you look up to the second floor, you will see she worked out a special surprise for you."

With the bitter bile of a complete loss of control rising in the back of my throat, I shifted my gaze upward. Micah loomed at the top of the stairs draped in a stunning sapphire gown and malevolent smirk.

"Hello, Mummy," she purred.

Carter tensed beside me, glance shooting in the direction where Rutherford had made his exit. "Suddenly, it feels like we chased out The Reaper and invited in Death."

FOLLOWING THE FLOW of traffic led us through the lush green menagerie of Rau's private conservatory, to a sprawling ballroom lined with marble pillars. Draperies in deep jewel tones separated the imposing space into smaller compartments occupied by various displays.

Keeping our smiles plastered in place for the milling masses, I questioned Micah through clenched teeth, "What the hell are you doing here? I thought we agreed you weren't ready for social outings."

Flipping her braids over her shoulder, Mics batted her mile-long lashes at a passing reporter. Poor fella tripped over his own feet in attempts to hold her stare just a moment longer. "*You* said I wasn't ready. I ignored you and called an Uber."

Catching her wrist, I spun her to face me, taking a quick scan of the crowd to make sure no prying ears were listening before I spat, "Do you remember how long you made me wait and all the training we did before you let me matriculate in any way? I remember *numerous* warnings about how dire the consequences would be if I risked venturing out before I was *completely* prepared."

Eyes wide and innocent, a malicious sneer twisted the corners of her bronze-painted lips. "And how did that first excursion go?"

Guilt tugged my gaze Carter's way.

"I thought you lined up a sitter for her," he offered, jerking his head in Micah's direction. "You know, to give mom and dad a night off from the kiddo?"

Ignoring his quip, I tried to swallow down the blame haunting me. "You know what happened, Micah, and that's *exactly* what has me worried."

"But that's the difference between you and me. You were a scrawny, inexperienced *pup* trying to figure out the hierarchy of an established pack. And me? Baby, I'm already an alpha dog."

While the response was still forming on my tongue, she sashayed off to join the party with her thick ass twitching, much to the delight of every red-blooded man she passed.

"She's going to get us all killed, isn't she?" Carter mused, scratching his chin with the side of his knuckle.

"That *does* seem to be her goal," I griped. "Best we can do is keep an eye on her and tether her if she starts getting feisty."

"In that case, I'm going to need another one of these." As yet another waiter breezed past, Carter swapped his empty glass for a full one.

"Sip and walk. I'm not losing sight of her."

Riding Micah's wake, we wandered through the displays of vampire life and lore. Thomas played presenter for the first, showcasing the latest in Nosferatu sleep pods.

"The VampNap allows us to rest and escape the sun's harmful rays wherever we may be." Pressing a button on the side of the sleep unit, Thomas opened its sliding canopy door. "With internal LED lighting, a memory foam mattress and a television streaming the latest Hollywood hits, you can see we've upgraded beyond sleeping in coffins."

"All right now, I gotta give this a try." A good ole boy with an expensive suit and happy-go-lucky smile ambled into the exhibit, hoisting his frame into the cocoon of the pod. Wriggling into the mattress, he grinned at the chuckling audience. "I need one of these for my office. Hell, maybe even for home. Bless her heart, my wife Barbara snores like a grizzly bear."

Lurching forward, the invited paparazzi set the moment ablaze with flash bulbs.

"Attorney General Berry, look over here!"

"Can we get a smile, Bob?"

"Will the NPI Bill get a Bob Berry endorsement?"

"Easy now." Closing his eyes, Berry pretended to be asleep. "I was looking for a nap, not to make a political statement."

Sauntering on, we let the lilt of laughter fade behind us. Elodie's demonstration was next on the tour. Draped in a heavy wool cloak, she stood before a stone basin filled with smoldering cinders. "These are ever burning embers, just as Vlad is everlasting. Lit from a torch at Castle Draculesti, where our lord lays, they are transported by our clergy and act as a reminder that one day he will rise again and walk amongst the worthy." Holding up a stone no larger than a sand dollar, she showed it to the onlookers. "With stones such as these we brand our forearms with the Draculesti crest, to bear his mark as true believers."

A middle-aged brunette with a loose bun and cat-framed glasses raised her hand. "With your ability to heal, the mark will vanish almost instantly, won't it? What, then, is the point?"

"It does heal and is then reapplied at our next sacred gathering," Elodie confirmed with appreciative nod at the question. "Consider it as you would communion for Christians. It is done often to reaffirm our faith."

Hitching one eyebrow, I quietly contested, "But instead of turning water into wine, our god opens a vein."

120

"Wine? And here I thought your drink of choice was an Old Fashion neat." I recognized the husky voice behind me instantly. Primarily because it awoke a deep loathing within me that yearned for violence and mayhem.

Linking my fingers with Carter's, in hopes of borrowing an iota of his serenity, I steeled my spine and turned to face the devil incarnate. "Carter, may I introduce my ex, Finn Danior, who slaughtered my family and left me for dead. Finn, this is my human companion, Carter ... who will be holding me back if I spontaneously lunge for your throat. Carter—Finn, Finn—Carter."

"Is ... is this the f-first time you've seen him since they d-died?" Carter stammered, eyes bulging in horror.

"We crossed paths once before," I admitted, scanning the room to locate Micah chatting up Judge Dean, "and reached the understanding that at some point, when I see fit, I'm going to kill him."

Carter's stare lobbed from Finn, to me, and back again. "Good thing you two have that understanding or this little interaction would be *insanely* awkward."

Silence.

"Yep, not uncomfortable at all." Carter drained his glass in one gulp and held it up before him. "Hey, look! My drink is empty and there's a bar in the corner. I'm going for a refill. Anyone want anything?"

Grinding my teeth, I begrudgingly granted Finn his momentary victory. "Old Fashion neat. But only because it sounds good, *not* because he suggested it."

"Atta girl." Carter tried unsuccessfully to fight off a grin. "If you can't be right, be petty."

The second Carter was out of ear shot, Finn took a brazen step closer. Raven locks falling across his forehead in an inviting disarray, he peered up at me from under his brow. "That dress designer should send you a formal thank you for how his work wears you. You have never looked better, Vincenza. If I haven't said it before, immortality suits you."

For a beat, I let myself drink him in. That chiseled jawline. The sculpted physique built with naughty promise in mind. Full, soft lips whose talents I could still taste.

Was I tempted?

Fuck no.

He killed my family!

That wasn't really an issue I was willing to work through.

"What about when my blood was pooling around me and I was begging for mercy? How did *that* look on me? Did you find it fetching?" I countered. Crossing my arms over my chest, I slaughtered him at least six different ways with my glare.

"We've talked about my lack of recollections of that night." Stare leisurely traveling the length of me, Finn dragged his tongue over his gums where the bulge of his fangs swelled. "Even so, that wasn't you. Not anymore. You've left the human foil. If there's anything I've learned, it's that our kind doesn't meld well with humans. Let our own tragic tale be proof of that."

My mouth opened with a sharp and cutting rebuttal, only to snap shut again.

When we engage the twat-weasel, we give it the attention it feeds off of.

"What do you want, Finn?" I asked, running my forefinger over the rim of my champagne flute. "I have a baby-vamp to watch and no time for your shit."

"What do I want?" Finn contemplated, sucking air through his teeth. "To see the fresh heaven that lies beneath that gown, followed by a weekend of debauchery. But ... I'll settle for a warning—among friends."

"Friends?" My eyebrows rocketed into my hairline. "How did you not choke on that word?"

Pursing his full, pouty lips, he feigned insult. "Come on, Vinx, we shared a near death experience. Surely, that earned me a bit of trust?"

"It earned you a bit of conversation," I corrected. Finding Micah on the move, I craned my neck to keep her in my eyeline. "Of which your time is running out."

"Even if it's about your boy, Carter?" Biting his lower lip, Finn's slate-colored gaze twinkled with wicked delight. "I've met him before. Not that he was in the state of mind to remember."

That was enough to draw my stare from my wandering progeny. "What the hell are you talking about?"

"Whatever draws humans and vampires together at first, in the end it all comes down to blood. A suck here, a nip there, and you either end up with a dead body ... case in point," he jabbed a hand in my direction, "or a human hooked on the rush of vampire blood. Whenever the vampire coalition feels anyone is becoming victim to their own demise, they offer them discreet treatment options. One of which your friend, Mr. Westerly, could tell you all about."

Scanning the room, I found Carter stopped in front of a display of vampire-themed artwork, where Rau most-likely was explaining the meaning behind it. Catching my eye, Carter offered me a boyish grin.

"I don't believe you. The coalition was holding him against his will. They planned to sell him to the highest bidder with the biggest appetite."

"Is that what he told you?" Plucking a drink from a passing tray, Finn polished it off in one gulp. "That after being hired to promote the NPI Bill, they imprisoned him and plotted his execution? And, since you whisked him out of there, that makes you, what? His hero?"

Come to think of it, Carter had never made any such claim. In fact, he never talked about his time among the Nosferatu at all. "Actually, yes," I lied.

Stepping in close enough for me to smell the faint tinge of blood on his breath, Finn dropped his voice to an intimate whisper. "I hate to shatter the knight with fangs for armor image you've constructed for yourself, but your friend was in rehab. He hooked up with a vampress by the name of Coraline and developed a greedy little addiction. I do hope his appetite hasn't flared since the two of you have been together."

"He's only drank from me once," I mumbled, struggling to swallow around the fist of unease squeezing my throat in a merciless vise grip. "I ... forced him."

"I'm sure that's exactly what he led you to believe." Finn chuckled, the cold chill of his touch jolting through me as he brushed his fingertips down the length of my arm. "I'm sure it's pure coincidence that his last two girlfriends were vampires, and not *at all* a twisted fetish."

Bobbing through the crowd, Carter drank me in, concern clouding his features.

"Oh! There is one more thing," Finn added, almost as if it were an afterthought. "His addiction? Coraline? Her skin was the hue of polished mahogany. Her hair as untamable as her spirit."

"Why are you telling me this?" I growled through gritted teeth.

"Because, Vinx, you met her. She was the same vampress who fed on you with me the night you were turned." Letting his words fall like stones in the chilling pool of his absence, Finn disappeared into the crowd.

"Everything okay?" Carter asked, gliding up beside me to hand me my Old Fashion.

Eagerly accepting it, I brought the amber liquid to my lips, prolonging answering him until I got to the bottom of the glass. A scent in the air rerouted my agenda, its magnetic lure igniting my veins with fiery longing. Dropping my drink to my side, I took a tentative whiff. Then another. The metallic tang of life filled the air, awakening my urgent ache to drop fang.

"I smell blood," I mumbled quietly to avoid causing a riot.

The mood in the room shifted. Every vamp fell silent. Spines straightening, their nostrils twitched at the perfume of temptation. The milling humans were oblivious ... so far. One flash of fang would change all that.

Even Rau, in the midst of a speech about the symbolism of a painting depicting a green demon seated in a garden, froze stone still. He only blinked back to an animated state when Thomas jogged up to whisper an urgent bulletin in his ear.

His nod of understanding countered by a troubled frown, Rau brought his microphone back to his lips. "Ladies and gentlemen, we are having a bit of a security issue. At this time, we will be concluding our activities and closing the doors to Lockwood-Mathews. We thank you for coming and hope you can visit us again very soon."

The triplets took their cue from that, ushering the humans out with comforting smiles and vague excuses.

Finding himself caught in the shuffle, Carter stumbled to stay with me in the crush of pushing him toward the exit. "Vinx?"

Visions flashed behind my eyes of him suckling from the bosom of the vamp I nicknamed the Black Mamba. "Go home. I'll meet you there."

Reluctantly, with dejection slicing lines between his brow, he gave in and let the surge drag him out. The moment the last beating heart—that they were aware of—had been escorted from the premises, Finn sealed the ballroom doors with a vacuum of finality.

Crossing the room in shadow form, Rau shoved aside the curtain behind the VampNap display. The previously muffled stench of death flooded the room, forcing a toothy reaction from all of us sharing the tainted space.

She sat hunkered against the wall. A black masquerade mask hooded eyes that stared fixed and unblinking into the hereafter. I recognized the red pants suit she wore in an instant. Its spiffy black trim had been ripped and splattered with gore. The discarded pile of meat before us had been the reporter questioning people outside only moments ago.

"Should we lock down the manor, my lord?" Thomas' chest swelled with purpose, his hands clasped behind his back. "And summon the police?"

Squatting down to check the woman's pulse, Rau chewed on the question. His hands fell between his knees, and he shook his head.

"It won't bring her back," he grumbled, hating the words tumbling from his tongue. "A murder on known vampire grounds would reaffirm the bigoted views of our opponents. That would be the death of the NPI Bill before it even made it to the vote. No, this was done for a reason. Someone was looking to send a message specifically for me."

"My lord?" Duncan edged up behind him, confusion creasing his face. "How do you know this to be intentional?"

Gently and respectfully, Rau slid off the accessory garnishing the face of the dearly departed. Cradling the black mask with vining gold trim in his palms, his top lip quivered into a vicious snarl. "This is the same style of adornment Joselyn wore when her body was fished from the river. Whoever did this, had insight into the death of my beloved and is choosing to taunt me with it."

Feeling the current of wrath from a centuries' old beast cracking and rallying around me, I did a mental head count of the vampires present and accounted for. Rau crouched by the victim. Duncan and Thomas hovered behind him, awaiting further command. Elodie shrugged off her cloak, letting it fall in a heap at her feet. Finn hovered by the door, undoubtedly hoping for a chance to slip out undetected. A few others I had yet to meet drifted nearby, seemingly as lost and bewildered as I was.

Dread prickled over my chilled skin when I realized one particular vamp was notably missing.

Micah was nowhere to be seen.

FOURTEEN
EXPERIMENT DAY 231: CAUSE

Experiment – A procedure carried out to support, refute, or validate a hypothesis.

Seated in the back of the Lincoln Town Car, I smoothed down the front of the ash-colored pant suit Micah coerced me into wearing. After months spent in breathable workout gear, the ensemble felt like it was trying to smother my crotch with the miserable fabrics of the mundane.

"After the Vesbon debacle, you said I wasn't ready to interact with other vampires yet," I pointed out for what felt like the millionth time, shoving a rogue strand of hair behind my ear. "You were quite adamant about it. I believe the phrase *will-power of a nympho at a nudist colony* was used."

"Oh, hell no, I won't be subjecting either of us to that again any time soon," Micah agreed, checking her file with the house address one last time. "If they didn't eat your eyeballs for sport, you would find some way to sneak in a weapon and take out as many of them as you could before they swarmed. That said, is your silver nail file on your person?"

"Yes, it is."

"Is there any chance I can convince you to leave it in the car?"

"No, there is not."

Filling her lungs with an exasperated breath, Mics exhaled through her nose, causing the delicate hoop of her nostril piercing to shimmy. "Try not to kill anyone with it."

"I will do my best." Head lolling in the direction of the white two-story boasting the American dream right outside our car window, I chewed on the inside of my cheek. "What makes you think I'm ready for *this?*"

"Basic conversation with a human being?" Pausing, Micah deliberated on the matter. "Absolutely nothing. But at least it is less likely to have fatal consequences."

"Worst pep talk, ever," I deadpanned.

In the front seat, 483, our latest assistant and driver, snorted his amusement. It had been two weeks since he replaced 972. We were still in an introductory period, yet so far he seemed a vast improvement from his predecessor who had an ever present toothpick lodged between his teeth and only communicated through gruff grunts.

Leaning over my lap, Micah opened the door and nudged me out with an elbow to the ribs. "All we need here is information. The man inside is Joselyn's father. My source says he was very involved in the search for his daughter. *Any* information that he could give us would be helpful. We know she paired with Rau. Whether it was willingly or by force remains to be seen. What we don't know is what atrocities she faced after that. If she called home, sent a letter, an email, or sent up a SOS signal, we need to know."

"Okay," I relented, swinging my legs out of the car. "If I'm not back in five minutes, it's because I'm suffering through a horribly awkward social interaction I will later need precarious amounts of alcohol-laced blood to recover from."

"Who are you kidding? You know you can't get drunk anymore. The bummers of rapid healing."

Sucking air through my teeth, I recoiled. "That is so mean. Why would you remind me of that in my moment of need?"

The instant I vacated the lush leather seat, she scooted into my place. Her hand closed around the door handle. "We don't want him to get stage fright having an audience. 483 and I will drive around the block, then park across the street. Your job is to smile, do your best impression of a pleasant human being, and let the guy pour his heart out. Simple enough."

With a casual lift of her shoulders, Mics slammed the door shut. They backed out of the driveway, gravel crunching under the tires of the Lincoln.

"Be a pleasant human being," I parroted. Standing in the driveway, twilight casting long shadows across the yard, I pivoted on my heel. With a wide, determined gait to get this over with, I strode to the navy-blue door with its polished brass fixtures and trim. "It's a conversation, Vinx. You've talked to people before. Used to thrive off it, in fact. Remember debate team? That was fun. Of course, that was before I drank blood and had a pulse that would make coma patients seems spastic, but that's neither here nor there."

Raising my fist, I delivered two sharp raps to the door.

Metal rattled and the knob turned.

"Oh, hell. Here we go," I muttered, fixing a toothy smile into place an uncomfortable second too late. "Hi, Mr. ..."

Son of a ... I never asked for their last name! Way to plummet from zero to completely inept in break neck speed.

"... Joselyn's dad. My name is Vincenza Larow. I was hoping I could talk to you about—"

"I know who you are," he interrupted. Standing a few inches above the six-foot mark, Mr. Joselyn's dad may have been a hottie in his younger days. Salt and pepper hair waved just past his ears. His features resembled that of Rhett Butler ... if the infamous star hit fifty and stopped giving a crap. "You're late. Hurry inside before my neighbors see you."

Stepping aside, he gestured me in with an urgent wave of his hand. I glanced over my shoulder, peering in the direction the car disappeared, wishing for some of the clarification it drove off with. "I … wasn't aware you were expecting me. Did Micah call you?"

"Yes, yes, come inside." As herded me into his foyer, the door clapped shut behind me, giving me a start.

The furnishings and décor of the living room to my left seemed an homage to the year nineteen ninety-five, wrapped in plastic to preserve its nostalgic charm. Every throw pillow, couch cushion, and inch of carpeting was covered with a thick layer of shiny, protective coating. Figurines and tchotchkes were safely tucked away in curio cabinets or display cases. This room was not for the living. It was a staged setting of a happy, functional family that no longer existed.

"Right this way," he instructed. Turning his back to me, he walked in the opposite direction, giving me time to notice his shirt tails hanging out from beneath his cardigan. It was a surprising show of dishevelment that betrayed his outwardly pressed façade.

"This will only take a minute. I'm fine right here," I protested, planting roots in that spot.

Opening a door in the hall, Mr. Joselyn's dad blinked my way, his expression vacant and haunting. "What you came for is down here. You can stand there staring, or you can see for yourself. Makes no difference to me."

In my human days, a suggestion like that would have made me bolt for the door in a blur of flying knees and elbows. Maybe it was the irregular beat of my heart that lured me into a false sense of security. Maybe I'm a moron. Whatever the reason, my dumbass fell into step behind him.

Don't judge too harshly, it's not like I believed myself invincible. I *did*, however, trust in the badass abilities I had been gifted with. One of our more generous benefactors arranged for me to train with the top MMA coaches in the field. Thanks to the teachings of Sa Bum Nim Dae and Grand Master Kwan, I could calculate what strike I would use if different circumstances were to arise.

If he lunges with a knife, I counter with an X block and use his momentum to drive the blade into the artery of his inner thigh.

130

Creepy bastard tries to grab me from behind, I use the side of my fist to punch him in the nuts as hard as I can. When he folds in half in pain, I slam my elbow into the bridge of his nose.

Or, if he lays a hand on me in any way, I rip his shoulders from their sockets and pin him to the wall with his own floppy appendages.

Okay, that last one was more vamp than martial arts. Still, the method of deterrent would be an effective one.

"And what's down there has to do with your daughter's disappearance?" Focused on his face, I didn't miss his flinch at the reminder that she was gone. A shroud of sorrow sagged his shoulders, stealing the dim light from behind his eyes.

"I don't have a daughter." Shaking his head, he left the door to the basement stairs hanging open, and shuffled into the kitchen with leaden feet. "Not anymore."

At the summit of the stairs, I peered down into the cavernous unknown. A bare bulb flickered from the ceiling rafters, threatening to plunge the basement into darkness at any moment. Music drifted up, the hypnotic drumming chorus of The Doors' "Riders on the Storm" easily recognizable. Heightened senses granted me the ability to hear the needle of the record player *shush* across the surface of the vintage vinyl. Beyond that, in a distant corner, something was alive down there. Their weak pulse and palpable terror called to the uglier instincts writhing within me.

It was those same inklings, comprised of dark shadows and unspeakable longings, that drew me down those creaking wood stairs. With each step of my descent, the music grew louder. As if Mr. Mojo Risin' himself was warning me to turn back. Ducking under the low hanging vent work, I scanned the dank and dusty space. At first glance, it looked like any other basement. Shelves in the corner were stacked with canned goods and paper products. The furnace chugged and whirred to my right. Boxes erupting with everything from Christmas garland to paint cans scattered the perimeter, situated to allow a workable path between them. Hair on the back of my neck rising in ominous warning, I reached into the pocket of my suit coat and closed my fist around grandma's silver nail file. Even if I encountered a malicious critter that fell into the non-vamp category, there were very few things that couldn't be taken down by a sharp object swung with purposeful intent.

A glance back up the stairs showed no sign of my host returning. Gritting my teeth to steady my nerves, I followed the cardboard trail around a bend to where it ended at a fruit cellar door. A sliver of light shone from underneath it, the source of the music trapped within. Nostrils flaring, I sniffed the air in a deep drag. The pungent metallic tang of old blood forced my fangs down with the *pop* of torn tissue.

Raising my hand, my fingertips brushed the chipped and tattered door. It opened with a breeze of a touch, swinging on its hinges at a snail's pace. I would have reveled in that last fleeting moment of sanity if I knew I was about to spiral into Helter Skelter.

In the center of the room sat an altar ... of sorts. A slab of meat, that had once been a body, was splayed across its surface. The chest was cracked open, the cavity within exposed. Wooden stakes pierced every quivering organ, except the heart. Bile scorching up the back of my throat, my fist flew to my mouth to squelch it. Every inch of available wall space was decorated with snap shots of bodies being tortured and mangled by nightmarish means. Inching closer to the pictures confirmed my chilling suspicion. They were all vampires. Immortal beings unable to die as someone tore them apart piece by piece.

Maybe Joselyn's father was heartbroken and seeking vengeance.

Maybe he was a psychotic mad man.

Neither option bode well for me.

He took great pleasure in torturing vampires, and I was wearing the most convincing vamp costume imaginable. The fact that he lured me down there to bask at his trophies led me to believe he wouldn't be open to the clarification discussion that needed to take place.

"Son of a bitch," I grumbled. Pulling out the file, I seized it in a tight overhand grip.

An anguished groan snapped my head around, instinct setting my muscles on a hairpin trigger to attack. The filleted body on the altar twitched, it's head lolling my way to prove there's no mercy for the damned.

Hair, crusted with blood, fell in a clump across a pallid forehead. Cracked, arid lips opened and shut, unable to form a single sound.

Ran through by the vicious blade of recognition, my mouth fell open with a gasp. I knew that vamp all too well. His face was burned behind my eyes, granting him a starring role in my every nightmare.

"Finn?" I rasped. For months, I dreamt of nothing more that subjecting him to unspeakable atrocities of my own creation. Even so, seeing him like that, I couldn't fathom *any* justification for that degree of suffering. At his side in two wide strides, I offered him my wrist. "Drink, *quickly*. We're getting the fuck out of here."

Black pupils, dilated by starvation, struggled to focus on me. Parched skin cracking and oozing, he forced his top lip to curl up. Two holes gaped at his gum line, his fangs ripped out by the root.

"You're going to owe me *big*," I grumbled, bringing my wrist to my mouth. "We're talking, like, *buy me a pony, and let me watch it nut-stomp you* level of gratitude."

Biting into my own flesh, I added the white-hot stabs of pain to the ever-growing list of things I hated him for. As ruby beads bulged from the wounds, I offered him my wrist a second time. Stifling a cringe, I looked away as his lips closed around the punctures and suckled life from my veins. While he drank in noisy slurps, I yanked the hand whittled stakes out of his exposed innards. With each shard of kindling I plucked from his torso, the tissue beneath began to knit itself back together.

Casting the last stake aside, I pulled my forearm away before he drank too much, and left us *both* too weak to escape. "Can you sit up? I need your help to get us out of here."

A bit of color returning to his fetid flesh, Finn closed the flaps of his mangled chest in a sickening soundtrack of cracks and squishes. "You're not here. Not real. Can't be. I showed you no mercy. That's why I'm here ... why I'm suffering."

Sliding my forearm under his shoulder, I forced him upright. "Later, when we are safely out of here, we will have a rousing chorus of *What a Monumental Ass Finn Is.* For right now, let's focus on working together to make sure we *have* a later."

"There is no later." Finn's hollowed gaze drifted over my shoulder, his crumbled form wilting further with defeat. "There's no hope. This is hell. If you're here, you're already dead."

Beaten, Finn rolled his head away from me in the same instant Joselyn's father stormed into the room, his face contorted in hate. Before I could shrug Finn out of my arms, the murderously bereaved father stabbed a syringe into my neck and emptied its contents into my vein.

"Vampire whore," he hissed against my ear, "I'm going to make you *beg* for death."

The mysterious solution coursed through me, scraping my veins with icy claws. Scream tearing from my throat, I spun into a low crouch, sweeping his legs out from under him. Instinct taking over, I pounced. Reduced to little more than a cornered animal, my lips curled from my teeth in a vicious snarl. In my right mind, I probably would have subdued him and called the cops. Sometimes, I dream that's what happened. That clearer heads prevailed ... and I *hadn't* lost myself to the enraged beast within.

But that candy-coated fantasy was not to be.

The tissue of his throat burst beneath my sawing fangs. Coppery warmth flooded my mouth, spilling from my lips in torrents that soaked the front of me. Pulling back, my palms cemented his shoulders to the ground.

"Should I make *you* beg for death?" I growled in a grating, demonic hiss foreign to my own ears.

Even as the color bleached from his skin, Joselyn's father shook with weak laughter. "You better kill me, devil bitch. Because, if there is even one ounce of life left in me, I'll use it to hunt you down. *You don't deserve to live.*"

Dipping my head to his, I murmured against his lips, "Neither do you."

I sunk my teeth in a second time, and his jugular popped beneath my fangs. A shudder. A choked gurgle. I felt the fight leave his body with a deathly rattle. Somewhere, in the darkest recesses of my mind, a train whistle blew and a primal part of my nature awoke.

"What *are* you?" Finn croaked, my healing offering having granted him the strength to roll onto his elbow.

The sound of his voice snapped me from my feral spell. Releasing my locked jaws, I shoved away from the now lifeless body.

"*What have I done?*" A wash of unshed tears stung my eyes, blurring my vision.

"You saved both our lives." With a grunt, Finn planted one palm on the slab and pushed himself up. "What makes no sense is *how.* He injected you with silver, and it didn't affect you. You smell like an immortal, but your blood doesn't have that flat, stagnate taste of death. What are you?"

I pulled my knees to my chest, unable to tear my gaze from the body of my first *human* victim. "You lost the privilege to question me when you left me for dead."

Gripping the edge of the slab, Finn rotated his lower extremities to let his legs fall over the edge.

"The first kill is always the worst." Reading my pained expression, his tone softened. "It was him or us. If silver didn't work, he would have found something else that did."

As I floated through a myriad of emotions, I slapped a hand to the paneling covered wall behind me and rose on unsteady legs.

"Call Micah," I murmured to myself. "She'll know what to do."

"Vincenza." Finn shifted his weight, wincing from the ache of the movement. "I can't walk on my own. Will you help me?"

Hysterical laughter bubbled up the back of my throat, threatening to erupt in a complete meltdown. The first time we met, he wore a plaid shirt with a russet leather jacket. Now, he was holding his torso together with both hands.

"Vinx, please?" he pressed.

I knew I had a shopping list of reasons to reject his pleas. Unfortunately, hovering over the slack meat of my fresh kill, my fumbling mind couldn't seem to recall them. Attempting to scoot around the body, the toe of my shoe bumped Joselyn's father's thigh. A whimper escaped me that I clamped my lips shut to suppress.

"All these pictures on the walls," Finn whispered as if offering confession. "He used them as part of his game. Covering his eyes, he would throw a dart at a wall. Whichever vile photo he landed on, *that* is what he would do to me. Once, he even made *me* throw the dart."

"Why are you telling me this?" I ventured, skin crawling with the visualization of that horrid torment.

"Mourn the loss of a part of you from this kill. Not the man you took down. We are cursed with the title of monsters. He *earned* it."

Edging up beside him, I eased Finn's arm around my shoulders and held tight to his waist. "Lean on me. Let's get out of here."

"You said you were going to call Micah." Finn's voice rose and fell with huffs and grunts of pain. "Who is that? Who are you working with?"

"An elite group of none of your fucking business," I answered, stare locked on the door.

"Wait!" Finn attempted to plant his feet with all the weak resolve he could muster. "The puppy, we have to get the puppy."

"Puppy?" I pulled up short, searching his face for signs he was kidding.

"There, in the corner. Little thing won't make it much longer if he's left here." I followed Finn's nod to a tiny French Bulldog pup cowered in the corner. Covered in his own filth, every rib was clearly visible through his patchy, black hide. Ears pulled back, his slight frame trembled in a combination of fear and starvation. "He used the dog as an hour glass, taunting me with the promise of a meal if I could just get off the table. He gave the dog water but no food and told me when *his* time ran out, so would mine."

"That's the heartbeat I heard." Helping Finn lean against the wall, I retrieved the frightened pooch. After letting him sniff my hand, I unhooked the chain wrapped around his neck and carefully folded him into my arms. Pointed ears perking, he thanked me with a feeble lick to the point of my chin. "You slaughtered my entire family, but your soft side comes out for a puppy?"

Giving me a minute to tuck the pup under one arm, Finn eased his weight back onto my shoulders. "No, I'm still starving. I was hoping you would cut the little guy's throat and let me drink him."

"*I'm not feeding you a dog!*" I yelped, tone dripping with disgust. "*Ugh* ... thank you for reminding me why I loathe you."

"If you loathe me, why did you save me?" Finn asked—his tone not one of accusation, but genuine curiosity.

Shuffling through the shadows of the basement, I tipped my face to the light beaming down from above. "Because, no one gets to kill you but me."

FIFTEEN

EXPERIMENT DAY 400 CONTINUED: EFFECT

Qualitive Data- Data that asks broad questions and collects word data from phenomena or participants.

The house was silent as a grave. The sounds of home, music playing, or devices streaming had all been ominously hushed. Most importantly, no pitter patter of little paws scurried across the floor to greet me.

"Find Batdog," I demanded, kicking off my shoes. Those were the first words I spoke to Carter since our rushed exit from Lockwood-Mathews. "If he's hurt, I suggest you get out of the house. That'll mean there's a colossal clash of fangs coming you do *not* want to get caught in the middle of."

Carter squinted into the darkness, his gaze on a constant swivel. "And if I run into our bloodthirsty scientist along the way? What should I do then? Because pretty much the only weapon I have at my disposal is screaming like a girl and soiling myself."

Lifting my chin, I sniffed the air. "You won't. She's upstairs."

I left the lights off as I prowled through the house, letting her scent lead me to the second floor. Creeping on tiptoe, the floorboards betrayed me by creaking underfoot.

"Tell me I'm wrong, Mics," I beseeched the darkness. "Finn had blood on his breath. Tell me you tripped over the body of his victim and panicked when you found your pretty party dress ruined." Pushing open the door to her bedroom with the tips of my fingers, a slight whiff confirmed no one had been in there all night and urged me farther down the hall. "Tell me *any* of the other vamps there killed that woman. I need your reassurance that you weren't stupid enough to drain a human at the home of Rau Mihnea ... *son of the Impaler.*"

Flicking on the bathroom light chased away any lingering hope with a flood of harsh reality. Blood smeared the white subway tile walls. Regurgitated gore filled the toilet bowl, and coated the seat. Micah sat huddled in the corner, her knees pulled tight to her trembling chest. Red-tinged tears streaked down her cheeks as she forced her stare to mine. The desperation etched on her face pleaded with me to save her from herself.

"I-I don't know what happened," she hiccuped. Wiping her face with the back of her hand accomplished nothing but smearing more of the ghoulish crimson. "I know I killed her, but I don't know how ... or why. I hated the taste. Hated myself for hurting her. I barely made it home before I puked. I keep trying to remember the details. But, it's just ... blank. All I know for sure is that I woke up beside her, panicked, and ran. What am I going to do, Vinx? The coalition will have me killed when they find out, and that would be the *merciful* alternative."

Maybe it was a ploy. Maybe I was kidding myself. She knew similar black-outs were something familiar to me. That was information she could easily use and manipulate. Truth be told, it didn't matter. Micah was the closest thing I had to family. After everything that had happened, I refused to lose her, too.

Padding into the bathroom, I took her by the arms and eased her up on wobbly legs. "The coalition isn't going to find out." I tapped her shoulder blade, urging her to turn her back to me. After pinching together the blood encrusted fabric, I unzipped her gown. "When I saw you were gone, I told Rau I sent you home because you were there against my wishes. Apparently, I'm the kind of sire that can't tolerate that kind of thing from my progeny." I ducked around her and turned on the shower. "I even used big words to make it more convincing."

Letting the straps of her gown fall over her shoulders, Micah held the bodice in place. An almost-smile twitched at the corners of her lips. "And you think he bought that?"

Rolling my fingers under the water, I waited for it to warm. "He's a few centuries old and has seen shit we couldn't *begin* to fathom. Of course, he was leery. I expected nothing less. Which is exactly why we need to meet this head on." Satisfied with the water temperature, I flicked the droplets from my fingers and turned to face her.

Sniffling, Mics did her best to collect herself. "What do you mean?"

"Rau has a local affiliate news station visiting one of the vampire refugee camps and he asked us to be there."

The second I uttered the words, Micah began shaking her head, slow at first but gaining in speed and intensity with each pass. "No. *No!* I can't. One look at me and he'll know—"

Catching her face between my palms, I forced her stare to meet mine. "You *can* do this, and you have to. Hiding shows guilt. Guilt makes you the enemy of the coalition. We are going to go, and you will admit to having spotty knowledge about what went on tonight, which is true. But, our *new* truth is that you only know what I reported back to you. That includes having any knowledge at all about Joselyn and her mask. Where did you get that, by the way? You know what? Even if you do know, don't tell me. It doesn't matter. Because as of this moment, you know *nothing* about her. For the first time in your life, Micah, you have to play dumb. That is the *only* way we're getting out of this alive."

"Nothing happened tonight," Micah repeated, her face crumbling as a fresh onslaught of sobs shook her shoulders. "I'm not a horrible person who deserves to die."

If she's horrible, what does that make me?

I knew firsthand what it felt like to be haunted by ghosts from my past.

Collecting her in my arms, I hugged her to me. "No, you're not a bad person. We don't know what happened, and even if we did, we can't change it. Our focus now is removing all doubt that you were anywhere *but* at home, pouting, tonight. Help me script your evening," I prompted, in hopes of distracting her from her strangling guilt. "What did you do when you got home in this alternate reality?"

Pulling back, Micah's chin fell to her chest to examine her ruined dress. "Hung my gown up neatly in my closet to honor it as the paragon of striking fashion it was."

"Let's hope he never rifles through your closet looking for it, because that thing is a lost cause in need of a funeral pyre," I countered, nodding to encourage her on. "And after that?"

"I don't know." Micah's tone bordered on hysteria. "Watched TV? What does it matter?"

Instead of arguing, I guided her back to the right path. "What did you watch?"

"I don't know!" Jabbing her palms to the ceiling, she let her hands fall to her sides with a slap. Her gown slipped down a little farther, revealing the lacy top of her strapless bra. "One of those stupid vampire shows, so I could mope about what a good sire looks like after you sent me home for a time-out."

"Good! That's great. Which show? The subscription channel one that's basically porn, or the teen one where everyone has perfect hair and spends all their time brooding?"

"Subscription channel ... for sure." Could it be? Had she actually relaxed an iota?

"Did you have a snack?"

"Mug of blood with cinnamon."

Recoiling, my nose crinkled in disgust.

"What? It's good."

"I'll take your word for it." I stepped around the splatter and retrieved a bath towel from the linen closet. "We've got a good start on our story. Now, we need to convince *you*. Take a shower and scrub it all away. I'm going to go change out of my dress, then I'll get this bathroom cleaned."

Accepting the towel, Micah attempted a grateful smile that landed closer to a grimace. "Thank you, Vincenza. I honestly don't know where I would be without you."

Probably inventing a cure for cancer, or engineering a Jeston's style flying car.

"But I *am* here, so you have nothing to worry about," I reassured her. Stepping out, I closed the bathroom door behind me to let her scrub the night off herself. Before reaching my third-floor oasis, I shrugged off the straps of my gown and wriggled it over my hips. After letting it fall in a heap at my feet, I stepped out of the confining fabric and walked to my dresser in search of my sweats. Clad only in a nude slip, a hint of my grandmother's file could be seen poking out from beneath, where I tied it to my thigh with a black, velvet ribbon.

A soft knock rattled my open door.

"Someone is looking for you," Carter stated, releasing Batdog, who scampered straight for me with a happy yip. "He was hiding under the dining room table, unharmed but—*wisely*—incognito."

Crouching down, I scooped up my wiggling pup. "There he is! There's my sweet boy."

Batdog's entire backside swung at lightning speed. Sniffing and snorting, he gave my face a frantic tongue bath.

Free of his suit coat, the sleeves of Carter's shirt were rolled mid-way up his forearms. His bowtie hung loose around his neck. Crossing his arms over his chest, he leaned against the doorframe, his gaze wandering the length of me. "So, I overheard that we're going to a vampire refugee camp. Do I need to find someone to watch our furry little friend for the outing?"

"You're not going," I corrected, the cold steel of my tone leaving no room for argument.

Nailing the smoldering, pensive look, Carter peered up at me from under his brow. "Can I ask why you've suddenly decided to break up the Three Musketeers?"

Giving Batdog one last kiss to the forehead, I set him down on the bed. He did three complete circles before laying down. "My freshman year of high school I went to see the school performance of *South Pacific*. A senior by the name of Thadd Montgomery played the role of Lt. Joseph Cable. The second I saw him, I was instantly infatuated. In that unrequited way only a fourteen year old with *no* experience with boys can be. His presence and charisma took my breath away, and I was hooked … for a time at least. Then, he graduated and faded from my sheltered existence."

"As much as I enjoy the insight into your past, I'm not sure that answered my question," Carter chuckled.

Ignoring his interruption, I untied the file from my thigh and set it on my dresser, carefully folding the ribbon under it. "My freshman year at Yale, I saw him on campus. Fooling myself into thinking I was an experienced adult, I got up the nerve to talk to him. What resulted was two whole days spent with him. I picked him up early afternoon … at his parents' house, and dropped him off in the wee hours of the morning … also at his parents' house."

"And, there, you got to live out your girlish fantasies?"

"Hardly," I scoffed. "Our time was spent with him talking and me listening like the enraptured groupie I was. We never kissed, never touched in any way for that matter. For all I know, he was gay. But, see, it didn't matter. I got off on the thrill of being with him."

Pushing off the wall, Carter edged closer. "Why are you telling me this?"

"Because," fingertips brushing across the top of my mahogany dresser, I turned to face him, "I am to you, what he was to me … a novelty."

"What? N-no," he stammered, pulling back.

"Who's Coraline?" I asked, pressing pause on his staged antics.

Expression icing over, he bought himself some time by dragging his tongue over his bottom teeth. "You uttering that name tells me you already know. So, I'll simply say she was an ex, and things got a little … out of control between us."

Moving in a blur of speed, I slammed my bedroom door shut. I caught Carter by the wrist and flung him onto my bed. Lip curling

144

into a snarl, I dove on top of him and pinned him to my mattress with my knees against his hips. I settled into my straddle, dropping fang for the *full* vampress effect. "All this time, all those doe-eyed looks, and all I am to you is a naughty little fetish. We can get that out of your system right now. I could ride you at a foamy gallop until you beg me to stop ... if that's what you're in to."

Desire and remorse battled for primary position in his desperate stare. "I was hooked on her blood. What's been forming between you and I is completely different. You know that, Vinx."

"Do I?" I mused, cocking my head. "And I should base all my trust and compassion on a *feeling*?"

Sinking into my mattress, Carter sagged beneath me and gave himself over to my limited mercy. "That's how these things work among the living ... and in love."

Leaning down, I breathed the words into him. "But I'm *not*."

Let him decipher which claim I was denying.

"When my family was slaughtered and I was left for dead, Finn didn't act alone. There was a vampire bitch beside him with wild hair and flawless mocha skin. I dubbed her the Black Mamba. *You* whispered her name on a lover's breath ... *Coraline*."

A wall of realization slammed into him, draining him ashen and swinging his jaw slack. Mouth opening and shutting, he hunted for an apology, an explanation, *something*.

"Don't bother," I coaxed, grinding my hips against the perked desire that betrayed him. "While *you* were caught up in your favorite kink, she was taking field trips to wipe out entire families. How does *that* play into your little fantasy?"

Repelling off the mattress, I flung myself across the room and steadied myself against my dresser. "Whatever this was, whatever we were on our way to being, is over. I'm more than a naughty fixation."

Carter pushed himself up on one elbow, struggling to stabilize his breathless reaction. "You have to know we're more than that."

"Yet, here we are." Pinching the silver file between my fingers, I flipped it over and back again. "I'll work beside you, I'll fight beside you, but from this point on, Carter ... stay the fuck away from me."

SIXTEEN
EXPERIMENT DAY 231 CONTINUED: CAUSE

Null Hypothesis – Rejecting or disproving a hypothesis.

Balancing grandma's silver nail file between the pads of my index fingers, I chewed over the idea of shoving Micah aside from her task of stitching Finn back together and driving it handle deep into his heart.

To the neighbors lining the street of what had once been Joselyn's home, it outwardly appeared a standard—albeit tragic—accident scene. Cop cars were parked on the lawn. Coroners loaded the body of Joselyn's father into the back of their van, after the "poor man" suffered a fatal "heart attack." All of it was staged. Every element, no matter how seemingly insignificant, was a cog in an intricate and well-oiled machine engineered by our enigmatic benefactors. Even the people, minus Finn, the lookie-loos, and the not-so-dearly departed, were on the payroll of the underground activists. Myself included. We would all play our part to sweep my crime under the rug for what was considered the greater good. But all the scrubbing and white washing in the world couldn't cleanse the fountain of blood tainting my soul.

Hidden away in the back of an ambulance, Micah tended to Finn's wounds, while I made sure he was gentlemanly about it. Even so, as I watched the red and blue lights from outside flashing in the gleaming edge of my file, I couldn't help but wonder if it would be better off used on me.

Snipping off the loose string from Finn's latest row of stitches, Micah glanced up at me over the frames of her glasses. "Get that look off your face. I saw the pictures. You would have been tortured and abused until he got bored. Then, he would have killed you in the most gruesome way he could think of just for fun. You did what you had to do to stay alive. Don't ever doubt that."

Lifting his head off the pillow of the gurney, Finn inspected the zig zag stitch work holding him together. "I tried to tell her the same thing. I doubt your declaration resonated any more than mine, and she hates me with the fiery blaze of hell's deepest circle."

"True story," I seconded, pointing the file skyward.

A soft whimper from the floor beside me was followed by smacking lips and the thumping of a wiggly little tail.

Despite my somber mood, I managed a smile for the scrawny little pup beside me. "Did you finish that already, pal? Want some more?" Plucking another slice of lunch meat from between the thick slices of deli bread, I tossed it down to my new friend. "It was so kind of that EMT to leave his sandwich in the cab for you. As a public servant, I'm sure it would please him to no end to know he's helping return Batdog to full strength."

Micah and Finn both glanced my way, wearing strikingly similar masks of bemused confusion.

"What?" I shrugged. "He looks like a bat. What else would I call him, Percival?"

As Micah stabbed the needle in yet again to close the last gash at Finn's ribcage, he let his head fall back and flung one arm over his eyes. "If those were your only two options, I understand why you went with the caped pup crusader."

"You've named him. You're feeding him. Why do I get the feeling we will soon be shopping for kibble?" Gritting her teeth, Micah forced the needle through Finn's tough hide.

"Because you're as beautiful as you are wise?" Pursing my lips, I made kissy noises at my little dark knight, who waggled his entire backside in response.

"The first time I step in dog shit, he's getting evicted," Micah stated, the smile in her tone contradicting her stern declaration.

Chest bobbing with a chuckle that made it hard for Mics to lace her thread, Finn appraised her with a slow, sweeping glance. "Maybe it's because you're tending to me, but you're quite fetching. Do you know that? You remind me of an ex-lover of mine. She was an ebony goddess with legs for days, and a fiery spirit … just like you."

The last of his wounds closed, Micah cut the loose thread and shriveled him with a glare. "First of all, comparing me to some random black chick you screwed is straight up racist. You're a few centuries old. Expand your mind. We don't all look alike. Secondly, my girl Vinx has told me *all* about you. You're a loathsome, disgusting troll. And, the fact that she hasn't killed you yet, proves she has the willpower of a saint." Rising to her feet, back slightly hunched due to the limited headroom, Mics pulled off her rubber gloves and threw them at him. Shaking her head, she met my stare. "He'll live. Although why we made that so still remains a mystery to me."

"Greater good and all that." Head on swivel, my gaze followed her out the creaking double doors of the ambulance.

"Whatever." Micah scooped up Batdog and tucked him under her arm. "I'm taking the puppy and shutting the door. Your ex is in one piece again. If there's nothing but ash and burn marks on that gurney when I come back, I won't have a thing to say about it."

The door slammed shut with the bang of a falling gavel.

Stretching my digits out, I wiggled my middle finger and ring finger to make the lights from outside dance across the file's edge.

"This is the crew, huh?" Finn asked, most likely filling the pregnant pause before it hatched homicidal thoughts I longed to nurture. "I expected an unmarked van, hazmat suits, and a little creativity. *This* involves expertise and extensive planning. What is it that's driving this escapade?"

"Because, there's an entire underground vein that knows what a dick you are."

Point of his tongue fiddling with his gum line where his fangs were beginning to grow back, Finn's gaze wandered out the window. "And yet there are things out there *far* worse than me. Why *didn't* you kill me, Vincenza? Or, leave me for dead? Vlad knows I deserve it."

"Yes, you do," I agreed, speaking in fact, not threat. "Fortunately for you, there's a few things I need first."

"Well," propping himself up on his elbows, Finn's head tilted expectantly, "I look like a patch-work quilt, and you're blocking the only exit. Shoot!"

"Was anything between us real?" I hated myself for asking, but with the film strip of our first meeting playing in my mind, I had to know. That day, with his tousled hair and over-sized hoodie, I found him adorably hot. Especially when, in the middle of his bumbled introduction, he tripped over his own foot and slammed down on one knee. I could still see the shy, embarrassed grin that graced his handsome face when he peered up at me from his crouch on the sidewalk. But vampires don't trip. Even that had been part of the performance.

Staring down at his snow-white fingers, Finn dragged one thumbnail over the other simply to have something to do with his hands. "If I said I loved you, or that I was sorry—"

"Don't." Raising one hand, I halted him out of fear I would lose my last shred of control and embed my file into his eye socket. "Just … *don't.*"

Lips pinched, Finn chanced death when he dared to push on. "I would say those things if I didn't know they would be as effective as a thimble of water against a roaring inferno. Instead of admitting *either*, I will tell you this. During my time as a human, I was one of the Romani people that have come to be known as Gypsies. In 1749 the Spanish Monarch led what was dubbed as The Great Gypsy Round-up, arresting my people and forcing us into labor camps. To say they treated us harshly would be a vast understatement. Between the lashings and starvation, I soon found myself on the brink of death. Instead of caring for me, my captors loaded my body up with those of the dead and wheeled me off to a mass grave that was little more than a crater in the earth. That is where Rau found me and saved me by siring me. I learned under his tutelage the ways, customs, and laws of the Nosferatu. I owe that man everything and have never disobeyed a word of his instruction ... until that night."

"Why then? Why us?" Swallowing hard, I forced the words from my throat that was raw with emotion.

Pushing off the gurney, Finn sat up. The intensity of his silver-ice stare bore into mine. "I have no idea. I deciphered what I could from fragmented, foggy memories. Still, I don't know how ... or why. I hate myself for it. I need you to know that. I never intended to cause you an ounce of pain. Since then, I have tried over and over to recall the details, what happened beforehand, why I would ever do such a thing, and my mind is just ... blank. I know this isn't what you want to hear, Vinx, but when it comes to that night, I'm as lost for answers as you."

Dragging my nail file over a blood-free spot on my pant leg, I buffed away the fingerprint smudges on it. I had no answers before, and I had none now. Nothing had changed, except for Finn being down a reason for me to keep him alive. "We aren't going to be in touch after this. Being around you threatens my resolve, and I can't allow that."

"I wasn't planning to invite you for coffee," he said with a lopsided smirk.

"At some point," I continued as if he hadn't attempted to slather on the charm, "we *will* cross paths in the vampire world. When we do, I need you to have my back at all costs."

Head listing, Finn measured me through narrowed eyes. "After everything that's happened between us, why would you even *think* to trust me in a situation like that?"

Lunging for him, I drove my knee into his chest. Back rounding in pain, a row of his stitches popped beneath my weight. I pressed the delicate point of my file to the tender skin under his chin, and dimpled his smoldering flesh with the lethal threat of silver. "You mean *other* than the fact you slaughtered my family, *and* I saved your miserable life? If that isn't reason enough, how about if we up the stakes? The *second* you fail in your task to help me, or prove yourself worthless, *that's* the day I kill you. It's not a matter of *if,* Finn, but *when*. You can help me, or you can resign your right to life. Your choice."

SEVENTEEN
EXPERIMENT DAY 413: EFFECT

Junk Science – Untested or unproven theories presented as scientific fact—often in a political context.

I hate arriving to a vampire refugee camp in a limousine," Rau muttered to the window, watching our posh ride glide under an overpass, past dilapidated houses. "It makes us look like ostentatious assholes."

The handful of times I met the vampire lord, he was a pillar of poise and affluence. That day, his demeanor landed closer to the dark and brooding persona of typical vampire lore. Only, instead of the flowing cape and sharp red collar, he opted for a gray suit and salmon-colored button-down.

Adjusting the waistband of my burgundy pencil skirt, my elbow bumped Elodie, who didn't register the contact or tear her stare from Micah's waxen face. As it turned out, my progeny's theatrical skills were sadly lacking. Guilt creased her face, tightening her posture to a tight rope of knots. Not that I could blame her—being seated between Duncan and Thomas was a potent lie detector of muscle and fangs. Lips trembling, Mics' twitchy behavior had me worried she was moments from blurting out a full confession. If either of us were going to make it out of this limo, we needed to name the elephant in the room and calm that big boy with some peanuts.

Wetting my lips, I took a beat to choose my words carefully. "This is the first time I've seen you since Lockwood-Mathews, Rau. How are you doing since that unfortunate incident?"

"Unfortunate incident?" Rau parroted, his tone sharp and cutting. "Is that what the youth of today call a guest in my own home killing a woman and taunting me with it?"

I met his gaze, keeping my expression a stoic neutral, and went for the mother of all sarcastic Hail Mary's. "No. We call that a BFB, a Big Fucking Bummer."

My risk paid off in a milli-second chuckle. In a blink, Rau's momentary reprieve from sorrow was over. Casting his stare back out the window, he resembled a forlorn music video from the eighties. "Working with my triplets to cover up the crime wasn't even the worst part. Don't get me wrong, it was horrible. Even so, it was that mask, *Joselyn's mask,* which gutted me." Attention shifting to Micah, he peered her way with the neutral indifference of a trained interrogator. "Tell me, Miss Walker, do you know of my lost queen, Joselyn?"

Lips pursed in a pinched white pucker, Micah shook her head. "Only what Vincenza has told me," she peeped.

"My rescuing her from a band of thug vamps was the beginning of our tale. I assumed she would base her opinion of our kind on the attack. I never dreamed she would be so open minded as to view it as the poor representation of a complex culture that it was. I didn't dare contact or pursue her after the whole sordid scene. It was she that sent cards and gifts of thanks, all containing requests that we meet so she may extend her appreciation in person. I relented only because I thought having her on my arm at a gala would be fantastic PR." Shaking his head, he scoffed at the memory. "Always on, always looking for an angle. That particular event featured ballroom dancing. After being charmed by her grace and poise, I thought to treat her to my old-world knowledge and skill at the poetries of dance. If I'm being honest, I meant only to impress her. Out onto that polished wood floor, we glided. With me guiding her in a flurry of grand twirls and chasse's. Despite years minus training or calling on my rusty skills, it went quite well. Right up until the point when I got a bit arrogant and attempted a Closed Change."

"You should know," I interrupted, "these terms you're throwing around mean nothing to me. You could call the move a Gorilla Headband, and I would completely take it at face value."

Micah looked moments from vomiting her ugly truth. My hope being that injecting a bit of wit would calm her nerves, or, at the very least, buy us some time before our grisly deaths.

"Apologies, child. In my day, those terms were as commonplace as today's Wi-Fi and tweet-book, or whatever the blazes it's called." Rau batted the concepts away with a flick of his wrist, his understated gold cufflink gleaming red as it caught the glow from a stoplight. "Anyhow, I fumbled with the footwork. The music played on, and I found myself utterly lost. *That* is when Joselyn picked up the lead and steered me back on track. The moment I caught up, she relinquished the role without missing a beat. Only when the song ended did she admit to being a trained dancer who studied at Julliard. Her eyes, the lush green of the Emerald Isle, gleamed as she explained that in a true partnership each in the pairing knows when to lead and when to follow. That is when I fell in love with her. To answer your earlier question about the *'unfortunate incident,'* I would like nothing more than to find the filthy worm who dared to shed blood on my threshold and disgrace Joselyn's memory. However, *now* is my time to lead. I must be the pillar of stability the vampire coalition needs. That is how I honor Joselyn: my love, my queen … my partner."

Seeing a door of opportunity open, I was damned sure going to shove my foot in it. "There are five vamps in this car who will take the lead if you stumble today. You're not alone in this."

The so-called monster covered my hand with his, a paternal smile lifting the corners of his lips. "Thank you, my dear child. Truly."

Across the aisle, Micah's shoulders sagged with relief.

MENTIONS OF A vampire refugee camp conjured images of crypts and mausoleums lit by dusty candelabras and furnished with all things red velvet. That romanticized melodrama version was a far cry from the war-torn setting I found myself in. As the sapphire cloak of night settled in, lights were positioned around the vacant junkyard that had been cleaned out to make room for what appeared to be a plethora of displaced vampires. Rows of ripped and tattered tents lined the space, the only shelter the Nosferatu had from the sun that would scorch their skin on contact. I couldn't help but picture them huddled in the corners, trying to sleep when even the slightest slip into the light would char their skin into agonizing blisters.

Parked behind one of the stocked tables, Micah and I handed out supplies to the seemingly never-ending line of vamps shuffling through. Each rose of vampiric beauty was a wilted, faded version of their once proud bloom. The look in each set of sunken eyes pleaded for a harsh world to show them mercy and kindness.

"Please, take a UV blanket," I offered the packaged bundles to each vamp that past, "a gallon of water, a personal hygiene pack, and one vial of blood."

"Thank you."

"Vlad bless you."

"Rau found good ones in you two," the steady stream of the displaced murmured as they collected their essentials.

Pausing to stretch out her back, Micah's stare traveled the length of the line still anxious for their turn. "There's so many of them."

"The slower we move, the longer it will take to get through them all," I pointed out, offering a polite smile and a hygiene pack to a waifish vamp with blue hair and enormous doe eyes.

Gaze flicking my way, Micah inserted herself back in the assembly line. "Thank you," she murmured, dropping her voice to a whisper meant for my ears only. A pointless act in a football-sized area filled with beings with superhuman hearing. "For what you did in the car. You didn't have to. I wouldn't have blamed you if you threw me to the—"

"Shut up," I snapped, cutting her off. "Did you turn your back on me after what happened to a certain father in the suburbs?"

"No," Micah uttered, her face shadowed by a storm cloud of bitter understanding and self-loathing.

"Then, why would you think I would do any different?"

Lapsing into silence, we focused our attentions on the task at hand.

A few feet behind us, Rau and a vampress with bird-like bone structure stood under the portable lights of a local news station, preparing for their on-air spot. The freshly pressed blouse the vampress wore hung off her slight frame, as if it had been donated and buttoned on to her specifically for the occasion.

"Vampires exiled from their homes without just cause." The glossy-haired reporter stated into the camera, her expression stern and stoic. "Landlords and hotels refusing to rent to them. Title companies denying them purchasing rights on property, because they are viewed as criminals who would present a risk to residents and lower property values. Ridiculed and banished, they are forced into camps just like this one, set up by political activists like Rau Mihnea, as their only safe haven. For many, the banks have even frozen their assets. Their punishment simply for being vampires in our current political landscape. Joining me today are Mr. Mihnea and Joyce Vos. Joyce was the CEO of VIN-Tech Engineering until her status as a Vampire-American was discovered. Forced from her corporate-owned home, she now relies on the kindness of the Vampire Coalition as she waits, with countless others, for the results of the voting on the NPI Bill. Joyce, you've admitted to being on the brink of starvation, yet you have refused to feed on humans. Where do you find the strength and will-power during these trying times?" Pivoting to face her guests, the reporter jammed the microphone in Joyce's face.

The former CEO's mouth pinched tight, the hitch of one brow hinting her displeasure. "If I was human, I'm fairly positive you wouldn't ask me where I found the strength not to eat my neighbor, but I digress. Through the kindness of Rau and his volunteers, our supply needs have continued to be met, thus far anyway, making a miserable situation slightly more bearable."

A twist of her wrist and the reporter redirected the mic. "Mr. Mihnea, some call you a hero. Do you feel that's a title you've earned?"

Another sharp jab of the mic transferred the power of free-speech.

A humble smile warmed Rau's colorless face, all traces of his earlier melancholy carefully tucked away. "I'm no hero. I am merely a man who believes in the importance of being a good Samaritan. If a vampire goes more than a month without feeding, they begin to suffer hallucinations. That is when dangerous accidents can happen. Through our *No Vamp Hungry* campaign, we work with local butchers and slaughterhouses to gather enough animal blood to provide a pint to each Nosferatu in need every two weeks. Organizations like this have been set up across the country, not by heroes, but by those that care to strive and make a difference."

"There you have it, vampires and humans pulling together in hopes of relief from a stifling oppression. This is Ariana Tole of Channel Eleven News, now back to Rod in the studio for sports."

Lip-service over, Rau gave a nod to the triplets to help the camera crew load up their equipment, said a polite good-bye, and inserted himself between Micah and myself. Much to my relief, my progeny managed to keep her posture relaxed and casual even with the vampire lord's elbow brushing hers. Any panic or unease was kept internally checked, for the moment at least.

"How are we doing on supplies?" he asked, clapping his hands together in enthusiasm to dig in. "We have more boxes in the trucks."

Glancing at the table, I did a quick scan of inventory. "We could use some more UV blankets, if you have them. I've been doubling up. Some of them need all the help they can get with those tattered tents."

Weirdest part of that statement? I meant it. These were the same beasts I had been training and plotting to bring down. Yet seeing them like this, as a downtrodden mass, slapped me with an obvious truth. These were creatures capable of violence potent enough to overthrow the government as we knew it. Even so, they were opting for the struggle today in hopes of a brighter tomorrow. That was a mentality I could get behind ... even if I did believe the whole thing to be a staged load of crap.

With a resolute nod, Rau rose on tiptoe to catch Thomas' eye across the milling crowd. "More blankets, if you would, please!"

As Thomas trotted off to fill the request, the flexing muscles of his back evident through the fabric of his cotton button-down, a caravan of limos and Lincoln Town Cars crunched across the gravel parking area. Paparazzi came out of nowhere. Bodies, I thought were there to help, suddenly pulled out cameras and phones to click away at the opening car doors. Outside the heart of the welfare center, the blatant propaganda arrived in full regale. Political officials stepped out of their vehicles like heroes returning from war, smiling and waving over their heads to each and every camera.

Rounding the table to greet the new arrivals, Rau squared his shoulders and fixed on a mask of humble sincerity that seemed a tight fit. "Brace yourselves," he muttered over his shoulder. "The show is about to start."

Pulling another box of hygiene packs out from under the table, Micah balanced it on her hip to restock our supply. "Too bad Carter isn't here. He could put names to the faces."

"We don't need Carter," I snapped with more force than was intended or necessary. Noting Micah's eyebrows had disappeared into her hairline, I cleared my throat and tried for a softer, less homicidal tone. "I recognize most of these people from Lockwood-Mathews."

"Is the *Will They or Won't They* pair leaning toward the friend zone?" Mics' lips screwed to the side, trying unsuccessful to squelch a smirk.

"Something like that," I grumbled. Finding vampire politics a safer topic than my abysmal love life, I rerouted her attention by jerking my chin in the direction of the frenzied spectacle. "The guy with the poof of white hair posing for pictures and shaking hands, is Judge ... *uh.*"

"Yeah, we don't need Carter here for this *at all*," Micah quipped, rolling her eyes.

"*Dean*," I pointedly finished, silencing her with a side-eye glare. "The pretty boy making a huge show of asking vamps the tragic stories that led them here, while wearing the *I'm listening and I care face*, is Representative Alfonzo Markus. Him I remember well, he made quite a scene. All the WASPS were in a titter. Oh! That weasel-faced guy with the glasses talking to Elodie ..."

The words died on my tongue. Something in the exchange between the two made me pull up short. So many opportunities to win political favor, and the man I remembered to be County Commissioner Rawling was locked in a heated discussion with the only female member of Rau's security team. Tendons of his neck bulging, Rawling's complexion was ruddy, a sheen of sweat dotting his brow and upper lip.

Elodie knew him, which was evident in the way she stepped in close, dropping her voice in hopes his agitated shouts would follow suit. When he failed to take the hint, her gaze flicked to Rau. Seeking his guidance or aid? No. She was making sure Big Daddy vamp was good and distracted before catching Rawling by the elbow and leading him around the side of one of the supply trucks.

Chewing on the inside of my cheek, I tried to decipher the soap opera playing out. "Huh. I think the composed and collected Elodie may be implementing extreme measures to sway political favor. Saucy little vixen."

"Right now, I'm more concerned about the water buffalo charging this way. Any idea who *this* guy is?" Nose crinkling, Micah's tongue played across her gum-line. "The sight of him makes my fangs ache."

"That's not a vamp exclusive emotion. That's Attorney General Bob Berry. He's a good ole boy who has made a career out of being the loud mouth who gets things done. You'll hate him instantly, now smile and play nice." Leading by example, I welcomed him with a grin wide enough to make my cheeks ache.

"Pardon me, ladies," he drawled. He hooked his thumbs in his belt loops and showed off his *American by Birth and Grace of God* buckle. "I'd like to get in here and help out for a tick, if ya wouldn't mind."

"Absolutely." Shuffling to the side to make room, I eyed the pleasant-faced baby boomer with balding blond hair and a thick paunch around his mid-section. Berry's mug was splashed all over the Internet. Every news channel and financial magazine debated on if he held aspirations for the oval office and, if so, if he stood a chance. Watching the expert way he played to the crowd removed any doubt that he could take his charade all the way.

"There you go, dear." Berry offered the next vamp in line a blanket and a smile. "Ole Bob likes nothing more than to help out those in need. Warms my heart and makes me feel a little better about those afternoons I waste on the golf course."

"H-how many pints of blood do we get this week?" a vampress clothed in rags rasped, her pallid lips dry and cracked.

"Take two, darlin'," Berry urged, dropping his voice as if it was a secret between them. "Like my mammi used to say, get some meat on them bones."

Drawn by their own desire to capture a bit of limelight, Judge Dean and Representative Markus swarmed the table. Offering smiles and supplies, they cast themselves good Samaritans for a cause they had still failed to publicly endorse. Micah and I were shoved aside, to make room for the grandstanding. A beat later, Rawling joined the team. Whatever robbed him of his composure moments ago had been restored, bringing with it a jaunty skip in his step. In a true testimony to how far the driven will go for their goals, they worked side by side until the very last vampire meandered through the line. In spite of their efforts, I could see the smiles that never reached their eyes, or the winces whenever cold Nosferatu skin brushed theirs. Of one thing I held no doubt: they would reach for the hand sanitizer the second they were safely back in their cars, to cleanse themselves of the filthy touch of the undead.

Rubbing his palms together, Markus blew on his fingers reddened by the cold. "That's the last of them, and a good day's ... my mistake, I mean a good *night's* work."

Early morning hour brightening the sky from cobalt to indigo, the Nosferatu retreated into their tents, happily hauling their cargo. Even the film crews were winding up their cords, storing away the last of their equipment.

Maybe I was tired.

Maybe I was peckish.

Maybe I was tired of watching them pretend to be evolved beings they most definitely were *not*.

Whatever my reason, the poison of my question slipped from my lips to slaughter their bolstered audacity. "I didn't realize you were all such friends to the fang. It would do a great service to our cause for you to go on camera with your *official* endorsement."

Shifting on their feet, the three politicos exchanged uncomfortable glances. After watching their antics from the sidelines, Rau edged in closer. His arms crossed over his broad chest, hatred wafting off of him in anticipation of their predictable response. The triplets guarded the perimeter, ready to move in if Rau so much as twitched.

After a measured pause, Markus spoke, his voice the silky timbre of an A.M. talk radio host. "We're all friends here. Surely, we can be honest. While we have nothing *against* the Nosferatu, it's a volatile time to publicly support the bill. The effect such a show would have on our careers would be immeasurable. You have to understand that."

"If the bill doesn't pass it will cost more vampires their lives," Rau rumbled. "Look around! You can't deny their suffering."

"I *am* looking around." Berry dragged a hand over his face, the jovial smirk he offered the crowds evaporating into stone-cold calculation. "I see this spectacle and my heart bleeds. It does. But then I remember most of these folks are hundreds of years old, giving them ample time to perfect this little act. It's a fantastic show. Well done. Everyone has a part to play, and they do so with practiced expertise. It's just that, well, I'm not buying a ticket."

It's a hard pill to swallow when you hear your exact thoughts uttered from the tongue of a closed-minded bigot.

Still, my reasons were real. My hate was justified ... wasn't it?

EIGHTEEN
EXPERIMENT DAY 365: CAUSE

Deductive Reasoning – Reasoning from one or more premises to reach a logically certain conclusion.

G ood boy!" Letting Batdog scarf the treat pinched between my fingers, I scratched him behind the ears. His entire backside whipped side to side with happiness. My sweet boy was growing and putting on weight—no longer did his ribs protrude from gaunt skin. Plus, he now wore a bright yellow collar with a bat signal tag to prove to the world he was the spiffiest little smoosh face around.

Curling my legs underneath me, I gathered the pup into my lap and gazed out the window to watch the glittering cloak of night descend. Just as the lights of the city below twinkled to life, a soft knocked rattled my door.

"It's open, Mics," I called.

Rising with a yip, Batdog hopped off the bed. He scurried over, offering Micah a frenzy of greeting sniffs. Leaning against the door frame, she crossed her slippered feet at the ankles and made kissy noises at our newest roommate. "How did you sleep? Any more nightmares to speak of?"

I arched my back, stretching my arms over my head, and tried not to call up the grizzly images that now roosted behind my eyes. "No. Thankfully, Joselyn's dad didn't visit me last night to skin me alive for my sins against him. But I did dream I was painting a wall beige while wearing a hot dog costume. What do you think that's about?'"

"No idea. I'm sure it's phallic in some way." She shuffled across the floor, curled one leg under her, and flopped down on the edge of my bed. Patting the mattress, she coaxed Batdog back up and welcomed him with scratches down his spine. "But I am glad you're making strides toward getting past what happened because we have a new development that demands your attention."

Talons of icy fear clawed at my guts, the mug of blood I finished only moments ago threatening to make a second appearance.

"I can't leave this room," I argued, as if suggesting otherwise was the most ludicrous concept imaginable. "Death and despair and all things bad are out there. Here, here is good."

Lifting her chin in that way she did whenever she was trying to make a point, Mics ignored my outburst and pushed on like I hadn't uttered a word. "Do you remember me telling you about one of my biggest sources, that reporter, Carter Westerly?"

"The one with the great hair and ass I wanna bounce quarters off of? Yes, I remember him, and no, even *he* couldn't get me out of this room. Although, I *am* game for him coming in."

Hand stilling on Batdog's side, she glanced up at me with a half-smile tugging back one corner of her mouth. "Glad to see your libido wasn't traumatized by your ordeal." Scratching resumed at the insistence of Batdog's plaintive whimper. "Recently, Carter aired a series of news segments hinting at a more sordid side of vampirism and how it could be connected to missing persons' cases ... namely, Joselyn's."

Kicking my legs off the bed, I crossed the creaking floor to my mini-fridge and pulled out a second blood bag. My moment of nausea passing had returned me to a normal famished state. "Wasn't he hired to be their boy and make them look like fuzzy teddy bears with fangs?"

Micah cupped Batdog's face between her palms, tickling his snout with the tip of her nose. "Exactly. They *couldn't* have been pleased. And now, Westerly is MIA. He has been noticeably absent from his segments, he won't answer my emails, and his voicemail box is full."

I took a pull from the blood bag and swallowed down a mouthful of metallic necessity. "Putting on our critical thinking hats, we can't ignore one glaringly obvious fact. He was taken by vampires. If they wanted to silence him, he's probably already been silenced in the eternal sense of the word."

"That's what I thought, too." My bed springs squeaked as Micah pushed off the pillow-top mattress. Scuffling my way, she dug a piece of paper from the pocket of her fuzzy pink robe. "Then, I found this."

I took the final slurp from my bag, then tossed it into the trash. After wiping my hands off on the front of my pajama pants, I accepted her offered paper. "The Vampire Coalition and their supporters present their annual celebrity auction. Join us at The Ballroom at LoRicco Towers to bid on an evening of fun with local celebrities, including *Start Your Day* host Chuck Kelly, *Political Outlook* vampire correspondent Mathieus Vaughn, and CYBC on-air anchor Carter Westerly. All proceeds will benefit the Youth Law Center, which provides abandoned children with safe and healthy living arrangements." Going off script, I added, "So vampires can feel better about themselves after eating people." Dropping my hands to my sides, my head lolled in Micah's direction. "This doesn't prove anything. It could have been posted weeks ago."

"Look at the time stamp at the bottom. The site was last updated last night. If one of their eligible bachelors weren't going to make an appearance, it seems they would have updated that at the same time they posted their vegan menu options. Which, by the way," Micah scoffed, "is *hysterically* ironic at a vampire event."

"Okay, so he's healthy enough to make social engagements. What's the issue then?" I asked, handing her back the paper.

"The issue," adjusting the frames of her glasses, Micah's lips pursed as she mulled over the issue, "is that they can't risk having Carter's blood on their hands when they're trying so hard to get the NPI Bill past. My guess? They are hoping auctioning him off to a room riddled with vamps will land him in the company of a Nosferatu with a loose moral compass and ravenous appetite. Which is why, pause for dramatic effect, we need to send you to the auction and make sure you have the winning bid."

Cue the blinding terror. "That's tonight and really goes against my whole *Not Leaving This Room* objective."

Crossing her arms over her chest, Micah planted herself firm and prepared for battle. "Vinx, if we don't help him, he could die. Add to that what an asset he could be to our cause. We want to walk the path Joselyn walked and find out her truth? He can show us the way, he's been there. You stay here, holed up in this room, and you are sentencing him to death. Or, you can shimmy into the ridiculously expensive gown one of our benefactors donated, get over your shit, and be a hero. Your choice."

"*How* ridiculously expensive?"

"If we sold this house, you *might* be able to afford one of your own."

Suddenly parched by fashion lust, I centered my argument on one undeniable truth. "You know I'm not ready, Mics. The fact that my last field trip ended in voluntary manslaughter is undeniable proof of that."

Stepping in close, Micah locked her stare with mine without wavering, her jaw tensed with resolve. "You were cornered and used your fangs to protect yourself. That's the most pure and basic display of vampirism I can think of. I have no doubts you're ready, Vincenza. Now, it's time to convince you. One last test. When it's over, if you still don't think you're ready, I'll let you hole up in here and rot. If that's what you think will *truly* keep the world safe."

One more test. And yet, I couldn't decide what the more terrifying outcome would be: an involuntary killing spree, or actually being swayed.

SWEEPING MY GAZE over what appeared to be a block of unmarked warehouses and industrial buildings, I tilted my head in suspicion of the obscure alley entrance that Micah claimed led to one of the most exclusive vampire clubs in town. "What did you say this place was called?"

"No name." Micah shoved her hands deeper into the pockets of her coat and raised her shoulders to her ears to battle the chilly night air.

"No Name? Meaning, like, be who you want, bite who you want, without being hindered by identity or consequences?" Nearby, a crow's wings beat the air. Following the sound, I watched it lift from its street light perch as if chased away by the building stormfront of my own unease.

"No name as in it's not a public establishment you're going to find on Yelp. It's privately owned and by invitation only. But way to go reading into the metaphor." Finding her pockets inadequate to the warming task, Micah cupped her hands in front of her mouth and blew hot breath on them.

"And, of course, I have an invitation," I grumbled under my breath.

How I envied her battle against the cold. Clad only in a miniscule, black slip dress, I longed to feel the frosty nip of night. If for no other reason than to distract from the harsh claws of terror ripping my insides to ribbons.

"Of course, you do," Micah confirmed, keeping her distance, careful not to crowd me.

"There's humans in there?" It was both a question and a warning of my slippery control.

A roll of her shoulders and Micah was all business—minor discomforts chased away by her pivotal mission to get me through that door. "Yes, there are bound to be humans. Consensual blood lettings are allowed. More importantly, there will be upwards of fifty vamps in there. All I want you to do is walk in through the front door, make your way through the club, and come out on the other side. Simple as that."

"And if they suspect I'm not what I claim to be?"

"Well, then that's going to make that last part a lil bit trickier, isn't it?"

As I risked a step forward, I blinked and that basement floor splashed with blood flashed behind my eyes. Wobbling on my designer heels, I let the wave of crushing regret crest and rescind. "Are you sure I'm ready for this?" I asked Micah ... and myself.

"I'm sure you have to be."

THE NONDESCRIPT EXTERIOR of the club opened up to a world of trendy opulence. Brick pedestals hoisted industrial iron posts up to reclaimed wood beams. To the right of them were intimate bistro-style tables, to the left cozy white leather booths. At the far end of the expansive space, a bar sat in the corner with different sized wicker lanterns hanging overhead. Positioned next to that was the dance floor. On slate tile, couples swayed to the latest Ed Sheeran masterpiece, the walls on two sides of them beautiful mosaics of repurposed barn wood. At first glance, it looked like any other hot spot where people went to be seen and feel better about their social status. Only upon closer inspection could I catch a glimpse of fang, or a wrist pressed delicately to another's lips, as the metallic tang of blood lingered in the air.

"You're new," a voice as decadent and smooth as warm maple syrup murmured against my ear.

A snarl brewed at the back of my throat. Spinning, in preparation to advise him in the most adamant of ways to back the hell up, I found myself face to face with lethal beauty. The kind that could

170

only be compared to a prowling panther, fluid elegance with chaos and carnage lying just beneath the surface.

There was no denying he was the most beautiful specimen of the male form I had ever laid eyes on. His skin, sun-kissed caramel, accented the deep blue eyes that mirrored a galaxy's starry eternity. My fangs ached to trace across his sculpted jawline, fingers twitching to weave into toffee-hued locks that fell in unruly waves just past his ears.

Still, sex appeal didn't grant him the right to lean-up on me without permission. A point I fully intended to press—by any means necessary—the first moment I was able to pry my stare away from his pecs.

Damn ... their outline is visible through his shirt and *suit coat. That's powerful peckage.*

"New," I managed, sounding more breathless than intended, especially considering my limited respiratory function. "But not a complete dumbass ... so, I suggest you back off."

One corner of his mouth tugged back in a winning smile that made merry little sparks of silver swirl in the depths of his stare. "Brave words for a girl alone. Don't you know, this is a den for lovers?"

"Oh yeah?" I countered, one brow lifting in challenge. "And yet here you stand, *alone*. Kind of a sexist double-standard, isn't it?"

Amusement crinkling the corners of his eyes, he chuckled. "I suppose it would be, but I'll let you in on a little secret." Dropping his voice to a seductive whisper, he risked life and limb by brushing a lock of hair behind my ear. "That rule doesn't apply to me. My name is on the lease."

I shifted my weight, cocking one hip, and slapped him with a bored glare. "Still, the rules of basic social conduct hold firm, and you're standing well inside my personal bubble. Do we need to have a conversation about boundaries?"

"I would much rather talk about you claiming to be undead, while the smell of sunshine still lingers on your skin. Were you made in the parking lot this same night?"

Fear of being detected, and having to battle my way out in a flurry of fangs, anchored me where I stood. A fact the brazen stranger took advantage of by tracing the knuckle of his index finger down my forearm.

"Does this place have an undead age restriction I didn't know about?" I asked with every ounce of manufactured moxie I could muster.

A little DJ magic and the music made a smooth transition to the soulful cords of "Take Me to Church" by Hozier, adding a hypnotic melody to a percolating yearning I couldn't name.

"Not in the least." Rocking back on his heels, the magnificent stranger fought back a grin. "It's usually the more mature vampires who visit us here. Newborns are far more interested in ... *ahem*, physical exploration of every conceivable kind. If you found your way here, you either are mature beyond your years or have well-connected friends."

Intrusive nature, wandering hands, slathered on charm; there was a growing laundry list of reasons to loathe this guy. Why then was I wishing it was *me* nibbling on his lip? "I tried the mature and responsible route and got my throat ripped out before my twenty-first birthday. Adulting is significantly overrated. Let's go with option two."

"In that case ..." Hooking his forefinger into the collar of his shirt, he pushed the fabric aside to give me a glimpse of his thick, throbbing vein. "Fancy a taste?"

Vlad be damned, I did. More than I had ever wanted anything in my life, I wanted to sink my teeth into him and claim every drop of him.

"Pardon me?" I coughed, choking on the words.

"Have you been part of a formal blood-letting?" he asked, with the casualness of requesting I pass him a napkin. One eyebrow rose in tempting invitation. "It would be my honor to grace you with a sampling."

Blood-letting, a tradition dating back to the days when Vlad still left boot-prints in the earth. It acted as a way for humans to show support for the immortal beings fighting to protect them from the

Turkish tribes thirsting to claim their lands and enslave them all. It was history I had studied. Repeatedly. Even so, hearing the suggestion of it slip from his luscious, ripened lips twisted the concept to the pornographic.

"I've never done it." The words hitched in my throat, wavering with desire. "But these clubs are all about blending, right? I'd love to do you. *I mean bite you.* Taste you! *Shit*, there's no way not to make this sound filthy."

Shoulders shaking with laughter at my expense, a dagger appeared in his palm as if from nowhere.

A symphony of hand-polished silver, it must have been tucked into the back waistband of his slacks.

"Come with me?" he softly coaxed, reaching for my hand.

A man, so sexy I could weep, brandishes a weapon, and asks me to take a walk with him.

Of course, my dumbass linked my fingers with his.

Micah told me to blend, make them think I was one of them. This was me playing the part—or at least that's how I justified it to myself.

Was it my imagination, or had the room gone silent?

Giddy apprehension seemed to crackle through the air.

Filled with equal parts morbid curiosity and gnawing desire to drop fang, I let him lead me to a private booth prepared in a quiet corner of the room.

"Something tells me this wasn't a spur of the moment decision," I jabbed, jerking my chin in the direction of his spread. "Would any vampress have done, or were you looking for someone *particularly* naïve?"

Emerald-hued pillar candles had been arranged in a circle, their wicks not yet lit. In the center sat a clay bowl containing a black book of matches. On its glossy black cover, a logo was imprinted. From where I stood, it looked like a silver D.G. encircled by braided vine.

Stepping in close enough for his chest to brush mine, he dragged his fingertip down my jawline and gently tipped my face to his. "If I said I was waiting *specifically* for you, would you believe me?"

"Not a chance in hell," I countered, and turned my palm skyward in invitation to his blade.

Eyes locking with mine, he wet his lips and dragged the curve of the dagger across my skin, splitting it in a silken ruby ribbon.

"What's your name?" he murmured, voice raspy with craving.

"Vinx." Shivering in anticipation, I fought against the demanding push of my fangs as he repeated the gesture across his own forearm.

Presenting me with his gifted essence, he spoke in a lover's whisper as my lips sealed around his wound to suckle in invigorating pulls. "Spirit lords, connect my ethereal cord with that of Vinx. Let us converge like the Moon's light and darkness. May we be one and the same in thought and in spirit."

The words struck a chord of discontent somewhere in the back of my mind. Unfortunately, I couldn't bring myself to care. Not with his blood spilling over my lips.

He tasted like a hard rain after an arid drought.

The first flower of spring that persevered after a harsh, unforgiving winter.

The lilt of a child's laugh riding a gentle breeze.

Life. Love. Happiness. Strength.

All intermingling in the heady brew of his gift to me.

Easing himself from my greedy hold, he held my bleeding hand over the bowl. Without offering explanation, he squeezed and manipulated my injured flesh, coaxing four fat droplets into the waiting clay bowl. "May my mind and will become one with hers."

That was it.

That was the skip in the record that pulled me from the magnetic rhythm of the moment. All the research Micah forced on me, all those hours toiling over every Nosferatu book I could lay hands on, *none* mentioned any kind of an incantation during a blood-letting.

Edging back, I snatched my hand away. "You're not human. Human blood tastes like it's already started to sour. What the hell is this?"

In place of an answer, he struck a match and lit each of the candles with care. "When I walk, she will walk with me. When I speak, she will echo each syllable. When I feel sorrow or lust, her heart will respond in kind. I thank you, my dark lords, for helping me. May you make the cord between myself and Vincenza strong like the chains ... of a prisoner." Casting a devious stare my way, he blew out the match. "Only when the sunrises after tomorrow's half-moon will we no longer be united. Her mind will again be her own, and no memory of any of this will remain."

Invisible tendrils coiled around me, chaining me where I stood. I could feel their chill slithering into my veins, binding my free will.

"*Who are you?*" Struggling against them was useless, still I thrashed for freedom. "Why are you doing this?"

With a carefree chuckle, he bent down to blow out the candles one by one. Each stole another chunk of my self-control.

"My name," *Puff.*

"Is Dorian Gray." *Puff.*

"I'm doing this," *Puff.*

"Because war is coming," *Puff.*

"And I crave chaos."

Puff.

A cloak of magic blocked out the world, and—for a time—I was gone.

"What can I do for you, Mr. Gray?" my subservient body queried in my absence.

Sucking air through his teeth, Dorian tipped his head back and let his lecherous stare wander the length of me. "Had we more time, I can think of a great many things. But for now, obedience is of utmost importance." Raising one arm over his head, he snapped his fingers at a middle-aged man with a pointy-chin and receding hairline.

The man darted over in an instant, a nervous twitch fluttering at the corner of his right eye. "Yes, Mr. Gray?"

"Vincenza," Dorian purred, ignoring the fact that his lackey had spoken at all, "be a dear and kill him for me."

Nerves contracting the side of his face into a pained grimace, the man's goose-egg stare lobbed from me to Dorian, and back again.

"No! You can't. I'm a necromancer. All your plans are for naught without me!"

To his great regret I was already moving, darting in on the attack at another's command. Tangling my fingers into his hair, I wrenched his head back and sank my fangs into the pounding pulse of his jugular.

"As anyone in any sort of competitive field will tell you, Hector," folding his hands, Dorian let them fall in front of him with waning interest, "there's *always* someone younger with talent that far exceeds yours. *Everyone* is replaceable."

Despite the geyser of vile coppery warmth gushing past my lips, I held firm. Only when the last of the fight seeped from poor Hector's artery, did I drop him in a crumbled heap on the floor. Retracting my fangs, I rose as the obedient little puppy I was.

"Good girl." Dorian licked his lips at the grisly sight of me. "Now, I'm going to need you to clean yourself up and head to that bachelor auction. You will get Carter Westerly back at any and all cost. I've padded an account for the transaction. Even lined up another vampire to help you convince Mr. Westerly. Go. Make a spectacle of yourself. And, by all means, have *fun*."

"Yes, Mr. Grey," I dutifully answered, turning on my heel toward the door.

"Oh, and Vincenza?" he called.

Immediately halting my stride, I glanced back over my shoulder.

"I meant what I said about the war. It's coming. And I want *you* right in the middle of it. That part, I truly hope you remember."

Silently, I blinked his way, mind absent of the gumption to press for details.

"You may go." He released me with a flick of his wrist in dismissal.

Feet clapping against the floor, I strode for the back exit. Crashing out into the alley, I found Micah huddled under the street light, dancing from one foot to the other to keep warm.

Whatever repulsive secrets were etched across my face, blanched her cheeks and widened her eyes.

"I'm going to need a gown," Dorian spoke through me, tone carving out each word with purposeful swipes that matched those of the blade that bound me to him.

"You know I have one for you, but—" Taking a hesitant step forward, Micah reached for me, only to reconsider and drop her hand. "Wh-what happened? Is that blood?"

Hand rising to my lip, I swiped at the spray of crimson covering my face. "Oh, that? I ran into one of our benefactors. Hell of a guy. Helped me find the confidence I was sorely lacking. More on that later. Right now, I have a reporter to find."

Micah's gaze shifted over my shoulder, as if expecting the bloody truth to come tumbling out behind me. "Uh … o-okay," she stuttered, teeth clenched tight with apprehension.

Not that I would remember any of this for a long time to come.

NINETEEN
EXPERIMENT DAY 505: EFFECT

Emerging Themes – Concepts which are closely linked in meaning.

Are you *sure* the red isn't too much?" Rau asked for what had to the be the millionth time. Having successfully lured him out of his dressing suite, we had made it as far as the top of the stairs before he launched right back into The Great Necktie Debate. "It's red. I worry it screams vampire."

"If that's your concern, you should try a little bronzer," I muttered, absentmindedly checking my phone to see how long I had been prepping Rau's wardrobe choices for his election day appearances. Two hours. That was one-hundred and twenty minutes of my undead life I wouldn't be getting back. "Your complexion looks like you haven't seen the sun since the crucifixion."

Silence.

Glancing up, I found Rau staring at himself in a hall mirror, inspecting his face by sucking in his cheeks and turning his chin one way then the other. "That's a form of women's cosmetic, right? I fear that would give me the appearance of a painted corpse. Should I reconsider?"

I tucked my phone into my pocket, pressed my palms together in a prayer pose, and brought them to my lips. "You're right, forget the make-up. But let's revisit the ties. Show me the red one."

Turning to face me, he brought the red slash of fabric to the collar of his white button-down.

"And the blue?"

Switching hands, the blue pinstripe took its place.

"Red again?"

Switch.

"Now the blue."

Switch.

"Let me see one over each shoulder."

After draping them as directed, Rau held his hands out awaiting my inspection.

Pursing my lips tight, I narrowed my eyes in contemplation. "Can I see the wave you're going to give to the voters? I can't really form an opinion until I see the tie in action."

Rau raised his right hand, and paused. "You're toying with me, aren't you?"

"You're, like, a million years old and freaking out about your wardrobe." Dropping my hands, I let him see the smirk I had been hiding. "You're darn right I'm messing with you. I think, and bear with me on this, that there's *a chance* you're overthinking this decision. It's … *a neck tie.* As long as you don't have entrails strung around your neck, humans will look at it, and see … *a neck tie.*"

Having successfully poked a hole in his inflating tizzy, Rau's shoulders sagged. An amused smile twisted the corners of his lips. "My darling, Vincenza, how did I ever get along without you? You truly keep me sane."

"That's why you keep me around." The chuckle died on my lips, chased away by the startling truth that I didn't begrudge my time with him. Not anymore. No longer did I force a smile simply to appease the "monster." Somewhere along the way, I had come to respect him. Which would make it that much more of a bummer if it turned out I had to kill him. Clearing my throat, I chased away that dreary thought. "Your press secretary sent over your winning and losing speeches. Let's grab a couple of blood bags, read them over, and take notes on needed changes."

"Fantastic plan. But first … did we decide on the red or blue?" he deadpanned.

Snatching the blue one out of his hand, I was tossing it over the bannister with a laugh when Duncan came thundering up the stairs.

"Lord Mihnea, you're needed in the foyer," he rumbled, nostrils flaring with the urgency of the situation. "It's Lawrence Rawling, sir. He's back."

Chin falling to his chest, Rau shook his head. "I worried about that the moment I saw him at the camp. I had hoped he would prove me wrong. Prepare a cocktail, Duncan, in case it comes to that."

Duncan moved surprisingly quick for a glacier-sized man, skirting around his boss to get to the fully stocked humidor across the hall.

"A cocktail?" I asked, following Rau down the stairs. "If all else fails, get him drunk? What is the guy, just a colossal bore?"

"It's a tranquilizer," Rau corrected, chest expanding at the scene he was walking into. "Rawling is a hardcore blood addict."

I recognized the man in question at a glance. He was the same pinched-face weasel who disappeared behind a supply truck with Elodie. With wild eyes and glasses askew, he grasped the front of Thomas' shirt in a white-knuckled grip. His scrawny frame quaked with the intensity of his shouts. "Please! I have money! I'll give you anything you want. Anything! I just need to see Elodie. I'm in love with her!"

"You are, huh?" Thomas glared down his nose at Rawling, lip curling to show a hint of fang. "And when you threatened her with a silver stake, that was your devoted adoration?"

"She was trying to leave me! She can't! We belong together … we belong …" Rawling's caterwaul melded into a quiet chant of self-soothing.

Leaning toward Rau, I asked out of the corner of my mouth, "Does this happen often?"

"More than it should," he grumbled. The moment his shoes connected with the white marble floor, he erased all emotion from his face and approached the twitchy addict.

"Rau!" Rawling yelped, as if seeing a flicker of hope for the first time. Red-rimmed eyes streaming with tears, a bubble of snot swelled from his nostril. "You have to help me! I need to see Elodie. We belong together. Let me have her. Let me leave with her, and we won't bother you again. I promise! You have my word."

"Lawrence," Rau *tsk*ed, clapping a hand on the man's shoulder to keep him at arm's distance. "You were doing so well, my friend. We got you treatment, and you were walking the road of recovery. What happened?"

Collapsing against Rau's chest, despite the vampire lord's attempt to avoid him, Rawling peered up at him with the adoration of promised salvation. "At the camp, I saw her. I ... I saw her and needed her. More than I have ever needed anything in my life."

"You have a wife and daughter," Rau countered. "What of *their* needs?"

"I'm no use to them or anyone without her," Rawling sniveled. I would have thought it a beautiful testimony of love, had he not added, "She let me feed from her at the camp. That pull, that rush ... it's why I need her."

Stepping back with disgust, Rau's face folded into a frown. He glanced to Thomas, he seeking confirmation to the claim. "Your sister fed him?"

Brow furrowed, Thomas shook his head.

"I think she did," I offered, cringing at the way Rawling drooled over me like a steak dinner. "I saw the two of them disappear together behind one of the trucks. If he keeps looking at me like that, can I bite him?"

"Not if I bite him first," Thomas' wide chest reverberated with a menacing growl.

"She fed me!" Rawling squawked, seemingly oblivious to our blatant threats. "She loves me, too. I know it!"

The stairs behind us creaked under Duncan's formidable weight.

"If she truly is your one true love and heart's desire, tell me her last name," Rau demanded, brows lifting in expectation.

Rawling's mouth opened and immediately snapped shut.

"Too hard a question?" Rau pressed. "Okay, how old was she when she was turned? Was it voluntary or forced? Does she have any human family members still alive?"

Again, silence was his only response.

Head bobbing, Rau acknowledged his made point. "You need to go back into a treatment program, Mr. Rawling. Do you consent?"

A sideways glance to Duncan signaled him to ready the tranquilizer.

Inching toward the door, Rawling's leery stare darted from one to the next of the three vamps slowly surrounding him. "No! I just want a taste. Please! I don't need a program, I just need the blood. It doesn't even have to be her. Any of you could help me, if you would just have mercy."

Darting around him in a blur of speed, Thomas caught Rawling in a bear hug from behind, holding him steady as Duncan moved in with the tranquilizer.

"Blood! I need the blood!" Rawling shrieked. He snapped his jaws at Thomas' face, narrowly missing lobbing off the tip of the vamp's nose.

Seizing his wrist, Duncan stabbed the syringe into his forearm and emptied the contents into a vein. Eyes rolling back, Rawling sagged against Thomas, who celebrated by dropping him in a heap on the floor.

"*This* is the society we fight so hard to be a part of!" Thomas bellowed, jabbing a hand at Rawling's slumped frame. "One that sees us as a fetish to exploit? We're better than them! It's the natural order of things, *the fucking food chain*! Yet we muzzle ourselves just to fit into their warped and jaded world?"

"We join them, that we may make changes from within of how they view us." Tone soft yet commanding, Rau looked on his men with the compassionate understanding of a long-felt oppression. "We cannot admit him to a treatment facility without consent. Duncan, please take him home. Tell his wife of his indiscretion and inform her that if he shows his face here again it will be viewed as trespassing and dealt with as such. Thomas, find your sister and bring her to me. She will take to the earth until the election as punishment for allowing him to feed. Vincenza and I will be in the study looking over my speeches."

Dragging our leaden feet through the fog of melancholy that had settled into the foyer, we each went about our charade of normalcy in a world longing to devour us.

"YES, I'M WELL aware he can't vote, Finn. I'm not a complete moron. He is, however, the face of this bill. When people go to the polls, Rau *needs* to make an appearance. I'll wait until just before sunset, slather him in SPF one million, and *get him there* to shake hands with voters. And while I'm doing that, you can do me a personal favor by crawling up your own ass." Pausing, I barely listened to the colorful insult he threw back. "Yeah, right back at ya."

Ending the "check-in" call with the first person on earth I deemed worthy of the title of my archnemesis, I yanked off my blue tooth headset and tossed it on the desk. The room I sat in, tucked in the back corner of the house, had once been my father's study. Now, freshly furnished with a cherry stained desk and matching bookshelves, it had become my fortress of necessity to maintain my deep cover.

"It seems you and Finn have found a palpable level of loathing that allows you to work together without bloodshed." Hovering outside the office's French doors, Carter leaned against the door jamb with his hands in his pockets. "Is that what the future holds for us?"

Wisps of blond hair fell across his forehead as his intense stare fixed on the curve of my lips.

"I don't hate you, Carter." Unable to maintain eye contact with him, my gaze flicked to the slew of papers decorating my desk.

Pushing off his perch, he braved the risk of crossing my threshold. "You aren't exactly *pleased* with me either. Which probably has a large part to do with the fact that I've never said I'm sorry. And I am, truly. I agreed to help you, because I thought it would get me back in the fold so I could find Coraline. That said, I need you to know that somewhere along the line, it stopped being about that. I should have told you the truth, but—"

I halted his long-winded ramble with one raised finger. "I understand, Carter. Really. You don't need to explain."

Especially after what I witnessed from Rawling earlier that same night.

He dragged his hands through his hair, causing flaxen strands to dart off his head in messy spikes. "You say that, yet I really feel like I do. I was weak, I got caught up, and that's not me. Actually, in some ways it is totally me, and I hate that. I don't want to be *that guy.*"

Realizing this purging of conscious was unavoidable, I leaned back in my leather chair and turned into the spin. "Close the door."

When he turned to oblige, I thumbed open the top three buttons of my blouse, allowing the lace camisole beneath to peek out. Spinning back around, Carter flinched in surprise, a blush of color warming his cheeks and neck.

Rising from my chair, I prowled around the desk with feline grace. "I mean it, Carter. I understand your situation. It's all science. Right now, you're experiencing vasodilation, or increased blood flow to your more sensitive regions. Your balls are tightening, dick twitching with primal impulse."

"Vinx, what are you doing?" Carter asked, his voice husky with a confusing blend of desire and uncertainty.

I closed the space between us, and the rise of my breasts brushed his chest. Tipping my head back to give him a grand glimpse of the money shot, I dropped fang.

Body rigid with desire, the breath caught in his throat. "Vincenza," he murmured, stare locked on the curve of my mouth.

"Now, the chronic beast of addiction is rearing its ugly head," I explained, mouth teasing over his. "What you feel is bigger than want. It's a compulsion. One that makes any potential consequences seem insignificant. With a vamp's legs wrapped around your waist, you're touching death. The thrill of it entices you to push farther, to delve deeper for that next fix. Personal limits mean nothing. Not a thing on earth can touch you when you're riding that high." Pressing into him, I pinned his back against the wall. The tip of my nose nudged his pulse point, urging his head back with a throaty moan. "Had you not got out when you did, you would have kept pushing that line until you ended up dead." Pulling back, my stare locked with his. "Like I said, I understand what you were going through and acknowledge it as the sickness it is."

"Th-thank you," Carter stammered, fingers curling into the bottom hem of my blouse.

"That said," I wove my fingers into his hair, wrenching his head back hard enough to illicit a yelp, and words tumbled from my lips in a menacing hiss, "I wasn't ready for *any* of this. I plunged into this snake pit to save *your* stupid ass. We thought you were being tortured, or worse. Instead, you were in treatment to stop yourself from boning your way into an early grave. Micah having to be changed? That's on you. We charged in, and shit went south. And all the while, your head was on swivel, looking for your undead booty call. So, yes, in scientific terms, *I get it*. But don't, for one second, confuse that with us being okay."

I released my hold, stumbling back to fling open the door in silent invitation for him to go.

Hanging his head, he strode toward the door, pausing before he stepped out into the hall. "You and Micah … you're my family now. You can hate me if you want, but I'm not going anywhere. You're going to have to make your peace with that."

Without another word, he stalked off.

TWENTY
EXPERIMENT DAY 508: EFFECT
ELECTION DAY

Narrative Fallacy – Limited ability to look at sequences of facts without weaving an explanation into them.

Thanks so much for coming out. Whether you support our cause or not, you are doing your civil duty by being here today. Next year I hope to be standing in this line with you." Rau Mihnea, the face of the modern-day vampire, worked his way down the line of folks patiently waiting to cast their votes. Oozing charisma and charm, he greeted each and every one of them. Not all among them were in favor of the NPI bill, but being that close to the infamous vampire was still a novelty they enjoyed. It was as close to a celebrity sighting as many of them would ever get.

To find the reality of the differing sides, one needed only to look as far as the sidewalks leading to the high school gymnasium housing the voting. The supporters were positioned on the north sidewalk. Waving their Vampire Rights banners over their heads, they chanted on a loop, "Movie monsters no more! Learn vamp history, not the lore!"

To the south were the loud and rowdy opposers with their signs that opted for graphic gore over sunshine and glitter. "Save your votes, save your lives! Don't be a meal! Let humans survive!" Over and over they chanted, as if anything with fangs wanted a taste of their cholesterol-riddled blubber.

No, thank you.

So far, the protests had been peaceful, but tension sizzled through the air as the long shadows of twilight stretched across the ground. The scales of civility threatened to tip at any moment. Nearing the end of the line, Duncan spoke into the mic at his cuff, calling for our limo. A beat later, it glided around the corner three blocks up.

All three of the triplet's hovered in an orbit around Rau, Elodie never wandering farther than arms distance away. A few days sleeping in the ground over her dalliance with Lawrence had her behaving like a scolded pup eager to win back favor—a situation I knew a little something about with Carter lingering at my elbow. I wanted Micah to be my plus one. She refused, making some point ladled with big words about Carter being a public figure and the benefits of having his recognizable face among us. Truth be told, I stopped listening. The setup to get us to kiss and make up wasn't even cleverly covered up, and I was nowhere near that point. Still, in his quest to mend things, Carter kept a smotheringly protective watch, eager and itching for the chance to prove himself.

Annoying as I thought it was at the time, it was that same diligence that drew his stare to a slowing Benz with its dark tinted window sliding down. Following his stare, I noticed the glow of the streetlight, which clicked on only moments ago, gleaming off a sliver of metal that emerged.

The world slowed to a deathly crawl as Carter formed the words, "*Gun! Get down!*"

Elodie threw herself at Rau, forcing his head down. Shielding him with her body, she hustled the vampire lord toward our approaching ride.

Dropping fang, which earned a chorus of shrieks from the stunned crowd, Thomas hurled himself at the brandished weapon. A lone shot rang out, slamming into his left shoulder. The force of it whirled him around. Protestors and voters hit the ground, screaming and sobbing in fear as the guard's arm exploded into smoldering ash.

"Silver bullets! Get down, stay down!" Carter hollered to anyone listening. Cocooning me in his arms, he rushed me toward the limo.

Brain moving at the speed of a turtle in peanut butter, I blinked his way in confusion. "I should be covering you. You're human and frail."

"Your gratitude is humbling," Carter countered, practically dragging me to the limo as it slid up to the curb in front of us. To whoever was inside, he shouted, "*Get the door open!*"

From within, it flung open wide.

Angling herself between Rau and the assailant's car, Elodie waved us in. "*Get in, I'll keep you covered.*"

Pausing, Rau glanced back, his desperate stare searching for me. "Vincenza!"

"She's right behind you! Go!" Duncan growled. Having appeared in a flash of superhuman speed, he gave Rau an insistent shove into the car.

Forcing my head down, the mammoth guard pushed me in next, Carter following a millisecond later. Gunning the engine, the limo started moving, forcing Duncan to dive in and slam the door behind us.

Only then, in the moment that should have been dog-eared for a sigh of relief, did we realize we weren't alone. Across from us, grinning in smug satisfaction, sat Bob Berry, Neil Rutherford, and Alfonzo Markus.

"What's happening? What is the meaning of this?" Rau demanded, searching their faces for answers.

Unease prickled up my spine, fangs aching at the tangible threat.

"We took the liberty of making plans on your behalf." Markus' calm, calculating tone dripped with malintent.

Swiveling in his seat, Rau glanced back at the voting site fading into the distance. "*No!* We have to go back. We must ensure no bystanders were hurt."

The rebuttal came in the form of one muffled *pooft!* A polished Beretta, fitted with a silencer, poked out from under Rutherford's coat, the contents of one chamber emptied into Duncan's barrel chest. Skin cracking and splitting, tar-black ooze seeped from the growing fissures until his body imploded, filling the cramped space with the scorching dust of his charred flesh.

The scattered embers cleared to reveal a wide smile spread across Bob Berry's ruddy features. A malicious twinkle brightened his sinister leer. "Hi-ya, Rau. Your calendar has been cleared, my friend. Your presence has been requested for a little side trip."

TWENTY-ONE

Kinesics — Analysis that examines what is communicated through body movement.

Our chorus of footfalls scuffed against the concrete floor of the aircraft hangar. The walls were painted pristine white, industrial lighting hanging overhead. Which of the tainted political elite owned the space and parked their lavish private jet there, I couldn't say. All of them seemed comfortable with that level of extravagance. These were pampered men of means ... yet here we were, *alone*. No bodyguards loomed at their elbows. No assistants scurried around to ensure their every whim was met. Not so much as a janitor with a broom occupied the cavernous space. Whatever they had planned, they didn't want an audience for it. That was far more off-putting than the gun Bob Berry kept trained on my back, jabbing it between my shoulder blades whenever my speed didn't meet his expectation.

Why me and not Rau or Carter?

Because the other two made the mistake of allowing their feelings for me to show. Every time Berry stabbed the barrel of his weapon into my back, both men tensed. All the lies and deceit that passed between us, yet I held no doubt either of them would swallow a bullet for me. The moronic beauty of chivalry.

"A little farther, darlin'," Berry drawled, giving my shoulder blade another rough poke.

"Actually, here is good," Markus corrected. Halting in the dead center of the hangar, his comfort in the space hinted he was either the elusive owner or a regular here. Overhead a jet engine roared past, screeching its departure into the night sky. Markus waited for the ruckus to die down before continuing. "Mr. Berry, Mr. Rutherford, if you would kindly keep our friends here company. I'll see to our guest of honor."

"Whoa now," Berry grunted his disapproval. "Where's that magic potion of yours? Load us up before you go strolling off."

Drawing attention his way simply by clearing his throat, Rutherford opened his coat to reveal two sterling silver darts in his inside pocket. Whatever the mysterious cocktail was, earned a fat-cat grin from Berry's puffy face.

Markus' determined stride hadn't wavered, the heels of his loafers clicking against the floor like hammer strikes. "I would go through the whole rigmarole that there's no use screaming, but ..." he called over his shoulder and pointed skyward. As if cued, another jet rumbled from above. Shoulders shaking with laughter, he disappeared into an office at the far end of the hangar.

A momentary hush fell in his wake.

Turning in a slow circle, Rau evaluated the layout of the space. "What exactly are we doing here, gentlemen?"

Rutherford shifted on his feet, his back hunched with palpable loathing. "Close your mouth, *bloodsucker*," he spat as if the title soured on his tongue. "I won't explain myself to a corpse."

Rau's head tilted with a mixture of interest and contempt. "I could explain all the fundamental flaws in that sweeping assessment, but

I would have to dumb it down with small words for your painfully simplistic human intellect."

While Rutherford glowered, Berry clucked his tongue against the roof of his mouth and waved his gun in Rau's direction. "I bet if I was a few centuries old, I'd be a pompous ass, too. Doesn't change the fact that we own this town. We are the kings of this domain! You want that bill of yours to pass? Only way that's happening is under *our* fucking terms."

"Come now, Berry, there's no need to be crass," Markus chastised from the office doorway.

No longer was he alone.

Carter edged in close, offering the only comfort he could by linking his fingers with mine. Whatever tension lay between us, in that moment I treasured the contact.

"Lawrence Rawling," Rau muttered, spine-straightening in steeping unease.

Elodie's twitchy-ex kept his gaze firmly fixed on the ground, hand clamped on the upper arm of a vision from the past. The young woman he clung to could have been Joselyn's twin. Same ruby-kissed lips. Same cascading curtain of golden hair. Same enchanting green eyes. It was hours spent studying Micah's file on Joselyn's death that allowed me to notice the subtle differences. The trembling girl's chin was narrower, and she lacked Joselyn's endearing dimples.

Seizing her by the other arm, Markus led their trio forward, only to be halted by his reluctant guest planting her feet and thrashing against them with all her might.

"Daddy, no!" she begged, adding a far more tragic spin to this unraveling nightmare. "Please don't do this!"

There was no need to guess which man held that title. Unable to look her in the eye, Rawling visibly blanched.

"Remember our deal, Lawrence," Markus clucked.

"She's his daughter? What the hell is happening?" Carter rasped.

Shushing him out of the corner of my mouth, I squeezed his hand to amplify the urgency of the suggestion. Whatever was about to happen didn't bode well for anyone with a pulse and no gun.

"I'm sorry." Tugging his own child forward, Rawling's voice dropped to a pained whisper, drowning in shame. "I truly am."

Watching her struggle against the two men, I lurched forward to help. The click of Berry's gun rooted me to the spot, my obedience ensured when he pressed the barrel to the back of Carter's head.

"That's a family matter, darlin'. Best we stay out of it."

Ignoring her captors, Rau beseeched the girl directly. "My dear, are you all right? Have they harmed you?"

Fingernails digging into her skin, Rawling yanked his daughter behind him. "You don't get to talk to her. She's not *for* you."

"*For* him?" The girl's voice hitched a nervous octave. "What does that mean? Daddy, what's going on? You're scaring me."

"So many questions, such demanding interrogation." Markus gifted us his most charming smile, but something dark and sinister roiled and writhed behind his eyes. "Let's handle the business at hand, then *all* will be answered."

A nod to Rutherford and his right-hand man lunged. Markus' public show of shaming him—the over the top acceptance of vampire culture—had all been an act. Having tucked his gun in his waistband, Rutherford drew a silver knife from the holster at his hip. He swung wide, throwing his weight into the strike. The fabric of Rau's clothing split to reveal a gash of gurgling black sludge that seeped from the sizzling edges of the wound.

Face contorting with vampiric rage, Rau's monster burst forth in a show of fang and fury. He dove for Rutherford, but Berry spun with his weapon raised to cover his spiteful cohort.

"The plan *was* to keep you alive." Head listing to the side, Berry closed one eye to peer down the sight at Rau's forehead. "But plans can be altered."

Palms raised, Rau backed down, his murderous glare frozen in place.

"Goodness, that was exciting, wasn't it?" Markus barked with laughter. Dragging the palm of his freehand over his chin dimple, he gestured to Rutherford. "Let's see the knife."

Rutherford retrieved his gun, training it on Carter and me as he skirted around the perimeter to deliver his bounty into Markus' waiting hand.

Pinching it by the hilt with his thumb and forefinger, Markus held it up for inspection. Rau's blood bubbled on the blade, hissing and spitting like a frying egg. "Mr. Lawrence, I believe this is payment in full: the blood of a descendent of Vlad the Impaler. Only son of the legend. I have no doubt the rush will be extraordinary." He adjusted his hold, then offered it to Rawling handle first.

He released his daughter, who was all but forgotten as Rawling smacked his lips and reached for his prize. A second before his fingertips brushed the hilt, Markus pulled it from reach. "And the terms of this arrangement are clear to you?"

"Crystal." Rawling nodded exuberantly.

Taking a step back, Markus' features sharpened with taunting cruelty. "On second thought, I really think you should be the one to explain it to her. After all, you *are* her father."

Dutifully, Rawling began reciting words that must have been drilled into his thick gourd of a head. "The knife and the blood is mine, in exchan—"

"*Ah-ah-ah*," Markus interrupted, pulling the dagger farther away. "Not to me. I already know what a loathsome failure you are. Look at her, your *only* child, and tell her what you've done."

Shuffling in front of his daughter, Rawling cast his gaze to the floor to avoid her pleading stare. "Am-bear—"

"*No*," she interrupted, the word slathered with repugnance. "Whatever you're about to say is well beyond the boundaries of pet names. Show me enough respect not to use those lame cop-outs."

"*Ooh-hoo!*" Head falling back, Markus' guffaw echoed off the ceiling. "She's a fiery one! Little Miss is having *none* of your shit, Lawrence. Better try a little harder."

Rawling shifted his weight from one foot to the other, the tendons of his neck contracting, left eye twitching with the strain of sobriety. "You're right. You deserve better than that." Wetting his parched lips, he focused on channeling enough humanity to produce a feigned ounce of compassion. "Amber, I've arranged for you to stay with these men in exchange for—"

"Your next fix," she finished for him, her tone a bluesy sonnet of melancholy and regret.

Anguish crumbled her face, her soul shattering while another red-eye flight roared off to its destination. The hollow cavity of my own torpid heart ached for her.

"You have to understand," Lawrence pleaded, stare locked on the dagger instead of her, "my blood burns in my veins. I can't think, can't help myself. I'm ..."

While he hunted for the wording of his paltry excuse, Amber arched back and spat in her father's face. The thick glob of her saliva trailed down his cheek, dripping off on to his shirt with a heavy *splat*.

"You sold me for your next high," Amber sneered. "You're disgusting. Just go. Get the hell out of here. Whatever depravity they have planned could never be as bad as you. You were supposed to love me, to *protect* me. Instead, you used me as *currency*."

For a beat, the twitching stopped. Clarity softened Rawling's features. "That's not true. I love you, Amber, more than anything. I need you to know that."

"More than anything, huh? That'll change the second you lick the blood off that knife." Tearing her glare from her father, she addressed Markus directly. "He doesn't need to be here anymore. I'm *your* property now."

That ever-present grin, which could make the devil wince, coiled the corners of Markus' lips. "You're absolutely right. Rutherford, would you please show Mr. Rawling out."

Crossing her arms over her mid-section, Amber folded in on herself, the fight having left her body. She wouldn't try to run, of that I was certain. Why bother? Where could she go? The best she could do now was batten down for the storm with the rest of us wayward souls.

Markus tossed the knife to the ground at Rawling's feet, sending the publicly respected County Commissioner scrambling to claim it as Rutherford seized him by the elbow and steered him toward the door. For Amber's sake, I wished he had done the inconsolable father act, screaming for his daughter until he faded into the oblivion; that his despairing cries could be heard for miles, resonating his heartache to the heavens. As it was, the only sounds leaving his lips were happy slurps while he dragged his tongue down one side of the blade, then the other.

"And you have the audacity to call *us* monsters," Rau marveled, shaking his head in disgust.

"What can I say," Berry chuckled, tempting fate by scratching his temple with the barrel of the gun. "We're a fickled kind."

The hangar door banging shut brought with it a clap of realization. Two stories, lining up in a way no outsider could see.

"The timeline was wrong," I muttered, acidic clarity burning up the back of my throat. "Joselyn's father wasn't trying to avenge his daughter. He never was. He hated vampires, to the point that dismembering them became his compulsion. To him, his daughter's public involvement with one was an atrocity." Catching Rau's stare, I held it in a cradle of empathy. "He sold her to keep his supply of victims flowing."

A fog of silence blew into the room, slowly turning Rau's head from Berry to Markus. "You were both in my home. Whoever bought her knew about the mask and planted it there."

Scream ripping from his chest, the vampire lord charged for Berry, knocking the gun from his hand with all the effort of an afterthought. Seizing the statesman by the shirt, Rau slammed him against the cement block wall, his forearm pressed to Berry's windpipe.

"In all my years, I have loved exactly *one* woman." Rau's voice dipped to a threatening whisper. "If I find out you had anything, *anything*, to do with her death, I will make you an immortal just so I can spend my days finding new and innovative ways to make you suffer."

"I suggest you relax, Mr. Mihnea. *He* had nothing to do with it." Sauntering behind Amber, Markus' hand lingered over her throat in an open threat. "I will admit to being the one who purchased your lovely inamorata. Even so, I viewed it as an act of mercy. Poor child's father held no value for her life. Lord only knows what kind of depravity she would have been subjected to in the hands of a lesser caring individual. Still, if you want to gaze upon the face of her killer, you need not look farther than the closest mirror."

Caught off guard, Rau loosened his hold, his exposed fangs dripping for justice. "No. I would never hurt her. I couldn't. It's not—"

Fffft.

Fffft.

Rau's adamant denial was cut off by two darts missiling into his flesh. One imbedded in his shoulder, the other his calf. A blink later, he crumbled to the ground.

Berry stumbled from the wall, eagerly gulping air by the mouthful.

"What did you give him?" Carter asked, breaking the hush I'd imposed on him.

Markus dug into the pocket of his suit coat and extracted a black masquerade mask vined with gold. "The first was a horse tranquilizer laced with silver to make him more susceptible to its influence." Ignoring Amber's whimper of protest, he fixed it over her eyes and tied it into place. "The second was an artificial sulfur substitute. It makes vampires particularly vicious, yet is completely untraceable once the effects wear off. It's the same concoction he was drugged with before ripping out the throat of his love. A few of your friends have experienced it as well. We find they make excellent hitmen under the influence."

"He's the son of Vlad the Impaler, the *ultimate* vampire," I warned. "You douse him with that and turn him lose, he'll kill us all."

"Not if you're already gone when he wakes up." Markus' expression was a sunny promise of the cotton clouds of freedom.

"And you'll let us just walk out," I huffed in wry disbelief.

"I will." Bowing his head, he glanced up at me from under his brow. The deepest, most vile pits of hell churned in the depths of his stare. "The second you kill this sweet child."

TWENTY-TWO

Scientific Method – Continuous process which implements a body of techniques to investigate a phenomenon, acquire knowledge, or correct and integrate previous knowledge.

Whoa, now." Berry's complexion faded chalk white. The hand holding his gun drooped. "Nobody said anything about killing humans. Stagin' a violent spectacle, I'm all for. But I draw the line at takin' an innocent girl's life. My mama raised me as a Christian, and I don't need her kickin' my ass at the pearly gates when I—"

His outburst was cut off by winging metal. Blood gurgled from Berry's lips, a choked gasp rattling from his lungs. Jutting from his throat was a silver knife identical to the one Rawling sauntered out with. Amber shielded her face, her shrill shriek reverberating off the walls in a deafening echo. Legs folding beneath his slack body, the pile of meat that had been Bob Berry slumped to the ground while Rutherford straightened his coat from where he extracted the blade for its fatal toss.

Strolling over to Berry's body, Markus shook a handkerchief from his breast pocket and used it to yank the knife out in a pulsing spray of crimson. "This will be destroyed," he explained. "The only weapon able to be tied to this will be the one Daddy Rawling insisted on taking with him."

"Why?" I forced the words through gritted teeth. "Why take out one of your own?"

Markus' head snapped up, eyes bulging with faux innocence. "Oh, *we* didn't. Rawling was your lap dog. Locked in the thralls of his blood addiction, *he* killed Berry when he tried to protect Amber from being drained dry by ... you." Clapping a hand over his heart, Markus saluted the corpse at his feet. "He died a hero's death."

Lifting my chin, I glared Markus down, frosting him over with my icy stare. "You hate vampires so much you would stage all of this at the expense of two lives?"

"On the contrary." Markus handed off the knife to Rutherford who would undoubtedly handle the disposal. "I don't hate any vampires."

"I do," Rutherford grumbled. Depositing the handkerchief and knife in a plastic bag, he tucked it into his coat pocket. "Bloodsucking parasites, the lot of you."

"And your opinion is completely justified." Markus stabbed a hand in his direction. "I'm simply of the mindset that the Nosferatu do not belong in civilized society. I had hoped voters would come to that decision all on their own, but the latest polls are leaning in the opposite direction. With your help, we're going to remind them what's at stake."

"You're putting a lot of stock in me playing along," I snarled.

Carter's chin dipped in my direction. "Vincenza, don't."

"No, I'm genuinely curious." Talking over him, I took a brazen step forward. "What if, instead of biting her, I ... don't? Then what? You kill me? Give Rau time to wake up so he can tear my throat out for you? I say we skip right to those options, because I'm not touching that girl."

"Ah, the naivety of youth." Markus nodded to Rutherford, who jabbed his gun barrel to Carter's forehead.

"Get on your knees," Rutherford commanded, his face vacant of remorse or hesitation.

Raising his hands, palms out, Carter obliged.

"Why go for the kill, when you can go for the hurt?" Markus asked, his tone conversational. "You *will* bite her, Miss Larow, or your friend's head will be hollowed."

"Please, no," Amber whimpered. Legs failing her, she sunk to the ground.

Catching my stare, a sad smile stole across Carter's features. "I told you I wanted to find a way to make things right with us. Call their bluff, Vinx. Show them they're the only monsters here."

"So noble! Such self-sacrifice!" Markus bellowed, throwing his hands in the air. Spinning on me, he let them fall to his sides with a slap. "That's the kind of guy you should hold on to. Or, you can do nothing and be haunted by the memory of being showered in his gray matter. The choice is yours."

"Don't make me do this," I beseeched the heavens more than the loathsome men lording over me.

Striding to Amber's side, Markus caught her upper arm and heaved her to her feet. "I wish there was another way, but sadly we're out of options. At pivotal moments in history, it takes horrendous acts to open the eyes of the public. *You* are that awakening."

"Don't listen to him," Carter said in a soothing whisper. "You harm her and you won't be able to live with yourself."

"Tick tock," Markus prompted, shoving Amber in my direction. "Don't let Rutherford make the decision for you. He's the impatient type."

"My trigger finger *is* getting itchy," Rutherford confirmed with stoic indifference.

Amber's frantic gaze lobbed from me to Markus, and back again. "Please, just let me go. I won't say a word to anyone, I swear." Her voice cracked with emotion, a fresh peal of sobs shuddering through her.

"One girl dies and the rest of you walk out of here." Maintaining a white-knuckled grip on her arm, Markus' fingers dug into Amber's flesh hard enough to sprout a rash of angry purple bruises. "I'll even help you detox Mihnea so he doesn't devour you. While I hate to sound like an infomercial, time *is* running out on this limited time offer."

"And then what?" Carter barked, face reddening with helpless frustration. "He paints you as the villain in this to the media? Your life would be over, with the entire country launching a manhunt for your head."

Closing my eyes, their shouts and pleas melded together into spikes of confusion that hammered into my temples.

"I don't want to die!"

"Don't let them make you into something you aren't."

"Smell her fear, give in to your desires."

"Let me do this, Vincenza."

"I'm begging you, let me go!"

"What's it going to be, Miss Larow?"

"I love you."

"*Shut him up!*" Markus ordered, his mask of calm finally cracking.

My eyes opened to Rutherford pistol whipping Carter, knocking him out cold.

Hands balling into fists at my sides, my fangs ripped from my gum line. "*Don't touch him.*"

"That's entirely up to you." Markus pulled himself up to full height, glaring down the bridge of his nose at me as if I had shown my hand. "That was just him losing consciousness, imagine how much worse it will be when he's dead. Time's up, Vincenza. Someone is got to die. Who's it going to be?"

Peering down at Carter's slumped frame, a red haze of fury clouded the edges of my vision. Amber filled her lungs beside me. A glut of questions rushed through my mind before she could expel it.

Could I get her out of the way and use Markus as leverage?

Was I quick enough to take both men out before they hurt anyone?

Would Rau truly be an enraged beast when he awoke? Was I powerful enough to subdue him?

So many questions, yet one crucial quandary completely escaped me: *Had anyone noticed the nail file in the pocket of my blazer?*

The failure to consider that detail is why it came as a complete surprise when Amber snatched it and buried it handle-deep in my chest.

TWENTY-THREE

Failure Analysis — The process of collecting and analyzing data to determine the cause of a failure.

The file slid in like melted butter, colliding with my ribcage and chipping off a shard of bone. Glancing down, I tried to make sense of the manicuring tool jutting out of my stomach or the searing ache that accompanied it.

Pain aside, I was still standing ... for the moment at least.

"I-It's silver," Amber stammered, staring at the file as if expecting an explanation. "Why aren't you burning?"

"Why indeed?" Tapping his chin with his index finger, Markus pantomimed confusion. "A vampire impervious to the effects of silver. Have you ever heard of such a thing, Rutherford?"

"It boggles the mind," the glorified yes-man responded without an iota of conviction.

"You knew," I croaked. Wobbling, I struggled to keep my legs under me. "You knew my parents, and you know what I am. You drugged Finn to attack us to make it look like vampires were ... killing those who publicly opposed them."

Closing the distance between us, Markus' shoes scuffed across the floor. "That would wrap this all up in a pretty little bow, wouldn't it? Grant you the closure your darkened heart needs? Unfortunately, answers to the questions truly worth knowing never come that easy." Hand closing around the file, he twisted it, and yanked it out in one smooth motion. Blood filled my mouth, seeping between my teeth. Dots danced before my eyes. All while Markus held the file up to the light, turning it over to admire the thick sheen of garnet coating it. "In this case, the truth is bigger than you or I. CliffsNotes version? Your parents were narrow-sighted innovators, taken out by their competition. Rumor has it you've even met the mastermind behind it, although I'm sure you don't remember. He has ways of remaining anonymous." Turning on the ball of his foot, Markus balanced the nail file between his index fingers.

Hands over my stomach, tepid stickiness soaked through my shirt and coated my fingers. "Please ... just tell me his name."

Ignoring my plea, Markus strolled across the hangar, pausing to impose instruction on Rutherford. "Keep an eye on both of them. If either try to run, shoot them in the leg."

"Gladly," the misguided coroner grumbled, adjusting his grip on the gun.

Energy fading, I glanced to Carter in desperation. Despite the pain and odds rapidly stacking against us, an almost smile tugged at my lips. Still pretending to be unconscious, he had subtly maneuvered his phone out of his pocket. Propped up against his supposedly slack hand, the brilliant bastard was recording every minute of our ordeal.

There was hope. It was grisly and covered in blood, but it was there.

A heartening prospect to behold even as Markus seized Rau by the hair and swiped the bloody file across his lips. The vampire lord's skin sizzled, but only for a moment before my blood shielded him from the burn. Rousing, Rau's tongue flicked out to taste the offering.

"He's waking him up. Why is he waking him up?" Amber yelped, trembling like an anxious Chihuahua.

Head rolling her way, I blinked through the haze of rapid blood loss. "Now you've got *two* vampires on your hands. Remember when I was the worst of your problems? Those were the fucking days, huh?"

Rau's eyes snapped open, unveiling ruby orbs of hunger and hate. His movement was paranormal poetry, floating him up to a defensive crouch. Features more beast than man, his lip curled into a vicious snarl. "All this time, you've been right beside me, and I never knew the truth."

Palms raised, I did my best to pump the brakes on the hydroplaning situation. "It's *me*, Rau. I'm still the same person." My appeal trailed off when Amber side-stepped to hide behind me. "Seriously? If you wanted me to fight for you, you probably shouldn't have skewered me."

Head slanted, Rau's murderous glare traveled the length of me as if seeing me for the first time. "You've *never* been one of us. Yet you infiltrated our hive, made us trust you."

"That's right, I did." Planting my feet firm, I owned my truth. "I started all of this looking for answers, and instead I found a place where I fit ... where I was needed. I hadn't felt that since my family died, and I don't want to lose it now."

"Shut up!" Jaws snapping, spittle flew from his bared teeth. "You know nothing of *family*. Family doesn't lie. It doesn't deceive. Anything that does is a *threat*, and threats must be eliminated."

Every cell of my body screamed for me to prep for the fight. Ignoring the pull of those instincts, I retracted my fangs. I would allow myself no show of aggression against the man who had inadvertently become my mentor. "Remember what I said to you in the limo? That I'd lead until you found your footing? I'm fumbling, Rau. I need *you* to lead."

"I can smell your blood now. How did you mask it before?" Rau asked, tongue teasing over the tip of one fang.

"One taste of her blood made you impervious to silver." Markus skirted along the perimeter of the room, injecting his venom from a more secure distance. "Imagine what you could do if you drained her. There's a chance you could feel the sun on your skin after all these centuries. Kill them. Kill them both, and taste freedoms you thought had forsaken you."

Sniffing the air, Rau's eyes rolled back with orgasmic delight. "I trusted you ... confided in you."

"You still can," I interjected with as much fervor as I could muster in my battle to remain upright.

"No," Rau rumbled, staring down at clawed hands that matched the silvery hue of a full moon on a cloudless night. "You don't know the pull of what's being offered. To feel the sunlight on my skin. To find sustenance from food, and not the pain and death of others ..."

"One last kill, to change your life forever," Markus pointed out. While the lift of his shoulder was casual, the intensity of his stare was fixed and demanding. "Embrace the hunger. Submit, *one last time.*"

As Rau prowled a slow circle around us, Rutherford mirrored his steps to keep us pinned in. "Talk to me, Markus. They usually go rabid dog by now. Why is he still up and talking?"

Markus beamed like a proud parent. "Because, he's older and stronger than the rest. He's fighting the pull. Rest assured, it will win in the end. It always does."

Amber's hands clamped onto my arms, clinging to me as she sobbed and snotted against my back. "He's going to kill us. We're going to die."

Rolling his head like a boxer entering the ring, Rau shivered from head to foot. "I don't want to hurt anyone. Never did. But, I ... am ... *famished.*" A sickening knot twisted in my gut, Rau's stare shifting from me, to Amber, and back again. "*Eeny, meenie, miny, moe.*"

"This is it. *Oh God, oh God, oh God.*" Amber hiccuped.

"Shut up!" I hissed over my shoulder. Planting my feet, I straightened my spine as much as the hot-poker of pain in my gut would allow and locked stares with Rau. "You don't want her. She's just another human. A meal and nothing more. You want to walk in the sun? I'm your best shot at that."

"You're like a daughter to me." As I watched, his pupils dilated to black pits of desire. "She's a question mark."

"A daughter that lied and deceived you," inserting the reminder, I tempted him by inching his way. "You said so yourself."

Saliva dripping from his fangs, Rau prowled closer. As his nostrils twitched, he closed his eyes to relish my scent.

Giving up his act, Carter pushed himself up on one elbow. Video capturing every moment, his stare darted around the room for some way to intervene. Mentally, I willed him to lay back down and keep himself safely out of the equation. Not that I thought such a flight of fantasy would do any good.

So fixated was I on Rau that I didn't notice Amber's building tizzy until she shoved me aside and ripped off the mask. "*It's too much. I can't take it. I want this over with!*"

One look, and I knew she was about to do something monumentally idiotic. "Amber, whatever you're thinking, *don't.*"

"If you're going to kill me, just do it!" Digging the pointed edge of the mask into her wrist, she dragged it up her forearm. Skin splitting in a bloody gush, a whimper seeped from her clamped lips.

Rau jerked with a jolt, head snapping her way with lethal interest.

"What an enticing development," Markus chuckled, dragging his tongue over his lower lip.

"Girl, you are a special kind of stupid." Forcing the words through my teeth, I shoved two fingers into my closing wound, tearing the tissue back open. Breakers of pain licked through my chest, setting fire to every nerve. Raising my hand over my head, I let the blood stream down my arm, falling to the floor in heavy splats. "I'm the one you want, Rau. Take your aggression out on me, but don't hurt her."

Rau paused mid-prowl, watery red eyes swinging my way.

"I'm already dead," I whispered softly. "My life ended on that attic floor with a train whistle blowing in the distance. Let this be my penance for deceiving you."

"Now or never, Mihnea," Markus boomed, drawing his gun from the back waistband of his trousers. "Choose one, or watch them both die."

If Rau heard Markus' threat, it bounced right off his slithering prowl.

Carter stayed hunkered to the ground, his phone captured every moment.

Hands falling to my sides, the weight of inevitability settled on my shoulders. "Prove your father wrong. You aren't a demon. You're not cursed."

Despite his swollen and snarling features, Rau's head tilted with something that resembled affection. "My dear child, if I hurt you, that's *exactly* what I am."

Before the scream could form on my lips, Rau moved in a dizzying blur. Pinning Amber's body to his, his fangs sank into the pulse of her offered throat.

TWENTY-FOUR

Breakthrough – An act or instance of removing or surpassing an obstruction or restriction.

Legs failing me in the same fashion I failed Amber, the ground rose to meet me. Whether it was blood-loss or the crushing weight of defeat that slammed my knees into the concrete, I couldn't say. But there I knelt, flummoxed in a growing crimson puddle. Casting my stare to Amber's discarded mask, there was no escaping the noisy slurps of Rau draining the life from her.

"I'm sorry. I'm so sorry," I professed, the words tumbling from my lips in a heartfelt confession. "It's all my fault. I thought I could do this. I thought I was strong enough … driven enough."

"Ugh, blubbering is so tiresome," Markus groaned. Plucking the tranquilizer gun from Rutherford's hidden holster, he aimed and delivered three darts into Rau's back. A squeak snuck from my lips as the feeding vamp crumpled over the body of his lifeless prey. Tossing the gun aside, Markus let it clatter to the ground. Its sharp crack resonated around me in a taunting echo. Hitching up the legs of his pants to allow himself ease of movement, Markus squatted down beside me. His husky voice dropped to a conspiratorial whisper. "You have to see this as the simplistic lesson in nature it is. This is a pure blood Nosferatu in their most real and brutal form. *Look* at what he's capable of. He was created for savagery. *This* is his true nature, what he was meant to be. Pull back the glossed-up mask of the wolf in sheep's clothing and marvel at the fanged beast beneath. *This* is why their kind has no place among civilized people."

Exhausted from the tears and gore raining out of me, I wilted back on my heels and met his hate head-on. "Civilized? Is that what you call what happened here?"

"This was done out of necessity." Markus shrugged. Purposely ignoring my aghast outrage, he jerked his chin in Amber's depleted direction. "That, on the other hand, was done out of pleasure."

"You drugged him," I slurred, blinking hard to clear my blurring vision.

"True enough." With a small chuckle, meant to appease me, Markus' lips twisted to the side. "But the drug can't bring out anything that doesn't already live within him. He's a pedigreed beast, thirsting for carnage. While you," catching a lock of my hair, he twisted it around his finger and gave it a tug, "you're a half-breed mutt that doesn't fit in their world or ours. It's good for you to see him like this—torn away from the illusion he cocooned himself in—to spare you from dying convinced of the lie." Standing, he shook out his cramping legs and gave the briefest nod to Rutherford.

The safety of a gun was released with a metallic clink in my ear and cold steal kissed my temple.

"And, Vincenza," Markus affirmed, Rutherford taking the position of executioner behind me, "you *are* going to die."

"That statement might be a tad premature." Pushing off one elbow, Carter, the forgotten about cast-off, lifted from the ground to assume a bold, wide-legged stance. Out in front of him, he held up his phone for all to see. "Smile, gentlemen, the world is watching."

FACE NOTICEABLY ABSENT of even a flicker of emotion, Markus hid his gun behind his back and gestured for Rutherford to do the same. Cheeks blooming the deep scarlet of repressed rage, Rutherford begrudgingly followed suit.

Phone balanced between his index fingers and thumbs, Carter performed a slow and steady side-step in my direction. "I'm guessing you boys have a lot of questions right now. Am I telling the truth? If so, how long has the camera been on? Is this the moment you got caught with your hand in the cookie jar? And, most importantly, how can you take Vinx and I out with the world watching? Let me give you a hint, the answer to that last one is ... you can't. You lay one hand on us, and your lives and careers are *over*."

A lesser man may have buckled under the weight of the heavy scrutiny forced upon him. Not Markus. A master of political manipulation, he didn't risk so much as a hesitation before launching into an oil-slick smooth spin. Tucking his gun into the back of his belt, he raised his hands palms out. Feigning sincerity with the expertise of a trained performer, he beseeched Carter along with any viewers watching. "You have done a service to your country by recording the truth. Rau Mihnea, public face of the Nosferatu Presumption of Innocence Bill, killed a woman. We have no doubt, had we not sedated him, he would have turned on the rest of us. As horrific as this tragedy is, we can take comfort knowing that the sheet has been torn and the truth revealed. Today's votes shouldn't matter. Not when the facts on this issue have been so carefully hidden. The executive branch needs to intervene, emergency action must be taken to veto this bill. The safety of the good citizens of the United States is at stake."

Heel bumping my leg, Carter took a protective stance in front of my huddled form. "You injected Rau with something that made him lose control. We all saw it. How do you plan to weave that into this story you're scripting?"

Jerking as if slapped, Markus blinked Carter's way in disbelief. "You watched that poor girl die in a rough and brutal manner no human deserves. How can you possibly rationalize that as anything *other* than the deplorable actions of a vicious animal?"

"What about the other body on the ground? I'm fairly certain any vampire worth their salt would find this level of waste Plasma Abuse. Plus, they have no need for guns, and District Attorney Berry is sporting a fatal bullet wound. Care to discuss that, Councilman?" Carter swiveled his phone to capture a shot of Berry slumped on the floor in a pool of his own blood.

"You're stunned by what's transpired." Markus clucked his tongue against the roof of his mouth, his practiced expression a picture of compassion. "Anyone would be. Hand me the phone, son. We'll call the authorities, and get you and your friend the medical attention you deserve." Reaching for the phone, his stare flashed with murderous intent.

"If it's all the same to you, I think I'll hold on to it," Carter countered. Shifting the device into his left hand, he extended the other to me. When I continued to sit slack and motionless, he nudged me with his foot. "Vinx, can you stand?"

Hatred flared Rutherford's nostrils. "This is bullshit. We did you a favor tonight, you ungrateful twat!"

Ever the pillar of serenity, Markus raised one finger to steady him. "Easy, my friend. After what these young people witnessed, it only makes sense for them to be confused and uneasy. Given time to reflect, they will have *no choice* but to accept the reality of this situation."

"That sounded an awful lot like a threat." Bending sideways, Carter's hand encircled my wrist. He ducked his head and draped my arm around his shoulders. "Vincenza, I need you to come with me. Markus and his guard dog won't do anything to stop us from walking right out of here. Will you, boys? Not so long as this camera is rolling."

Battling to keep his rage at an impassive neutral, the tendons of Markus' neck bulged. "I doubt that the police will look favorably on you fleeing the scene of a crime. Why don't you stay here, and we'll all alert the authorities together?"

"You've got the County Coroner on a leash. I'm not deluded enough to believe that's where you're influence ends." Breath warming my cheek, Carter murmured against my hair, "Lean on me as much as you need, but I need you to get up."

Forcing one foot under me, I eased a small portion of my weight onto it. The traitorous limb collapsed, driving my knee into the floor with a sharp bark of pain. Call it guilt, or affection, but as I fought for the strength to try again, something dragged my blurring stare back to Rau. Once a regal prince of the media. Now, prostrated and covered in gore.

"I can't leave him," I croaked. "He needs me."

As Carter struggled to hold the phone steady, he hoisted me up on wobbling legs. "There's nothing we can do for him now. The camera is our key out of here. He would want you to take it."

"Rau is a proven killer." Clapping his hands as if in prayer, Markus' predatory glare searched for a weak point to strike. "Thanks to you, the world has seen that. If you even tried to leave with him, you would be thrust into a nationwide man-hunt. Still," his shoulders rose and fell in a casual shrug that sharply contradicted the waves of malicious desire wafting off of him, "if you'd like to hand over the phone, you could drag him out of here. I find him far too dangerous to throw myself in front of if he was attempting to leave. After all, I am a family man."

Ignoring Markus' posturing and posing, Carter risked a glance my way. His stare pleaded with me for an ounce cooperation. "We have to go. There's no time for choice or debate. I *promise* you we will find a way to come back for him, but right now we need to go."

As if to further prove his point, the screen of his phone flashed its warning that the battery life was at twenty percent. The lights of the device dimmed enough to be notiecable.

"I'm sorry. I'm so sorry," I chanted to Rau and Amber, while Carter yanked me from the ground and tucked me tight against his side.

"Everything okay?" Markus folded his hands with staged concern, eyes narrowing with a vulturine gleam. "Don't feel you have to rush off. If the girl needs medical care, we would *happily* see to her."

Carter stabbed the phone out in front of him with the lethal intent of brandishing a machete. "You're not getting anywhere near her." While he edged us toward the door, his gaze remained on a swivel for possible threats. Adjusting his grip to gather me more firmly in the fold of his arm, he muttered against my hair, "We *will* see Rau again. For now, I need you to stay with me."

"And what, pray tell, is your plan when that door bangs shut behind you?" Markus queried, looping his thumbs into the pockets of his suit coat.

Battery at ten percent. Any second now, the lights would shut off and it would be open season for our hides.

"I'm going to keep the camera rolling as long as possible, you son of a bitch," Carter bluffed. Kicking open the door with the heel of his foot, he scooted us through it. His voice dropped to an urgent whisper as he muttered into my hair, "Can you run?"

"I-I don't think so," I stammered, tipping my face up to his. Up that close, I could see a small mole next to the bridge of his nose, directly under the corner of his eye—a slight imperfection that added an element of approachability to an otherwise flawless face. It seemed extreme blood loss had me waxing poetic. "But I'm willing to die trying."

"No one else is dying. Not today." His phone picked that moment to make the effective counter point of shutting off. Spinning on the ball of his foot, Carter launched forward, catching my wrist to drag my stumbling mass behind him.

Rutherford charged our way, only to be halted by Markus' hand slamming into his chest. "No, you can't be seen. Call the boys. Make sure they don't make it off this airfield alive."

Door banging shut behind us, we were thrust into the blanket of night. Steering us in the direction of the row hangars to the east of us, Carter screamed to be heard over the deafening boom of jet engines roaring overhead. *"Go! Run!"*

TWENTY-FIVE

Disproven Theory – To prove to be false or wrong by finding a single observation that disagrees with the predictions of the theory.

Clamping my arm over the hemorrhaging hole in my gut, I stumbled to keep my feet under me. Each forced stride sent a fresh wave of the pain searing through my core and bile scorching up the back of my throat. I was physically broken and emotionally shattered. For so long, I ached to return to what I once was: another hapless mortal blind to elements of the world I didn't understand. Now, seeing firsthand the atrocities humans were capable of, I found myself relieved to be rid of that narrow-minded affliction. If I died this night, in the final sense of the word, I would do so not as a monster, but as an evolved being capable of understanding, compassion, and mercy.

The limo that dropped us off reappeared around the side of the hangar we hobbled to escape, screeching to a halt in a spray of loose gravel. Two heaving gorillas in suits stormed from the car, slamming the doors behind them. "Do a sweep! Find them!"

Carter's head whipped around, searching for a safe haven. "They haven't spotted us yet. We're too exposed here. Between the hangars, move!" Dragging me onward, he pulled us both around the side of the closest hangar.

I collapsed against the metal sheeting of the structure, bequeathing it the majority of my weight in effort to keep myself upright. Glancing to Carter, I watched his chest rise and fall, and envied him for the relief he could derive from a calming breath.

Engines of luxurious private jets rumbled from the hangars housing them. Noses of posh liner's poked out, taunting us with the promise of escape. Silently, I said a prayer of thanks for their thunderous symphony. At least I didn't have to hear the footfalls of our approaching doom. My heavy lids were falling shut in resignation of the inevitable, when wind rushed past my cheek. The hair was blown from my face by the wings of a low-swooping crow.

No. Not *a* crow.

The crow.

The same avian creature of darkness that had inadvertently become my totem since my transition. Times of crisis or unease, it always seemed to lurk nearby. That couldn't be a coincidence. Streaking into the open hangar opposite us, it seemed to be guiding me onward like a beacon in the night.

"The crow, follow it." As I pushed off the hangar, a dagger of white hot pain twisted my gut, folding me in half. My stumble forward morphed into a stumble onward. "I can't ... just go," I croaked. Sinking to the ground, one fist collided with the earth as spots swam before my eyes.

"Like hell I will." Carter scooped me into his arms, hooking one hand under my knees and the other around my back. Breaking into a sprint, he didn't let a little thing like my head bouncing against his shoulder slow his stride to the welcoming maw of the beckoning hangar.

Skirting around the nose of a *Hawker 400,* my slipping consciousness allowed me pivotal glimpses of the otherwise mundane. Carter wove behind a row of pallets stacked with shipping crates and silently melted to the floor with his back against the wall.

"Normally," chest rising and falling in frantic pants, he fought to catch his breath as pearls of sweat dotted his forehead, "I would launch into the whole *stay awake, stay with me* routine. But now, more than ever, being still as the dead would really work in our favor."

If they found us, our only option would be to bend to their will and pray for mercy. Fingers curling into the fabric of his shirt, I peered up at Carter's face to await our fatal end.

"I'm sorry," I rasped. The pain was less now. Somehow, that seemed like a bad omen. "For everything I said. I wish—"

"Don't." Pressing his forehead to mine, he lowered his voice to a husky whisper. "We get out of here alive, and we'll take turns confessing for all of our asshole tendencies. My list will be a lengthy one. Right now, let's focus on a quiet survival."

Lips parting with a sticky pop, I tried to coerce sentimental words of forgiveness and loyalty from a swollen, lethargic tongue.

"Shhh," Carter soothed, holding me to him with one gentle hand supporting the back of my head.

Outside the fleeting safety of our thinly veiled cocoon, heavy footfalls thundered into the hangar.

"Around the sides of the jet! Find them!" a deep baritone, with a hint of a twang, boomed.

Blame it on the blood loss, but I swear I heard the ruffle of feathers.

"Can I help you, gentlemen?" a calm, familiar voice asked, growing nearer by the second.

Carter's head swiveled away from mine, leaving behind a lonely chill. "*Thomas. It's Thomas,*" he breathed.

"Two people may be hiding in your hangar. We fear at least one of them is armed and dangerous. If we could search the area, we will make sure the space is clear of threats for you." One of the henchman lurked close enough to make the hair on my arms rise. Still, I couldn't pry open my weighted lids. His words seemed to echo down a stretched tunnel, pinging off the fog encapsulating my slipping mind.

"Didn't see anyone come in here." The smile in Thomas's tone was audible. Fabric rustled in three steady swipes.

"No?" the guard with the gravel voice pressed. "One was bleeding and there's a spot of blood right here on your floor."

"Lost my arm in a hunting accident recent enough for it to still ache on the regular. I popped one of my stitches trying to work on the engine like I used to." I could see Thomas behind my eyes, edging closer to position himself between us and danger. Ever the regal sentry, prepared to sacrifice himself for the cause he deemed worthy.

"Sorry to hear that, friend." At the long pause that followed, I envisioned the guard craning his neck to sweep his gaze over as much of the cavernous hangar as he could. "In your injured state, wouldn't you feel better letting us have a quick look around? Just to be safe?"

As if arguing otherwise, the jet's engines purred to life.

"It would seem the pilot is ready to take off." Thomas hollered to be heard over the deafening roar. "Which means I need to lock the hangar down and board. I'm afraid I can't jeopardize my employment by delaying departure to allow strange men with guns to scope the place out."

Tires rumbled across the ground, the iron eagle gliding from its nest.

"It'll only take a moment," one of the guards injected into the hush that followed. "I'm sure your boss would understand."

"You think so?" Thomas sounded close enough to touch, his presence pushing against the intruders to herd them back out the wide flung doors. "He's a *Fortune 500* businessman, with a private hangar for his opulent jet. Does that sound like the type of man with an abundance of patience?"

"I'm sure if you explained the situation …"

"That was a rhetorical question." Thomas's tone hardened, his earlier playful lilt replaced with a swiping blade of annoyance. "The answer was no, he does not. If this plane isn't waiting for him when he's ready to leave, the entire flight crew is out of a job. That means we all have to move in with *you* gentlemen. Are you prepared to extend your families to include a few grown ass adults over this matter? I should warn you, I've been known to sleepwalk naked."

"I really must insist we take one minute." Even as the guard attempted the demand, his voice grew more and more distant.

Huddled in Carter's arms, my teeth chattered as a vicious rash of shivers ravaged me to the bone.

"A minute is exactly what I don't have." Tone sharp and cutting, Thomas slid one half of the hangar door shut in a screech of metal. "I promise you, boys, I've been staring at these four walls all day, and no one that didn't belong wandered in—except for you. I would have reveled in a little company or excitement, even if it was some gun wielding maniac."

"We're actually talking about an injured vampire," one of Markus' boys tried to implant in an ominous threat. "One that would make a gun-crazed maniac look like a fuzzy bunny."

"Bunnies must be terrifying in your world." Catching the other side of the door, Thomas yanked it across its track, preparing to close it in their faces. "Now, I would suggest you boys scurry off and find that blood sucker of yours. Every minute you've spent with me, they're getting farther away."

"If you *do* see anything—"

"I'll scream like a tiny little girl so you two can burst in, guns ablazin', and be heroes. Until then, off you go." Metal rumbled over metal and the outside world was shut out in a reverberating clang.

Exhaling a trapped breath, Carter peeled me from his chest. "Vincenza, can you hear me? *Vinx?*"

I wanted to answer, to wrestle my eyes open and peer into the languid pools of his cerulean stare, but that was not to be. My body locked me in an icy prison within, where the chill of death sucked the morrow from my bones.

Carter readjusted his hold on me, freeing one arm. Sucking air through his teeth, he muttered a colorful stream of expletives. The coppery scent of blood wafted to my nostrils, awakening a scorching burn in my veins. "Vincenza, you need to feed." Sticky warmth dripped on to my lips, streaking salvation down my chin. "It's right there, baby, just open your mouth."

It was a beautiful, self-sacrificing moment, ruined by the hourglass of my borrowed time running out.

A long shadow fell over us, Thomas' frame blocking out the glare from the industrial lighting. "Noble as that act is, son, all it accomplished was getting you a step closer to needing a Tetanus shot. That's not going to help our girl. If she were a traditional vamp, a little bite-n-bleed would do the trick. But Vinx here is the new and improved Ferrari model of Nosferatu. You feed her premium, not regular, if you want her to run right."

Still, Carter kept his wrist hovering over my mouth, in hopes of a blood sucking miracle. "I'm not going to let her die. I'll slice open every artery if I have to."

"I appreciate a gory martyrdom as much as the next vamp." Crouching down, Thomas forced open one of my plastered lids. The dam of darkness broke, flooding light in with a blinding flash. "I would advise, though, that your efforts may be better served getting her aboard the jet. We need to evaluate her injuries. Even for a hybrid, she should be healing far quicker than she is."

"Y-you know the t-truth ... about h-her?" Carter stammered. Gathering me in his arms, he stumbled to his feet.

"Brother, I have insight that would blow your brain out the back of your head." Slapping a hand to Carter's back, Thomas strode back to the doors, opening one far enough to poke his head out. "Looks like the Dynamic Duo took the hint. We're safe to hustle your sweetie aboard."

"Whose plane is that? How did anyone know we were here?" Seemingly cemented in that spot, Carter took a tentative step forward.

"Whoever the plane belongs to, they should be proud it took Elodie as long to hot-wire it as it did. She normally does it in half that time. We tracked the four of you here from the high school

... Vlad rest Duncan's soul. I will gladly answer more questions, and we can play catch up, just as soon as we are safely aboard the stolen vessel. And, I would walk fast if I were you. There's a thin line between undead and just-dead, and she looks like she's about to trade *Vera Wang* for a body-bag."

TWENTY-SIX

Inquiry – Diverse ways in which scientists study the natural world and propose explanations based on the evidence derived from their work.

"Lay her down over there," Elodie commanded. Side-stepping to allow Thomas to take her place in the cockpit, she pointed to a table in the middle of the seating area. A sweep of her arm cleared the makeshift gurney, the mess clattering to the floor as Carter eased me down onto its surface.

Teeth chattering hard enough to chip a molar, my muscles locked to stone. Consciousness came in rippling waves of coherence. It took Carter and Elodie's combined strength to pry my arms from their rigor state curled against my core. Outside, the engines roared louder still. The jet lurched forward to begin our voyage.

"She was stabbed with her silver nail file." Carter's mask of concern floated before my fluttering lids. "But silver doesn't affect her. I don't know what's happening."

"Silver may not affect her the way it does *traditional* vampires," Elodie corrected. Curling her fingers around the collar of my blouse, she tore it open to better assess my wounds. "However, there could still be a sensitivity there. A milder form, but not nonexistent. If, for example, someone were to *oh, say* stab her in the chest with it, she could still have a reaction. Think of it like a bee sting. If you're not allergic, it's just an irritant. Unless, the entire hive swarms and you suffer a thousand stings all at once."

Wadding up my tattered shirt, she used it to wipe away the excess of blood. Carter hovered at her elbow, brow pinched with concern. "What can I do?"

Elodie peeled one of my eyes open, peering down to evaluate my pupil dilation. Whatever she saw folded her face into a stern scowl. A jerk of her chin gestured to a designer satchel pooled in the corner. "In my weekender, there's I.V. bags of serum and blood. Grab me one of each, two packages of tubing, and a needle. We're going to hit her with everything we've got."

"Do you always travel with medical supplies?" Spinning in the tight space, Carter was on the bag in two strides.

Applying pressure to slow the bleeding, Elodie blew her bangs from her eyes. "My employer insisted one among the triplets have those items on hand whenever we traveled anywhere with Rau and Vincenza."

"The undying loyalty implied *Rau* was your boss." Carter offered her the retrieved items.

"I could take the time to explain all that now. Or, I could save your friend. You pick." Not waiting for an answer, Elodie threaded the stainless-steel I.V. needle into a vein at the crook of my elbow. Attaching the tubing, she connected it to a bag of the serum that made me the undead American I was and ran it wide open. She peeled open the second package of medical tubing, unraveled it, and pinched one end between her thumb and forefinger. "She won't be able to feed on her own. Open her mouth and tip her head back."

Doing as instructed with quaking hands, Carter averted his gaze as she threaded the thin tube down my throat and into my stomach.

The chills subsided into an oppressive blanket of numbness, granting me clemency from the pain attributed to the invasive procedure. Matter of fact, I felt nothing at all. It was as if my spirit checked out and floated above my tattered body to patiently wait for a less traumatic time to return. Stabbing the other end of the tube into the blood bag, Elodie gave it a gentle pulse to get the flow started.

The second the first drop of vampire blood settled into my stomach, the fires of hell tore through my gut. Launching off the table, my body seized in spastic convulsions. I clawed at my face, tearing the tube out, gagging as it hurled it from my gullet. Unimaginable pain and torment punched through my core, a scream rattling from my raw and raspy lungs. Slamming to the carpeted floor, I twisted into a tight ball as a fresh onslaught of spasms claimed me.

The intercom clicked on with a sizzle of static. "What's happening back there?" Thomas bellowed.

"Unless you're coming back to help, I don't have time to explain!" Elodie screamed. Leaning over me, she rolled me onto my back. "She's reacting to the vamp blood. There has to be silver left inside of her. Part of the nail file must have broken off."

"Do we have tweezers or surgical tools to pull it out?" Carter dropped to his knees and eased my head on to this lap.

"You want to use silver implements to get silver out? Not sure that would help our cause if we had them. Plus, you wouldn't be able to feel for it. You're going to need to use your fingers to find it and dig it out." Crawling across the floor, Elodie claimed a bottle of scotch from the mini-bar. She yanked the cork out with her teeth, spat it aside, and sloshed the amber liquid over Carter's hands and my wound. Its sting barely registered over the unmistakable feeling of my guts being turned inside out.

Carter's sapphire eyes bulged to volleyballs. "*Me?* Why me?"

Shoving him aside to take his place at my head, Elodie stretched my arms out and pinned them to the floor. "Because I have the strength to hold her still and you don't. All you have to do is stick your fingers into the wound until you feel the fragment, then pull it out. A monkey could do this, a human shouldn't have *too* much trouble."

"*You're coaching skills lack conviction!*" Reluctantly positioning himself at my side, Carter's frantic shout bordered on maniacal.

"I'll save the coddling moments for when we're *not* trying to save your girlfriend. Now, sit on her legs to stretch out her torso."

Gingerly doing as he was told, Carter yelped at the shriek of pain that escaped my paling lips. "I'm so sorry, Vinx," he muttered through his teeth. Closing his eyes, he forced his middle and index finger into the oozing gash.

Tissue popped.

Tendons ripped.

Head falling back, I screamed until my lungs ached.

"Don't fight it," Elodie whispered, her thumbs tracing circles of comfort on my wrists. "You don't need to be here for this. If you want to pass out, you go ahead and do it."

Planting the seed of the suggestion into my mind, it quickly took root. The last of my strength drained from my body, and I escaped into sweet oblivion.

I WOKE IN a world I no longer recognized, and that had nothing to do with the cloud-soft bed and terrycloth robe I found myself in. Thankfully, the sawing pain was gone, and none of my friends had any of their appendages crammed into my guts. Thank Vlad for that small blessing. Untying the belted robe, I parted the plush fabric to assess the damage to my battered core. Only a puffy pink scar remained; my rapid healing had been hard at work to knit me back together.

Easing myself off the bed, I stretched to full height. A slight tug of my stomach muscles injected the reminder to proceed with caution. Securing the knot of my belt, I padded out of the jet's private quarters in search of my saviors. I found Elodie and Carter one room away, perched on the edge of overstuffed leather recliners.

Both of their stares were fixed on the flat screen mounted on the wall. Before my mouth could open to croak out a greeting, my attention was stolen by the somber-faced reporter speaking directly into the camera. At the bottom of the screen, a *breaking news* banner scrolled.

"*It has been confirmed that the footage came from the phone of known reporter Carter Westerly. However, officials have yet to locate the whereabouts of Mr. Westerly. What they do know is that the young woman seen in the footage has been identified as Amber Rawling, daughter of New Haven, Connecticut County Commissioner Lawrence Rawling. Commissioner Rawling has yet to release a statement, however we have received word that he did provide a confirmation that the body recovered from the airplane hangar was, in fact, that of his daughter. A manhunt is now underway in search of Rau Mihnea, the vampire activist who spear-headed the Nosferatu Presumption of Innocence Bill. Mihnea was recognized in the footage leaked by the authorities, in hopes that it will lead to his immediate capture. Before we show this footage, we must warn that this is not suitable for all viewers.*"

The footage Carter captured with his phone was patched in to the feed. On screen, Rau paced a slow circle around me. Despite the blood seeping from my gut, I matched his every step to keep myself between him and Amber. A wound far deeper than that inflicted by the file tore open within me. My soul bled to turn back the clocks and change the script of what was about to unfold. Blood-tinged tears blurred my vision as I watched Rau dodge around me to claim his victim. Latching on to Amber's throat, he was riding her body to the ground when the video cut away.

"What the hell?" Face reddening with rage, Carter seized the chair's armrests in white-knuckled fists. "Markus and Rutherford weren't even *mentioned*! They edited the footage. No one even knows they were there."

Sitting still as stone, Elodie's nostrils flared. "They have friends in high places. But they aren't the only ones."

"Is that the boss you mentioned?" Trying on my voice, I found it tender with a sandpaper grate. Both their heads snapped in my direction. The matching shock on their faces prompted me to double check my robe was closed. "I ... heard you say something about that, right before Carter tried to touch my spine from the front."

Carter bolted from his seat in a blink. "We didn't expect you to be up so soon, or to remember any of that. How are you feeling? Can I get you anything?"

"You can explain that hot mess." I bobbed my head in the direction of the TV.

The suggestion was met by nothing but heavy silence.

With a groan of annoyance, I let my shoulder sag. "I'm fine. I swear. You both did a great job putting Humpty Dumpty back together again. Now, can we get back to the more pressing issue of Rau becoming public enemy number one?"

Lips parting to protest, Carter was cut-off my Elodie's monotone timbre. "My boss is Father VanHelsing, sentinel to Vlad the Impaler. My brothers and I were assigned to protect Rau Mihnea at all costs. As he is being held captive by the humans he was so desperate to integrate with, I'm sure his father would find this a matter of great concern." Picking up the polished ivory phone from its pedestal beside her, she typed the number one to connect with the cockpit. "Reroute us to Romania. We need to pay a visit to the home office." Pausing, she pulled the phone slightly from her ear where Thomas' rants could clearly be heard. "I don't care *where* we have to stop to refuel, just fly the damned plane and get us there."

"Romania?" Carter squawked, tone bordering on a whimper.

Returning the receiver to its cradle, Elodie folded her hands in her lap. "Castle Draculesti to be precise, birthplace of the Son of the Dragon. It's situated on the border between Transylvania and Wallachia. Unless you have some reason you can't travel to the birthplace of the Nosferatu?"

Sinking back into his seat, Carter suddenly seemed to find the carpeting beneath his feet fascinating and fixed his steadfast stare on it. "I just ... don't have my passport with me," he murmured.

"I assure you, that won't be an issue," Elodie replied him, her lips twisting to the side.

The lighthearted moment of reprieve was ruined by a special alert chime from the television. Finger to his ear, the reporter listened with his forehead creased. After a resolute nod of understanding, he addressed his viewers once more. "*We're receiving word that the NPI Bill has been vetoed by emergency executive order. Across the country, violent protests are breaking out in a rash of vampire hate crimes.*" Over his shoulder, footage from a chopper camera caught a horde of humans dragging a vampress out into the sunlight. The instant she burst into flames they danced and cheered around her decimating corpse.

"Where is Micah?" I demanded, maternal flames licking up my spine.

"As soon as we got you stabilized, Elodie called Finn. He hustled her onto a plane to meet us. Our pilots have been exchanging coordinates." Dragging his tongue over his teeth, Carter braced himself for a blow up. "I know you hate Finn, but we needed to utilize—"

"No," I interrupted, stare locked on the screen, "he needs to bring her. Everyone needs to come together, and run."

The news footage cut to a vampire refugee camp, not unlike the one I visited. Tents of the displaced were set ablaze. When the inhabitants tried to flee, they were gunned down with semi-automatic weapons loaded with silver bullets. The final scene was outside one of the voting stations, where vials of acid, laced with silver, were thrown at human and Nosferatu pro-vamp picketers alike.

Elodie melted from her seat, crumbling to the ground in a heap as blood-stained tears dripped from her cheeks. "They're hunting us. We sought acceptance and were answered with the drums of war."

Sinking down on the armrest of Carter's chair, the ache of my heart made that nail file to the gut seem like a papercut. "How do we help them? What can we do?" Voice breaking with emotion, I gratefully took Carter's offered hand, thankful for the warmth of the contact in a world capable of such chilling hate.

"I-I don't kn-know," Elodie stuttered, swiping at her cheeks with the back of her wrist. "We ... need to wake up Vlad. He's seen this kind of hate before, when people first learned of our kind. It forced us back into the shadows then, for so very long. He might know of something we could do different. Some way to stop history from repeating itself."

"To be clear," Carter pressed his lips together, choosing his words with care, "our master plan here is to unleash a man known throughout history for his panache of impaling the bodies of his enemies on spikes, in hopes he can somehow *end* the up rise of violence? Are we sure about this? It has a very 'adding fuel on the fire' vibe to it."

"We don't have a choice." Stare locked on the screen, my jaw twitched with the threat of battle. "We can stand back and watch more die, or we can go back to where it all began and arm ourselves with the ugly truth. We need to—"

As if to counter my point, the news channel panned back to the apathetic reporter. *"With the true nature of Rau Mihnea revealed, victims of the vampire lord are now bravely coming forward with their own stories of his brutality."*

My attention was diverted from those trumped-up allegations by an emblem that appeared at the bottom corner of the screen. Occupying the spot for broadcast sponsors were the letters *DG* scrawled in a swirling silver font and encircled by a braided vine. Something about them scratched at the surface of a memory. Unfortunately, I was unable to dig deep enough to uncover it.

"Vinx?" Carter ventured, peering up at me with hopeful expectation. "I believe you were saying something about how awakening a man capable of mass genocide would *benefit* our cause?"

Dragging herself up off the floor, Elodie adjusted her knee-length skirt and smoothed the wrinkles from her blouse. "It will. It's our only plan, and a sensible one. However, if we're going to do this, we do it by unanimous agreement. Whatever follows, whatever we unleash, will be on *us*. I'm in with a venomous passion that makes my fangs ache. What say the two of you?"

"I say, the idea being balls-out crazy, I'm understandably leery." Dragging a hand over the back of his neck, Carter filled his lungs to capacity, expelling the breath from puffed cheeks. "That said, desperate times being what they are, it seems balls-out is the only way to go ... so to speak."

In the background, the TV rambled on. "*The first victim to come forward, who recently sat down with our in-field correspondent Dean Mason, was left for dead after surviving a vicious attack by Mihnea.*"

"Vinx, you want to weigh in on this?"

"*He took me from my home after killing my parents.*" The voice of a ghost lured my attention to the television screen.

No. It couldn't be. Blinking hard, I willed the image to change. Prayed my eyes were deceiving me.

"*For a year I was held against my will, tortured day and night. In the end ... I begged for death. Even that he denied me, turning me into a monster instead.*"

"Vincenza?" Carter pressed.

It was no sudden drop of altitude that forced me to my knees, but reality whirling around me in a dizzying tailspin.

Darting to my side, Carter caught my elbow to keep me upright. "What is it? What's happening?"

"Jeremy?" His name left my lips in a hopeful whisper, beseeching the universe to offer an alternative explanation for the nightmare swelling before me.

Elodie's stare lobbed from the news footage, to me, and back again. "Who is that?"

"*If it wasn't for the efforts of DG Enterprises and the state of the art medical advancements they have access to, I wouldn't be alive today.*" The interviewee, with the face I knew so well, peered into the lens—his sheepish, lopsided grin undoubtedly winning over viewers everywhere. "*I owe everything to them.*"

Mouth creaking open, terror tied my tongue. "That's ... *my brother.*"

SCIENTIFIC THEORY

Well-substantiated explanation of some aspect of the natural world, based on a body of facts tested and confirmed through observations and experiments.

The comfortable world I once knew was gone. Stolen from me by vile men committing deplorable acts for what they believed to be the greater good. Yet there, drowning in the despair of icy reality, I found new hands to lift me up.

Micah.

Carter.

Rau.

Thomas.

Elodie.

Knowing they were there, my wayward band of misfits, gave me the strength and courage to kick for that emblematic surface. Whatever fresh wave of hell crashed down upon us, we would crest that watery tomb in a spray of victorious truth.

No longer did I fear the spiral into darkness. That's where my kind lived. Where we reveled. Our enemies sought to imprison us there, chasing us back into the shadows with lashes, threats, and posturing. But we would meet their fight head-on, with fangs bared. The Nosferatu had clawed their way out of the toxic sludge of oppression, and I would gird for battle alongside them to ensure that slaving effort wouldn't be undone.

The journey was far from over, yet the destination had shifted.

Listen close and you can hear the trumpets of war. Blood from both sides surges within me. Yet no longer do I harbor resentment for either. My fury is a special brew, bottled for those who corrupt and manipulate for their own devilish delight.

I am not death.

I am hope.

I am a scientifically proven fact that humans and vampires can peacefully coexist. If it's true in the blood sluggishly pumping through my veins, I have faith the same applies to the world around me.

First, the fraud and exploitation pitting the two sides against each other must be eradicated. My fangs throbbed for a taste of that task. Rau had been taken. What had become of my brother concealed. With flames of unease licking up from all sides, I vowed to save them both by finding the thread of truth woven into a tapestry of lies.

Lifting my chin from my chest, I rose to my feet, steeled for the fight. A slight smile tugging at the corners of my lips, I realized that when it came, I would be toting a weapon that would make the world tremble.

I'm coming for you, Markus, and I'm bringing the Son of the Dragon with me.

The Veiled Series will continue with Book 2, Vlad.

ABOUT THE AUTHOR

Stacey Rourke is the author of award-winning books that span various genres, yet maintain her trademark blend of action and humor. She lives in Florida with her husband, two beautiful daughters, and two giant dogs. She loves to travel, has an unhealthy shoe addiction, and considers herself blessed to make a career out of talking to the imaginary people that live in her head.

Connect with her at:

www.staceyrourke.com

Facebook at www.facebook.com/staceyrourkeauthor

or on Twitter or Instagram @rourkewrites

Sign up for her newsletter at: http://eepurl.com/c56flr

Made in the USA
San Bernardino, CA
21 May 2020